HOME TO PARADISE

THE COMING HOME SERIES

HOME TO PARADISE

BARBARA CAMERON

THORNDIKE PRESS

A part of Gale, Cengage Learning

GALE
CENGAGE Learning·

Farmington Hills, Mich • San Francisco • New York • Waterville, Maine
Meriden, Conn • Mason, Ohio • Chicago

GALE
CENGAGE Learning·

LIBRARY OF CONGRESS CATALOGING-IN-PUBLICATION DATA

Names: Cameron, Barbara, 1949– author.
Title: Home to paradise / by Barbara Cameron.
Description: Large print edition. | Waterville, Maine : Thorndike Press, a part of Gale, Cengage Learning, 2017. | Series: Thorndike Press large print clean reads | Series: The coming home series ; #3
Identifiers: LCCN 2017008928| ISBN 9781410499653 (hardcover) | ISBN 1410499650 (hardcover)
Subjects: LCSH: Amish—Fiction. | Paradise (Lancaster County, Pa.)—Fiction. | Large type books.
Classification: LCC PS3603.A4473 H66 2017b | DDC 813/.6—dc23
LC record available at https://lccn.loc.gov/2017008928

Published in 2017 by arrangement with Abingdon Press

Printed in the United States of America
1 2 3 4 5 6 7 21 20 19 18 17

For Barbara Scott and Ramona Richards
and for women who share their love
of quilting with others

A NOTE TO THE READER

Many readers who are familiar with the Amish allowing their children to join the church in their adulthood ask me how many actually decide to stay in the community.

The number is surprisingly high — statistics say as high as 90 percent. I believe this is because Amish families form very strong bonds because of their commitment to their faith, to each other, to extended family, and to their community.

Remaining apart from the outside influences of those they call the *Englisch* means the family and community can influence values important to them.

But to make sure that their children have free will to join, the Amish allow their teenagers to explore the nearby *Englisch* community. It's a period they call *rumschpringe* or "running around."

The idea came to me to write a series about three brothers who leave the Amish community and the three sisters who love them and want them to return. The sisters love the brothers — have for years — and want them to return to their family, their friends, and their church.

The series made me think about what home, family, and the place we live mean to us. The loss of those people and places also interested me and found their way into the series.

Lavina Zook loved David Stoltzfus and brought him back to the Amish community in *Return to Paradise,* Book 1, and Mary Elizabeth, Lavina's sister, convinced Sam, David's brother, to return as well in Book 2, *Seasons in Paradise.* Now, in *Home to Paradise,* Book 3, Rose Anna has a real challenge bringing John, the third Stoltzfus brother, back to the Amish community.

Someone once said, "Home is where your story begins." Abingdon Press has been my writing home since 2009, helping me bring my stories of hope and faith and love to readers. I will never be able to thank all the wonderful people for their hard work bringing my words to readers in beautiful editions. Few writers get an opportunity to work with such dedicated and caring staff. Thank you to all of you.

I also want to thank Tom Vickers and

Monica Peters for their tireless encouragement.

And, as always, thank you to God for giving me life and the inspiration to share His faith and belief in us.

1

Snow fell quietly, cold and white. Inside the big old farmhouse where Rose Anna had lived all her life it was warm. A fire crackled in the hearth, the only sound in the room.

Rose Anna glanced around the sewing room. Usually she and her three *schweschders* sat chatting and sewing with their *mudder,* sometimes singing a hymn as they worked. Today it was just her and her *mudder.*

She sighed. "So here you sit with your old *maedel dochder, Mamm.*"

Linda laughed. "I hardly think you're an old *maedel* at twenty-three, Rose Anna."

She knotted a thread, clipped it with scissors, and squinted as she rethreaded her needle. "I feel like one," she said, pouting a little. "Both of my *schweschders* are married, and so are lots of my friends. I have been a *newehocker* at so many weddings!" She made a face as she began stitching on her quilt again.

"*Guder mariye!*"

Rose Anna glanced up. "*Ach,* here comes my newly married *schweschder.*"

The three Zook *schweschders* were often confused for each other because they looked so much alike with oval faces, big blue eyes, and hair a honey blonde. They'd been born just a year apart, so they'd grown up close. Rose Anna was the youngest — something her two older *schweschders* never let her forget.

"Mary Elizabeth, it's *gut* to see you. *Kumm,* sit by the fire and get warm. You look cold."

She leaned down and kissed her *mudder*'s cheek. "Lavina's on her way up."

Linda brightened and turned to look in the direction of the door. When Lavina walked in a moment later, her face fell. "Where's Mark?"

Lavina laughed and shook her head. "You mean you're not glad to see me?"

"Well, *schur,*" Linda said quickly. "But I thought you were bringing my *grosssohn.*"

"He was fussy and stayed up most of the night, so now he's sleeping." Lavina sank into a chair. "Waneta said she'd mind him so I could get out for a bit. She told me she wouldn't let him sleep all day so he'd keep

12

us up again."

"You look like you need a nap," Rose Anna told her.

"It's tempting, but I need to stay to my goal of finishing this quilt," she said as she threaded a needle.

"Could he be teething already?"

Lavina shuddered. "I hope not. He's not three months old yet. I've heard about teething from my friends."

Soon it was like it had been for so long, everyone chattering and sewing, the mood as bright and cheerful as the fire.

But Rose Anna felt a growing restlessness. She put her quilt aside, went downstairs to make tea for their break, and found herself staring out the kitchen window. The trees were bare and black against the gray sky. Snow had stopped falling, coating every- thing with a white blanket that lay undis- turbed. She found herself pacing the kitchen as she waited for the kettle to boil.

Finally, she knew she had to get out and burn off her restless energy.

"I'm going for a walk," she announced when her *mudder* and *schweschders* came downstairs. She pulled on rubber boots and her bonnet, then shrugged on her coat. "I won't be long."

"But, *kind,* it's cold out there," her *mud-*

der protested.

"I need to walk. 'Bye."

"She'll be fine, *Mamm,*" she heard Lavina say behind her before she closed the back door.

Funny, her older *schweschder* reassuring their *mudder.*

She started off down the road, watching for cars and staying well to the right. Smoke billowed from chimneys as she passed farms. Fields lay sleeping under the snow. The only sound was her boots crunching snow.

Usually she loved this time of year when life was slower, easier. All the planting, harvesting, canning was over. Farmers spent time in their barns repairing harnesses and equipment and planned their spring planting. Women occupied themselves with sewing and knitting and mending clothes. *Kinner* grew restive being cooped up and begged to go outside and build snowmen.

The Stoltzfus farm came into view. Lavina had married David, the oldest *sohn,* and lived there now. Mary Elizabeth had married Sam, the middle *sohn.* And she, the youngest Zook *schweschder,* had hoped to marry John, the youngest *bruder.*

John's truck, a bright red pickup, was parked out front of David and Lavina's

14

farm. She wondered what he was doing home during a workday. Her feet slowed as she frowned and worried. Was his *dat* ill again? Surely Lavina would have said something. Amos had been cured of his cancer for quite some time now.

John came out of the farmhouse carrying a box of clothes and walked toward the truck, then he saw her. "Need a ride?"

"Nee, danki," she said, lifting her chin and walking past him. She might have to be pleasant to him in front of family, but she'd never forgive him for not wanting her anymore.

If she was honest with herself, though, she didn't need to see John to be reminded of him most days. The three Stoltzfus *bruders* looked so much alike they could have been triplets — tall, square-jawed, with dark blue eyes so often serious. John wore his brown, almost black hair in an *Englisch* cut because he still lived in that world.

Rose Anna heard the truck engine start, and the next thing she knew John was pulling up beside her. He stopped and the window on the passenger side slid down. "You're sure you don't want a ride?"

"I said *nee, danki,"* she repeated, and her words sounded as cold as the air she was breathing. She'd rather freeze to death than get into his truck.

His driving the *Englisch* vehicle was one of the many sources of friction between him and his *dat*. John was the last of the Stoltzfus *bruders* who had moved to town after not getting along with their *dat* and the last to reconcile with him and rejoin the Amish community. The only reason he was living here now was because Sam and Mary Elizabeth had married, and John could no longer afford the apartment he'd shared with Sam.

Mary Elizabeth had confided to her that she and Sam had asked John to move in with them. She wondered if that was the reason for John carrying the box out to the truck just now.

It was nice that they had offered when they'd only been married a few months and moved into their own farm down the road.

But whether he lived at his old home, or with Sam and Mary Elizabeth instead of in town, it meant that she was going to have to see him more often and that rankled.

Rose Anna glared at the truck. Later, she'd chide herself for childishness. She found herself reaching down to a drift of snow at the side of the road, packing it into a hard ball in her hands, and throwing it at the truck as he accelerated away.

16

It hit the glass window of the truck cab, dead-on — no surprise since she was great at softball. He slammed on the brakes, then he got out and stood staring at her, his hands on his hips.

"Why'd you do that?" he demanded.

She turned on her heel and began stomping back toward home.

And that was when she felt something thump her on the back. She turned and saw him forming another snowball with his hands.

Frowning, she bent, quickly scooped up snow in her hands, formed another ball, and hit him in the center of the chest before he could lob another at her. She took off running toward the Stoltzfus farm and made it to the front door just as he got her with another ball of snow. Doors here weren't locked in the middle of the day. She slipped inside before he could hit her again and found herself staring at Amos sitting in his recliner reading the newspaper.

"*Guder mariye,*" she said politely. "Is Waneta home?"

He closed his mouth that had fallen open at her abrupt entrance and nodded. "In the kitchen."

Rose Anna brushed the snow from her coat and wiped her feet before walking

17

there. Waneta stood at the big kitchen table kneading bread.

"I was just out and thought I'd stop by," she said brightly. She spun around when she heard footsteps behind her.

John strolled in just then. "I think you forgot something," he said, pushing a handful of loose snow in her face.

"John! Whatever are you doing?" his *mudder* cried, looking appalled.

"She started it," he told her and he strolled out, chuckling.

Rose Anna wiped the snow from her face and grinned at Waneta as the older woman hurried over with a dish towel to dry her off. "He's right. I did. I don't know what got into me."

She did know, but she wasn't going to tell the woman she'd hoped would be her mother-in-law one day. It just hurt too much to share with her how badly her *sohn* had hurt her when he turned his back on their relationship and left the Amish community.

John knew he was going to hear from his mother about what he'd done when he returned for the rest of his things. And undoubtedly, if she told his father, he'd have a word or two or three with him for sure.

But it had been worth it to see the look of utter shock on Rose Anna's face and to rub the snow on that cold face of hers.

Boy, the woman sure could hold a grudge.

Icy water dripped down his neck as the snowball she'd hit him with melted. He found himself grinning as he turned up the heater, slipped his favorite CD into the player, and turned the volume to full blast.

He jumped when he heard the siren behind him and caught a glimpse of flashing lights in his rearview mirror. A quick glance at the speedometer sent a chill down his spine that had nothing to do with Rose Anna's snowballs. *Great,* he thought, hitting the brakes and signaling that he was moving over onto the shoulder of the road.

The police cruiser pulled up behind him, and an officer appeared at the side of the truck. John lowered the window, and a blast of cold air rushed in.

"Do you know how fast you were going?" the officer asked him, sounding testy.

"Uh, no sir. Not exactly."

"Twenty miles over the speed limit."

He winced. "Sorry."

"Let me see your license and registration, please."

John handed him the license and leaned over to get the registration out of the glove compartment.

"Truck's not in your name." The officer peered at him with suspicion.

"I'm buying it from my brother."

All he got was a grunt. "Sit tight. I'll be right back."

John shivered and rolled the window back up. Minutes ticked by. Long, long minutes. Was he going to jail? He tapped his fingers on the steering wheel and shivered. No way was he starting the engine to turn on the heater and having the cop think he was going to make a run for it.

Make a run for it. Now he sounded like one of the shows he'd watched on the tiny television he and Sam used to have in the apartment they'd shared in town.

Another police cruiser pulled up. Oh man, he thought. Two officers? I must be in big trouble.

The officer who appeared at his driver's side window wore a bulky jacket over the police uniform, but he saw it was a female — a familiar one.

"Hey, John," she said, pushing up the brim of her hat so that he saw it was Kate Kraft. "How's it going?"

"Not so well. I didn't realize how fast I was going."

"There's a lot of horsepower under that

hood," she told him easily. She turned as the male officer strode up and joined them. "I know John," she said. "He *is* buying the truck from his brother Sam."

"Thanks," the man said, handing John his identification. "I'll let you off with a warning this time," he told him. "Get that paperwork straightened out as fast as you can."

"I will. Thank you, Officer."

The man nodded and returned to his car.

"Everything okay?" she asked, studying him.

"Yeah. I thought I was in big trouble when a second officer showed up."

"Officer Smith called me when he saw your name on your license. I'm often called in if an officer thinks he needs someone who knows Pennsylvania *Dietsch.*" She tilted her head. "So, speeding?"

"Yeah, I just wasn't paying attention. The truck really moves."

She grinned. "Faster than one of the buggy horses you used to drive, huh?"

"Yeah. Lots."

A gust of wind tossed a flurry of snow at Kate's jacket. "Well, I better go. Keep an eye on that speedometer. Officer Smith gives just one warning."

"It won't happen again."

21

"Good. Okay, I'm headed home. Drive careful."

"You, too," he said, then wondered if he should have said it. Police officers always drove carefully, didn't they? Since she didn't make any comment and was walking away he decided he hadn't offended. After rolling up the window, he started the engine, checked for traffic, and drove out onto the road.

John pulled into the drive of his family home and was careful to park to one side. No way was he giving his father an excuse to fuss if he needed to pull the buggy out the next day before John went to work. Not that his father went anywhere early, but he'd fuss anyway if he was blocked in.

He parked, locked the truck, and hurried toward the house. The wind was picking up, slapping snow into his face. He grimaced, remembering how Rose Anna had thrown snowballs at him earlier.

When he opened the door to the kitchen, he let in a blast of cold air. His mother looked up from a pot she was stirring on the stove.

"Wipe your feet."

"I always do," he responded as he stamped his boots on the rug before shedding his jacket and hat.

"Don't backtalk your *mudder*," his father said as he walked into the room.

John glanced over at her, and she cast him a beseeching look. *Don't argue,* her look said.

"Sorry, Mom," he said. "Something smells good."

"Always shows up for a meal," Amos grumbled as he took a seat at the table.

"So where's David and Lavina?" he asked as he walked over to the stove and looked over his mother's shoulder at the contents of the pot she was stirring.

"They'll be home soon. They went to visit some friends." She glanced at the kitchen window. "Snow's really starting to come down."

"So what were you doing having a snowball fight with a *maedell*?" Amos demanded, his bushy black eyebrows drawn together in a frown. "Aren't you a little old for such childishness?"

"She started it," John told him. He endured his father's steely gaze and shrugged. "We were just playing around."

"What if the bishop had been passing by?"

"He doesn't need to be bothering people having a little fun."

"Now you're telling the bishop his job?"

John felt his temper rising. "Look, can we

23

drop it?"

"Sounds like home," David said as he strolled into the room.

"Your *bruder* here —" Amos began and then abruptly stopped when he saw Lavina walk in with her *boppli* in her arms. He jumped up and crossed the room to take his *grosssohn* from her so she could shed her coat.

"He fell asleep on the way home," Lavina told him. "I'm going to take him upstairs and put him in his crib for a nap."

Amos frowned. "I was hoping to spend some time with him."

She smiled. "He won't sleep long. I promise you'll have a visit with him before he goes to bed tonight." She carefully lifted Mark from his arms and went upstairs.

"He likes Mark because he can't talk back yet," John muttered to David as he took a seat next to him.

"I heard that." Amos sat at the table again. "John, could you go down to the basement and get me two jars of green beans?"

"Happy to."

Relieved to get away from his father, John went on the mission even though the basement was cold. He grabbed the flashlight kept at the top of the stairs and walked up and down the rows of shelves until he came

24

upon the Mason jars of green beans canned during the harvest. With them tucked in one arm he went back upstairs and found Amos engaged in a conversation with Lavina.

"Here you go," he told his mother and put the jars on the kitchen counter next to the stove.

And that's when he saw green beans warming in a pot on top of it. "What do you call that?" he asked quietly, pointing to the pot with steam rising from it.

"Keeping the peace," she said, smiling. "Supper's ready!"

Feeling chastened, he took his seat at the table.

Rose Anna sang along with the congregation during the long worship service. She glanced around the room, absorbing the peace, wanting to carry it with her until the next service.

It was so *wunderbaar* to be with friends and family and celebrate their faith.

The trouble was she found her attention wandering as the minister spoke. She couldn't help remembering her childish behavior earlier in the week.

She couldn't do something like lose her temper and do something so impulsive like pelt John with snowballs the next time she saw him. What if someone had seen her the other day? But she couldn't help smiling as she remembered how it had felt to surprise him. It had been worth his retaliating when she escaped into his house. She had a feeling that his *mudder* had chastised him *gut* when he came home later.

"Something funny?" her *schweschder* Lavina whispered.

Rose Anna wiped the expression off her face. *"Nee"*

"I'm going to go check on Mark. Waneta's watching him and several *boppli* while they nap in a bedroom."

She slipped from her chair and left the room. Rose Anna found herself studying the faces of family and friends gathered in the Miller home for the service. She loved it that church service took place in a home in her community. Home was church, and church was home. Gathering to worship in the home of a member was something that was such a part of their lives she couldn't imagine anything that touched her heart as much. What had started as a way for her ancestors to avoid religious persecution had strengthened families and enriched the lives of all who came after them.

One day, if she married, she and her *mann* would host services in their home, and their *kinner* would grow up with church services in their home as she had. And she hoped that they would make their faith as much a part of their daily life — not just on alternate Sundays — as she had growing up.

A slight movement in the men's section of the room caught her attention. Peter smiled at her. She smiled back. He was such a nice man. They'd known each other all their lives and had gone to *schul* together. She might have dated him sooner if she hadn't had eyes only for John Stoltzfus. Stung by his leaving their community to live in the *Englisch* community in town, and his refusal to have anything to do with her, she'd decided to move on.

And practically no time later she'd walked into Sewn in Love delivering craft items sewn by the women in the shelter where she volunteered. She had taken one look at Peter, seen him in a different light, and they'd started seeing each other.

Her *schweschders* accused her of flirting with him to make John jealous, and maybe she'd been a little guilty of that in the beginning. It felt *gut* to have a man pay attention to her. John had enjoyed his time away from the Amish community a little too much in her opinion. When she'd confronted him and wanted to know when he was coming back, needing so desperately to know if he had any feelings at all for her, she'd found that he didn't.

Remembering how she'd felt being rejected still rankled. After all, she and John had dated for more than a year before he left home. Any *maedel* would have been hurt by his behavior. She took a deep breath to calm herself, then another. And reminded herself she should be paying attention to the church service and not thinking about her dating life.

She'd see Peter soon enough. They were having lunch after church today. He'd told her he was taking her to her favorite restaurant. She'd argued with him about it. The restaurant was pricey, and with him working two jobs, she didn't think he should be spending the money. But he'd overruled her objections so charmingly that she'd said okay.

Thinking of an afternoon spent in his company in one of her favorite places put her in a *gut* mood. She joined in another hymn and must have done so a bit too enthusiastically because Mary Elizabeth nudged her with her elbow and frowned at her.

As soon as the service was over Rose Anna stood and went to help some of the women in the kitchen. Everyone had a job to do after the service — the men converted pews to seating areas, and the women served and cleaned up after a light snack. She was hungry, but she had volunteered to help serve so she could leave right afterward. It was hard to resist the church spread. The peanut butter–marshmallow spread on a slice of bread smelled so *gut,* but she was determined to save her appetite for the restaurant. She'd eaten there four times now — twice with her *schweschders* on special occasions and twice with Peter.

Today she thought she'd order the chicken cordon bleu. The name just rolled off her tongue. It was so rich. So fancy.

Seeing how much she'd liked it Lavina had looked up the recipe and made it for her birthday supper. She'd told Rose Anna the recipe wasn't hard. Just a chicken breast rolled around a slice of Swiss cheese and ham and baked to a golden deliciousness. It was sweet of her oldest *schweschder* to prepare it, but Rose Anna liked having it at the restaurant as a special treat. Followed of course by a fancy French pastry. That was even more special than the chicken.

And she really enjoyed going out with Peter. It felt *gut* to have him smile at her the way he did every time he saw her. What *maedel* wouldn't feel her self-esteem restored by having a handsome Amish man like Peter waiting in his buggy outside to take her to lunch when she finished in the kitchen?

She could tell Peter liked simpler food and surroundings more than her favorite place. He'd teased her about her favorite chicken saying, "Fancy name for chicken stuffed with ham and cheese." But he indulged her.

Peter was tall and lanky, but he ate like he had a hollow leg. He ordered the baked chicken and ate hungrily. When he eyed her plate, she pushed it toward him so he could finish the last few bites of her meal.

"You can't still be hungry," she told him indulgently. "I saw you having a snack earlier."

He chuckled. "*Mamm* says I'm a growing boy."

They were both twenty-three, so he was hardly a boy, but it did seem as if he had grown taller over the previous summer. Was that possible? Before she could ask him his attention was drawn to the dessert cart their server wheeled beside their table.

He ordered the chocolate cake — here it was called *gateau au chocolat* — and she got her favorite, a napoleon.

They lingered over dessert, and then he

30

took her for a long drive in the country. Of course, whenever they traveled through a covered bridge they had to stop midway and do what all Amish couples did and share a quick kiss.

It was a pleasant afternoon. Peter was charming, attentive, and a wonderful man to date.

But as she stood on the porch and watched Peter drive off, she found herself looking in the direction of the farm where John lived and wondering what he was doing.

2

If there was anything Rose Anna loved more than quilting, it was teaching the twice-weekly quilting class at the women's shelter in town.

She'd started volunteering there with her *schweschders,* and now whether or not they were able to come, she continued because she enjoyed it so much.

The shelter was a big, rambling house just outside the town proper. There was no sign in front. People passing by wouldn't know it was anything but a family home. That was because the women and *kinner* inside wouldn't be safe if the husbands and boy-friends the women fled from knew where they were.

She knocked and Pearl, the woman who ran the shelter, answered the door herself and greeted her with a big smile.

The shelter should have been a sad place. Actually it had been at times when she first came with Lavina. She'd never seen women with bruised faces or *kinner* with eyes full of fear who hid behind their *mudder*'s skirts. It wasn't that abuse didn't happen in the Amish community. But it wasn't something that she had come into direct contact with like she saw here.

Gradually she'd seen the women's shelter as a place of hope. Because the place itself had changed.

The quilting classes taught by Kate Kraft, the police officer and quilting enthusiast, had made a difference.

Once by one, women climbed the stairs to the second floor of the shelter to a room Pearl had converted into a sewing room with long tables and donated sewing machines. Kate had volunteered to teach the quilting classes, and being Kate, she'd convinced others to join her.

Lavina hadn't believed she could contribute anything, but Kate showed her that she could. And then Lavina had gotten Mary Elizabeth to come.

So, of course, Rose Anna had to see why her two older *schweschders* took time off from their work and daily chores to teach quilting at a woman's shelter.

And she'd been hooked.

Kate had made a difference, and then

Leah, an Amish woman who owned the Stitches in Time shop in Paradise, had seen a way to help the women even more. The two of them had come up with the idea for Leah to open a second shop called Sewn in Hope to sell the crafts they made.

Now the room was filled with women who happily sewed their way out of despair and financed a way to build a future for themselves and their *kinner.*

Today, many of the women were sewing Thanksgiving and Christmas crafts. They were the most popular items offered at Sewn in Hope at any time of the year.

Rose Anna stopped by the table near the window where a new resident sat staring at the quilt block handed out at the beginning of the class. The woman looked small, her chin-length brown hair falling forward over her thin face. She wore a faded T-shirt with an Army slogan and camouflage pants.

"Hello, I'm Rose Anna."

The woman jerked and stared up at her with frightened green eyes. "I — hi. I'm Brooke."

"Would you like some help with your block?"

"No, I think I can handle it."

She bent over it again, and Rose Anna couldn't help wondering if she was intent on working on it or trying to hide the yellowing bruise around one eye.

And Brooke kept glancing nervously at the windows at her side as her fingers plucked at the fabric block.

"Just let me know if you need anything," Rose Anna said quietly. "And welcome to the class. I hope you enjoy it."

Brooke nodded jerkily and kept her eyes focused on the block.

Rose Anna walked a few steps away, and suddenly something bright and round whirled at her like a child's Frisbee and chucked her on the chin. She grabbed at it and frowned at the fabric circle. "Why it's a yo-yo."

"Sorry, Rose Anna."

She grinned at Jason, a little boy who'd come to the shelter last month with his *mudder* and two *schweschders*. "It's okay. It didn't hurt me."

"That's not a yo-yo. Yo-yos are toys."

"My grandmother made these," Edna told him. "I thought about making a quilt with them, but then I came up with something different." She waved a hand at her table, and Rose Anna saw that she'd made various sizes of them, stacked them from largest at the bottom to the smallest at the top. Then she'd sewed a fabric ribbon at the top to hang them. They were little trees of fabric.

"They're darling," Kate said as she stopped at the table and held one up. She smiled at Edna. "I think they'll sell well at the shop."

"They're easy to make and don't take much fabric."

"Speaking of fabric," Kate announced as she continued into the room. She held up a shopping bag in each hand.

"I thought you had court this morning."

"I did. We finished early, and Leah's shop was on the way here."

"Ha!" said Edna. "You know you find every excuse you can to stop by there."

"Guilty!" Kate laughed. "So I guess this means you don't want to see it?"

Edna jumped up. "You guessed wrong." She turned to the other women in the room. "Kate's got new fabric!"

They swarmed over, eager to check out the new fabric. Kate stepped closer to Rose Anna.

"I see we have someone new," she said quietly, jerking her head in the direction of a woman who sat at a table near the windows.

"Her name's Brooke. She didn't want to talk much," Rose Anna told her. "So I told her to let me know if she needed any help and just let her be. Sometimes it takes a while for a person to feel comfortable."

Kate nodded. "I'll put my things down and say hello."

A woman walked up to ask her a question, and after she left, Kate turned to Rose Anna.

"Where'd Brooke go? I didn't see her leave the room."

Rose Anna glanced around. "I don't know."

"Could I have this piece, Kate?" Edna asked, her eyes bright with excitement. "It'd go great in a lap quilt I want to make."

"Sure. Take whatever you want." She smiled at the women milling around the table admiring the fabric. "Malcolm said if I brought more fabric home he'd have to build an addition onto the house."

Rose Anna laughed. "My *daed*'s always saying things like that. But I noticed that he always smiles when he says it, and he keeps building more shelves in our sewing room."

There was a tug on her skirt. She glanced down and saw Lannie, a little girl who was three, clutching at her skirt.

Lannie popped her thumb out of her mouth. "Lady," she said, pointing at the table by the window. "Lady," she repeated and pulled at Rose Anna's skirt to indicate she should follow her.

She let the child lead her over to the table, wondering what she could be trying to tell her. "Lady," she said again. She pointed under the table.

So Rose Anna obliged and looked under the table and into Brooke's terrified gaze. The woman had her arms wrapped around herself and was shaking.

She knelt down. "Brooke? What's wrong? Are you feeling unwell?"

"Window," she managed. "I can't. The window."

Rose Anna turned and gestured to Lannie. "Get Kate, Lannie. Get Kate."

"So how are things going?"

John dumped the shovel of manure in the wheelbarrow and grimaced at his older brother.

"Couldn't be better. It's the weekend, and here I am helping my brother clean out a stall. As if I don't shovel enough of this on my job."

David laughed and slapped him on the shoulder. "Well, Lavina'll make it up to you. She's fixing us lunch, and you know she'll give you enough leftovers to feed you for a week. I heard she made an extra pie."

"Apple?"

"Ya."

John paused and considered. "That makes me feel a little better."

"Still eating a lot of ramen noodles?"

He laughed. "My specialty."

"Sam must be missing them now that he's married to Mary Elizabeth."

"The two of you are getting to be soft old married men," John jeered.

"Marriage is great," David told him as he set his shovel aside. "You should try it."

"Not me. Not for a long time. It's up to me to keep up the Stoltzfus reputation now." He grinned. "It's hard for one man to carry the load, but I'll try to do the job."

David frowned. "Sounds like you're enjoying your *rumschpringe* a little too much."

"No lectures, big brother." John picked up the handles of the wheelbarrow and started out of the barn. No way was he going to admit that he didn't have the time — or the money — to enjoy the single *Englisch*-guy lifestyle.

He dumped the contents of the wheelbarrow and returned to the barn.

"Seriously, you and *Daed* couldn't get along? It would have saved you from having to get your own place."

"I tried."

"Did you?" David asked quietly.

John felt his defenses leap up. "It's not me!"

"Nee?"

"No." John refused to use Pennsylvania *Dietsch* since he'd left the community. "I just seem to . . . irritate him. Nothing I do, nothing I say is right."

"Yeah, I always felt that about you."

"Gee, thanks."

"I was joking, John."

He stared off into the distance and sighed. "I know Mom was happy I was here, but I just can't handle it anymore. And if I stayed, I'd just be pressured to join the church. You know that. So I found myself a place."

"Something you can afford on your own? I thought you and Sam looked before he got married."

"A friend of my boss has a caretaker's cottage he hasn't been using. It needs some fix-up so I'll be doing that to reduce the rent."

"Well, I guess that's *gut*," David said doubtfully.

"Why wouldn't it be?"

"I'd hoped you'd work out the problems with *Daed* if you stayed here."

"Well, I couldn't." He pinched the bridge of his nose. "I think it's for the best. I appreciate you and Lavina having me here."

40

"Anytime." David laid a hand on his shoulder. "Anytime. I mean it. And I know Sam and Mary Elizabeth asked you to stay with them."

"Yeah, just what a newly married couple needs. A brother hanging around so they have no privacy."

"You're forgetting *Mamm* and *Daed* live with us, and they don't intrude on our privacy."

John shuddered. People always said things could be worse. And they could. He could be an old married man like his brothers and have his parents living with him. He was just twenty-three. He wasn't ready to be a married man anytime soon.

"Look, I'm glad you and Sam are happy being married. But I'm not ready. I'm not sure I'll ever be ready."

David paused shoveling and regarded him. "I thought you were interested in Rose Anna for a long time."

John shrugged and shoveled up more manure. "That was a long time ago. And I can safely say we're not going to get back together now."

"Now?" David straightened. "What happened?"

"You mean Dad didn't tell you?"

"Nee."

41

He stopped and propped his arm on the shovel handle. "She has quite a temper, that Rose Anna." He told David about the snowball fight.

"You didn't! Right there in the kitchen?"

"She started it!"

"*Ya,* and you didn't have any trouble finishing it, did you?"

John looked hard at him, trying to see if David was judging him. But David was grinning.

"She's sure holding a grudge," John said as he went back to shoveling.

"The Zook *maedels schur* never held back on letting us know how they felt."

"But Lavina forgave you. Mary Elizabeth forgave Sam."

"*Ya.* But we met them halfway."

"You know Rose Anna. She wants all the way — and everything her way."

"She reminds me a lot of you."

"I don't have to have everything my way."

"Nee?"

"No!"

They went back to shoveling and didn't speak. When the wheelbarrow was full, David stood with his hands resting on his shovel. "Lavina forgave me. And then she saved my life. She persuaded me to come home. It was hard at first. *Daed* was as miserable as he ever was when I first came back. He'd always been hard. But he was angry at getting the cancer."

"I know all this."

"*Ya.* But maybe you're forgetting that things changed for the better. And it's because of Lavina leading me back home, back to church, back to God."

"I'm happy for you," John said quietly. "But I don't need the same things."

"*Nee?*"

"No. And I don't need you trying to bring me back to the church. I know that's what you and everyone in the church is supposed to do to save me. I don't need saving."

He propped the shovel against a wall, pushed the wheelbarrow outside, and dumped the contents. Turning, he started back and then stopped. He took a deep breath to steady himself, then another. It was no good getting mad at David. They'd both gone to church since they were babes in their mother's arms. They were taught that if someone strayed from the church, you had to try to save them or they couldn't go to heaven.

By the time he went back inside David had spread bedding in the stalls for the horses. "I gotta go," he told him. "I promised to put in a couple hours with Peter."

"Eat first. Please. Lavina will be so disappointed if you don't."

John hesitated.

"Please."

He nodded. It was tough to say no when he brought up Lavina. "I can't stay long."

"I'll tell her you have to eat and run."

"Well, that doesn't sound very gracious."

"She knows how you are." David grinned at him and slung an arm around his shoulders.

"Think you're pretty funny, don't you?" John grabbed him in a headlock, and they tussled for a few minutes before David managed to throw him off.

"I'm not so soft, am I, *bruder*?" he asked, chuckling.

"I let you go," John said. "I'm hungry."

But just to make sure David didn't try to prove him wrong, he took off to the house.

"How are the quilting classes going at the shelter?" Mary Elizabeth asked as they sat working on their quilts in the sewing room of the Zook home later that week. "I was so sorry to miss them the past two weeks."

"We had some excitement the other day."

"Not an angry ex-husband —"

"*Nee,* nothing like that." Rose Anna knotted her thread, clipped it with scissors, and looked at her *schweschder.* "We have a new resident who came to the class and had an anxiety attack."

"Quilting class made her anxious?"

"Kate says she has PTSD as well as being abused by her ex-husband. She hadn't been out of her house in months, then she had to leave when he beat her."

She frowned. "She came to the class and couldn't handle sitting by the window. She was hiding under her table. It was so sad."

"What's PTSD?" their *mudder* asked.

"Post-Traumatic Stress Disorder. Kate said Chris Matlock had it after he served in the military. You remember, he used to be *Englisch* before he came here and married Hannah, Matthew Bontrager's *schweschder.*"

"So this woman was in the military?"

Rose Anna nodded. "Kate said she served in Afghanistan."

"Imagine, women in the military," Linda said.

"Kate was in the Army before she came here to work as a police officer," Rose Anna reminded her.

"I forgot. Seems like she's been here so long she's always been a part of Paradise." Linda got up and put another log on the fire.

"So what happened?" Mary Elizabeth sat, needle suspended over her quilt, looking at her. "Kate got under the table and talked to her awhile and got her to come out. Then they went downstairs. When Kate came back she told me that when Brooke returns we should find her a table away from the window."

"Sad."

"I think it's time for a cup of tea," their *mudder* announced a few minutes later. "I'll go put the kettle on."

"We'll be right down." Mary Elizabeth watched her leave the room then turned to Rose Anna. "So, how's Peter?"

"He's fine."

"Just 'fine'? That doesn't sound so *gut.*"

Rose Anna stared down at the quilt in her hands. "I like Peter. I really do."

"But?"

"But I don't feel the same way about him that I do about John."

"Well, from what I hear, Peter might be happy about that."

"What?"

Mary Elizabeth tried to fight back a smile. "You've got really good aim."

It took a moment, and then Rose Anna realized what her *schweschder* was talking about. She rolled her eyes. "How did you

46

find out? *Nee,* let me guess. Waneta told Lavina, and she told you."

Mary Elizabeth just grinned.

"Are you going to tell *Mamm?*"

"Do I look like a tattletale?"

"Ya." She paused then shook her head. *"Nee.* That would be our older *schweschder.* She was always telling on us."

Mary Elizabeth laughed. "Well, if I don't there's no guarantee Lavina or Waneta won't, you know."

"I don't know what got into me," Rose Anna said, remembering. "He was getting into his truck, and suddenly I just saw red. Before I knew what was happening I was making a snowball and throwing it at him."

She sighed. "And you know John. He didn't just keep going on his way. He got out of his truck and started firing snowballs back at me."

Mary Elizabeth shook her head. "The two of you have always gone head to head."

"Hey, I'm not the one who does that."

Her *schweschder* just looked at her.

"Anyway, when I ran inside his *haus,* he followed me. He actually followed me into the kitchen and rubbed snow in my face. In front of his own *mudder.*"

"Bet he got a lecture from her," Mary Elizabeth muttered.

Rose Anna grinned. "And hopefully his *dat* heard about it from her and he had something to say to John."

"Now that's just mean! You know he and his *dat* don't get along. I bet Amos burned his ears off."

"I know." She giggled. "I wish I could have been there for that."

"Shame on you." Mary Elizabeth tried to look stern. Then she giggled, too.

"Are you going to tell *Mamm*?" she asked her again.

Her *schweschder* stared at her for so long Rose Anna felt apprehensive. "If she asks me, I have to tell her," she said finally. "But I won't go telling her. That would be gossiping."

Rose Anna nodded. *"Danki."* She sighed. "But like I said, Lavina or Waneta could." She set her quilt down. "That's what I get for my behavior. It's just that John makes me so mad sometimes."

"Now he doesn't make you anything," Mary Elizabeth chided as she put her quilt down. "It's how you choose to react."

"Look out," Rose Anna told her as she narrowed her eyes. "I'm feeling like reacting right now."

Laughing, Mary Elizabeth ran for the stairs. "You'll have to catch me first."

Linda looked up as they clattered down the wooden stairs. "Well, well, there's two dainty, ladylike *maedels.*"

She turned to her *mann* sitting at the kitchen. "Do you know these hooligans, Jacob? They look like our *dochders,* but I'm not *schur.*"

He chuckled. "Sounded like heifers coming down the stairs, but *ya,* those do look like our *dochders.*"

Their *mudder* shook her head and smiled as she poured boiling water into mugs. "I wasn't *schur. Kumm,* have your tea."

Rose Anna pulled out a chair and sat primly. "Mary Elizabeth was chasing me."

"Really?"

She stared at Mary Elizabeth, then her *mudder.* She'd learned her lesson about impulsive behavior, hadn't she? *"Nee,"* she said after a long moment. "I was teasing her."

The four of them shared a break with cookies and tea — well, her *dat* was having his usual coffee. He *never* drank tea.

After a few minutes he got to his feet, saying he had to get back to his chores. He shrugged into his jacket and grabbed up another cookie before heading out the back door.

Linda went upstairs shortly afterward,

leaving Rose Anna and Mary Elizabeth alone at the table.

"You're being awfully quiet."

Rose Anna stared down into the contents of her tea cup wishing she could find an answer there. "I can't — Peter — I can't —" she lifted her hands, let them fall as she shook her head. "I tried to fall in love with Peter. I wasn't just flirting with him the way you and Lavina thought."

She shook her head. "Well, I did flirt with him, and he flirted with me. It felt *gut* to have a man want to be with me after John didn't want me."

Mary Elizabeth just sat listening.

"But I don't feel Peter is the *mann* God set aside for me."

"And who is?" Mary Elizabeth asked her cautiously.

"John."

"If he is — and I'm not saying he isn't — don't you think things would have worked out before now?"

"Sometimes it takes more time," Rose Anna said firmly. She got up and put her cup in the sink.

Then she turned to face her *schweschder*. "And sometimes God needs a little help."

3

Mary Elizabeth snorted tea out her nose. "God needs a little help?" she gasped.

Grabbing a paper napkin from the basket on the table, she dabbed at her streaming eyes. "Rose Anna, sometimes I can't believe what comes out of your mouth!"

Rose Anna sniffed. "I don't see anything wrong with saying that!"

Her *schweschder* scooted her chair away from her.

"Why'd you do that?"

"When He hurls down a bolt of lightning, I want to be out of the path."

"Very funny. God wouldn't do that."

"You're *schur* of that, are you?" Mary Elizabeth selected another cookie and bit into it. "Let me know if you're going to make outrageous statements like that so I don't choke, *allrecht*?"

Rose Anna made a face at her. "I just think since things haven't happened the way

I want, maybe I need to do something about it."

"You don't think you have? What do you call talking to John about it?"

"I must just not be going about it the right way." She tilted her head as she studied her *schweschder.* "You and Lavina both got the *mann* you wanted. You went after them. So why shouldn't I?"

Mary Elizabeth opened her mouth and then shut it. "I don't think we went after them the way you're talking about doing with John. Almost as if you're . . . hunting him down."

"I'm just talking about being determined. I'm not going to hunt him down." She got a mental picture of doing that and almost grinned. After all, she'd been pretty aggressive about pelting him with snowballs.

The back door opened letting in a blast of cold air. Lavina rushed in carrying a blanket-covered bundle in her arms. The bundle let out a cry.

"Look who's here!" Rose Anna rushed to take the *boppli* from her *schweschder.* She walked over to the stairs. *"Mamm?"*

But footsteps were already clattering down the stairs. "Did I hear Mark?" She rushed into the kitchen and held out her arms. "There you are! I've been waiting all morning to see you!"

"It's *gut* to see you, too, Lavina," Lavina said with a rueful smile.

Linda laughed as she crossed the room to her eldest and kissed her cheek. "It's *gut* to see you, too." She cradled Mark in her arms. "He's getting so big!" She turned to them. "We're going upstairs to visit. We'll see you later."

Lavina watched her *mudder* leave the room. "I'm feeling kind of unnecessary here."

"Oh, *nee,* you came at a *gut* time," Mary Elizabeth told her. "Rose Anna here was just saying you and I got the *mann* we wanted by going after them, so why shouldn't she?"

"I didn't say that!" she protested.

"You *schur* did."

"I didn't mean it quite that way."

Lavina shed her coat and hung it on a peg by the door, then walked over to the stove to pour herself a mug of hot water. She took a seat at the table opposite Rose Anna and chose a tea bag from the bowl on the table.

"So what *did* you mean?" she asked as she dunked the bag in the water.

"Just that you wanted David, and Mary Elizabeth wanted Sam, and you didn't let yourselves get discouraged when things were tough. You went after them."

" 'Went after them' sounds like they were big game or something," Mary Elizabeth pointed out.

Lavina chose a cookie and nodded. "It does."

"Want to hear something even worse?" Mary Elizabeth asked. "She said she wants John, and she figures, since she doesn't have him, God needs a little help from her."

"That's not exactly what I said."

"Close enough," Mary Elizabeth said with a smirk. "I moved my chair away from her. You know, just in case God sent a bolt of lightning down at her. You might think about it, too."

Lavina laughed. "I don't think He needs to. He's like us. He's used to Rose Anna being outrageous."

"I'm not outrageous!"

"Well, outspoken, anyway."

"Can't argue there," Mary Elizabeth muttered.

Rose Anna folded her arms over her chest. "The two of you just can't stop treating me like a *kind.*"

"Once the *boppli* of the family —" Mary Elizabeth began.

"Always the *boppli,*" Lavina finished.

The two of them giggled and looked at

her indulgently.

Rose Anna stood. "I'll just take my immature self off so the two of you don't have to bother with me," she said huffily and flounced over to the refrigerator.

"Now no sulking. We didn't mean to hurt your feelings," Lavina came over to say. She patted her shoulder. "We were just teasing you. Weren't we, Mary Elizabeth?"

"Ya."

"I looked up teasing in the dictionary once," Rose Anna said, lifting her chin. "It means to annoy in fun."

"Kumm, sit down." Lavina led Rose Anna back to the table. "I suppose it might look like I pursued David," Lavina began. "You know he and his *dat* couldn't get along, and when David had enough and moved out, I was devastated. We were supposed to get married, and here he left the community and it looked like we'd never see each other again let alone get married."

She closed her eyes and shook her head. "I never prayed so much in my life for him to return."

"If all it took was praying, John and I would be together," Rose Anna told her.

"I'm sorry." Lavina paused for a moment. "But then one day I found out that David's *dat* was seriously ill with the cancer. His *mudder* asked me to find David and tell him and ask him to come home and help with the farm. So I found David and he returned home, and eventually he and *dat* gradually made up their differences. And David returned to the church and we got married."

"And are living happily ever after," Rose Anna said and did her best not to sound resentful. She didn't envy her *schweschder* — she really didn't. She loved a happy ever after. It was why she read the romance novels she kept hidden under her pillow.

Lavina smiled. "Well, mostly. We have our differences now and then. But we work them out because we love each other. But my point is that I didn't hunt him down, but I did let him know that I loved him and wanted to have a life with him."

"Sam left home not long after David did," Mary Elizabeth said. "Even after their *dat* had been told he'd beaten the cancer, by then there was still such tension between Amos and Sam. You know that Sam was just as resistant to returning home and to our church as David."

She took a deep breath and looked at Rose Anna. "All I'm trying to say is that like Lavina, I couldn't stop loving Sam, so I let him know and didn't give up on us. But I didn't set out to hunt or entrap him."

"Well, that's all I'm saying I'm going to do," Rose Anna said stubbornly.

"Allrecht," Mary Elizabeth said, but she exchanged a doubtful look with Lavina.

Rose Anna was glad when they went upstairs a few minutes later. It gave her some quiet time to come up with a plan.

Her two *schweschders* might be acting like their relationships had just happened, but clearly that wasn't working for her and John. She needed a plan, a way to get what she wanted.

Lavina and Mary Elizabeth didn't just tease her for being the *boppli* of the family. They also teased her for getting what she wanted — whether it was to be treated to a fancy lunch as she'd gotten Mary Elizabeth to do not so long ago. And she was *gut* at finding a way to get out of chores she didn't want to do as well.

She hoped they were right this time about her getting what she wanted.

John couldn't believe it, but he found himself looking out for sneak snowball attacks for the next several days.

Talk about silly.

But he wasn't letting Rose Anna catch him unawares like that again. He climbed into his truck and drove home. Despite telling his brother he was enjoying his time as a bachelor, tonight — just like many other nights — he was going home to a solitary supper of some version of ramen noodles and some time renovating his current living space.

The small caretaker's cottage was a step down from the apartment he'd rented with Sam. The walls hadn't been painted in years, there was only a sagging single bed in the one bedroom and an assortment of lawn furniture in the living room.

And he'd found evidence of mice in the cabinet beneath the kitchen sink.

But it was cheap, and he didn't need much. He had talked the owner into quite a price break by offering to do painting and repair.

The trouble was it meant adding more work onto a busy day making deliveries in his truck for one business and doing part-time construction jobs he picked up.

He knew some local Amish found jobs in tourism and such, but he preferred what he was doing for now.

When things were tough back home, his *mamm* had always said God would provide.

Sometimes John felt as if God had forgotten him.

He shook off the thought. No sense thinking about that now. And he sure didn't want another *dat* — the important one — angry at him.

So he heated some leftovers Lavina had sent home with him the other day and tried not to think about how it must feel to be the settled husband he'd joked with David that he didn't want to be.

He ate the meal on a metal tray and watched the small television set. Both had been thrift store finds.

And then he spent the next two hours repairing the kitchen cabinets. Finally, exhausted, he took a shower, and when the water ran cold after just a few minutes, he wondered if he'd be talking to the owner about replacing the water heater soon.

The bed, even lumpy as it was, felt good to his tired body.

As he began to drift off, he found himself wondering what Rose Anna was doing right now.

Was it his imagination that when she thought he wasn't looking at her the last time he'd seen her that she'd looked . . . lonely?

No, that had to be his imagination. He'd heard through the Amish grapevine that she was seeing Peter.

There was an expression about making

59

your bed and lying in it. Well, he'd done that. He'd left his community, left the woman he loved, and now here he was lying in this lumpy bed all by himself.

Suddenly he was wide awake.

Rose Anna caught her attention wandering several times during church service.

This had to stop, she told herself.

The plan to win John Stoltzfus kept intruding. The plan. She almost giggled with joy at the thought and just caught herself. Oh, she wouldn't ever dare to call it that out loud. She'd written it in her journal and tucked it under a loose floorboard in her closet in her bedroom. She didn't dare tuck the journal under her pillow. It wasn't that her *schweschders* would go looking for it. Journals were sacred after all. No one snooped. But this plan was just too private, too daring, to risk anyone seeing it.

Her *schweschders* loved to tease her about being the *boppli* of the family, tease her about being immature, tease her about just about everything. They'd had quite a time laughing at her about pursuing John that day not so long ago.

Wasn't there a saying about anything worth having was worth working for?

The woman sitting on the bench in front

of her moved restlessly. Then she got up. Rose Anna had been absorbed in her thoughts and hadn't noticed who had sat there.

Now she saw that it was Jenny Bontrager. Jenny rose and slipped from the room, moving with a limp so slight only those who knew her detected it. Rose Anna knew that every so often sitting on the hard bench for three hours was too much for Jenny, and she'd leave the room to walk around and ease her back. As she walked past Rose Anna, Jenny gave her a smile that seemed strained at the edges.

So Rose Anna found herself getting up and following Jenny out of the room.

"Are you *allrecht*?" she asked her when she caught up with her near the front door.

Jenny turned, and Rose Anna saw how pale she looked. Her face was pale, her gray eyes shadowed as though she hadn't been sleeping well. Rose Anna knew Jenny was in her forties, but today she moved as if she was older, not her bright, energetic self.

"I'm fine," she said quickly. "Benches and my back have never been close friends. When I woke up this morning, it was aching. I should have taken something for the pain before I left the house."

"Do you want me to get Matthew?"

61

"No, the service is almost over."

"I can ask *Mamm* if she has any aspirin or ibuprofen."

"I can wait. Moving around helps. I thought I'd get my bonnet and coat and walk around the porch a bit."

"I'll join you. If you don't mind the company."

"I'd love it."

They walked into the front room, got their things, then stepped outside.

"How are the quilting classes going at the shelter?" Jenny asked.

"Very well. We'd love to have you join us again someday soon."

"I could come next week. I'm not the quilter you and your *schweschders* are, but I enjoy helping where I can."

"The women enjoy having visitors since they can't get out much." The memory of what had happened in the last class came to her. She hesitated.

"What is it?"

"I — well, there's this new resident. She reminded me of you when you first came here to Paradise. After you were hurt in the car bombing overseas."

"She was injured?"

"Well, I can't see any physical injuries . . ." Rose Anna trailed off, frowning. "Kate said she has something called PTSD."

Jenny nodded. "Post-Traumatic Stress Disorder. I see."

"Sitting next to the window scared her. I found her huddled under the table, shaking and crying. Kate got under there with her and talked to her."

Then she pressed her fingers against her lips and shook her head. "Oh, if you come to the class, you won't say anything to the woman? I wouldn't want her to be embarrassed."

"No, I won't. Promise." Jenny paced the porch, and her steps seemed to get easier. "You know, if Kate talked to her she'll know what to do to get her the help she needs."

"*Ya,* when *Mamm* and I talked about it she said Kate's been here so long we forget she was in the military before she became a police officer. And her *mann* was in the military, too."

She glanced at Jenny. "I can't imagine going into a war zone voluntarily."

"It took me a long time to adjust when I came here," Jenny said. "I felt guilty being back home and safe when I knew the children were still there living with fear and hunger and their parents and siblings were being killed around them."

Rose Anna didn't know what to say. It was

63

so far outside her experience, this talk of war and of innocent *kinner* being hurt.

They sat, silent for a long moment, hearing the sounds of a hymn being sung inside the house.

"May I ask you something?" Rose Anna broke the silence between them. "Not about war. About, well, about . . . well, about men."

Jenny laughed. "I'm not much of an expert on them."

"But you've been married a long time."

"True. But I'm not sure that even makes me an expert on one man." She paused. "I might have been married to him for even longer if things had worked out years before," Jenny mused, looking thoughtful.

"Really?"

She nodded. "You know my *daed* decided not to join the church and left the community. But he let me visit my *grossmudder* every summer. I fell in love with the boy next door, but I went back home and went to college, and the years passed. It just didn't work out for us at the time."

She sat in one of the rocking chairs and stared out at the fields surrounding the house. "And then I got hurt. While I was lying in the hospital, my *grossmudder* sent me a quilt with a note. It said to come home and heal. I did, and there was Matthew, and I was attracted to him all over again. I thought at first that it wasn't fair, he was married. But he was a widower. I think I fell in love with his *kinner* before I fell in love with him again."

Rose Anna sighed. The story touched her romantic heart. Then she realized Jenny was watching her with a faint smile on her lips. "Is there a reason you're asking about men?"

"I'm trying to understand them."

Jenny laughed. "One in particular is my guess."

She grinned. *"Ya."*

"So what is it that's troubling you?"

It was tough to know what to ask. She felt she could trust Jenny, but she didn't want to say too much.

"I just . . . how do you know if someone's the *mann* God set aside for you?"

"I haven't thought about that for a long time." She smiled and fell silent. "When I first knew Matthew I was convinced he was the one for me. Things didn't work out. We went our separate ways — I went off to college. Matthew stayed here, married, had *kinner.* We didn't see each other for years."

She shifted in her chair. "Then I got hurt and came here to recuperate. I could barely

65

walk, was suffering from depression, and didn't know where I was going with my life. And there was Matthew still next door. This time with three adorable children. And he was a widower. This time things worked out, as you know."

Rose Anna absorbed what she'd said. "So what you're saying is it came down to timing."

Jenny smiled slowly and nodded. "That's the perfect way to put it. God's timing."

They went back inside, and Rose Anna thought about what Jenny had said.

Timing. Just how much time was she supposed to give John? It felt like she'd been waiting for him for forever.

4

"Thanks for the ride," Rose Anna told Kate as she got into her car. "*Mamm* needed the buggy today."

"It's no problem," Kate said cheerfully as she pulled out onto the road and headed toward town. "I wanted to talk to you about Brooke."

"Is she okay? I haven't seen her for weeks. Is she ever coming back to the quilting class?"

"Yes and yes." Kate glanced at her then back at the road. "I've stopped by to talk to her a couple of times, and a friend from a counseling center did as well. When she does come back we should put her at a table in the back of the room, away from the windows. Pearl said she has an additional table she can set up in the room."

She paused. "The thing we have to do is help her feel comfortable when she comes back. She's embarrassed she had an anxiety attack so bad she climbed under the table that day."

"I've never experienced what she has, but anyone can have an anxiety attack. I remember someone I knew had one years ago. She was afraid of going to the hospital for an operation."

"I wouldn't wish one on my worst enemy."

Rose Anna remembered her conversation with Jenny on Sunday and told Kate that she might stop by for a class sometime soon.

"That would be nice. They enjoyed her last time she came. It can get to be isolating at the shelter. They can't come and go as they'd like since so many of them are hiding from their husbands or boyfriends until we can put the abusers in jail."

She shivered. "I can't imagine living like that." Then she looked at Kate. "I'm not saying we don't have abusers in my community. That would be lying. You and I know it's not an *Englisch* problem." She thought about how Lavina had told her Amos, John's *dat,* had talked to his *fraa* when she visited their house one day. A man didn't need to raise his fists to hurt a woman. Cruel words were almost as bad. Thank God Amos had changed, had learned before it was too late.

Now if he would only repair the rift

between himself and John, his youngest *sohn.*

She sighed.

"You okay?"

Rose Anna nodded. "I'm fine. I was just thinking about something."

"I've been told I listen well."

She tilted her head and studied Kate. "I know you do." She bit her lip.

"It's an open-ended offer. Any time you want to talk about anything just let me know."

"You're a good person, Kate Kraft."

"You, too." She pulled into the driveway of the shelter and turned off the ignition. "If you're not ready to talk about whatever made you sigh so sadly, let's go have some fun quilting."

Relieved, Rose Anna nodded. Funny how someone so different from her had become such a good friend, one who understood her so well. "Let's go."

They went inside, climbed the stairs to the quilting classroom, and found it full of women who were already sewing and chatting happily.

And sitting at the table at the very back of the room, away from the windows, sat Brooke staring very seriously at a quilting block in front of her.

"Go help her," Kate suggested.

"But wouldn't you be better?" Rose Anna asked. "I —"

"Go. She needs to start feeling normal. Show her how to quilt. We know what happens when women come to this class and start sewing."

So Rose Anna walked over to Brooke. She smiled. "Hi. I'm glad you came back to class. Would you like some help with that block? It's one of my favorites."

"I could use all the help I can get. I don't have any experience sewing. Well, other than sewing up a gash in my leg one day when the medics had bigger injuries to take care of."

She grinned self-deprecatingly. "Guess I should thank that home economics class they forced me to take in high school. I'll show you my stitches someday."

Rose Anna stared at her as she slid into the seat next to Brooke. "You really did your own stitches? I was the biggest baby you ever saw when I had to have stitches at the emergency room. I can't imagine putting a needle in my skin. Or going without that shot they gave me before they did the stitches."

She glanced at Kate helping a student at the front of the room. "You and Kate have lived such different lives than me. Mine has been so . . . boring compared to yours."

"I'll take boring," Brooke said fervently. "Boring sounds pretty good to me right now."

Rose Anna nodded. "Let me show you how to piece this block. Sewing is very soothing once you get the method. I think you'll like it. The class has been very popular here at the shelter. Especially since Leah started a shop in town to sell what the women create."

Brooke watched her pin the block. "I doubt I'm going to get good enough to sell anything."

She glanced around and frowned at the windows. Rose Anna saw her hands shake. "I hope I won't have to stay here long. Home became a prison before I had to leave it. I don't want to feel I have to stay here a minute longer than I have to. I don't want this place to become another prison."

Rose Anna's fingers faltered on the straight pins she was using to hold two pieces of material together. Home had become a prison? How sad. And sadder still to have to be here at the shelter. Pearl made it as safe and pleasant, homelike, as she could, but it still was a hiding place no matter how homey she'd made it.

Home should be a place to feel safe and happy and loved. She knew she'd been lucky to have a good home with her family all her life. She wondered if she had ever told her parents how much she appreciated what they'd given her.

Brooke slid the material under the foot of the sewing machine and then fumbled looking for the lever to set the foot down. Rose Anna showed her. These machines were electric, different from the treadle ones they had at her home, but some things were the same.

She sewed a seam and examined it. "Oh, it's so crooked."

"I think it's a pretty good effort for a first time. But if you're not happy with it, the seam ripper here is a great tool to rip the seam out and do it again."

She showed Brooke how to use it and nodded approvingly when she sewed the seam again.

"That's nice and straight," Rose Anna told her. "Good job."

Brooke smiled briefly but avoided her eyes. "Thanks."

"Sometimes I wish there was a tool to do that with bad decisions." Rose Anna frowned. Brooke looked pale, and a fine sheen of perspiration had covered her face.

"Are you feeling all right?"

"Excuse me. I have to go." She bolted from the room.

"Problem?" Kate asked quietly.

She turned. "I thought she was doing really well, and then she said she needed to go and ran out of here."

"I'll go check on her."

Rose Anna roamed the room greeting other women and helping with projects. When Kate returned fifteen minutes later she came alone.

"She got a little overwhelmed," Kate explained quietly. "She just needs to take things slowly for a while. I told her to come back today if she wants, and if not, we'll look forward to seeing her later this week or next week." She smiled at Rose Anna. "I think she will. She told me to thank you. She said she enjoyed talking to you."

"I get to meet such interesting people in the class," Rose Anna mused. "I'm glad you asked Lavina to help you or none of us sisters would have done something like this. *Mamm* told me that there's not as much contact with those outside our community in other places. I suppose it's because we have more tourism and less farming here so we see more of each other."

"It's a unique place for sure," Kate said.

"I'm glad I settled here after I separated from the Army."

The hours passed quickly, and before she knew it, the women were packing up their sewing in their project boxes, stacking them on the shelves and chatting about what was on the lunch menu on their way out of the room.

"If you have time I thought we could stop for a few minutes at Sewn in Hope on the way home, drop some crafts off."

"Sure. And remember what you said earlier? That I should just let you know when I was ready to talk? I have a question for you."

Kate picked up a box from a nearby table. "I'm all ears."

John walked into the kitchen and checked out the contents of the refrigerator.

Nothing new had appeared.

Now that he lived alone he couldn't expect anything new unless he shopped for it. When he and Sam shared an apartment, Sam would sometimes bring home groceries or — even better — something that Mary Elizabeth cooked.

His stomach growled, and he found himself envying the supper his two brothers were undoubtedly eating right now. Both of them had married women who not only possessed sweet personalities but were wonderful Amish cooks. He enjoyed helping both his brothers with their farms because their wives always insisted on him staying for supper after a workday and then sent him home with a bag full of leftovers.

When his stomach growled again at the reminder of the last time he'd enjoyed a second-day feast, he told himself having regular — delicious — home-cooked meals was *not* a good reason to get married.

Actually he couldn't think of any reason to get married. His brothers had good marriages, but the memory of his parents' relationship was still too vivid for him to contemplate. An Amish marriage was forever. He didn't want to chance getting into one and not being able to get out.

He got a paper plate and plastic fork from the cupboard, found a package of ramen noodles. A check of the freezer revealed some hamburger patties from Sam's last barbecue. All he had to do was defrost them in the microwave, then add some bottled spaghetti sauce and serve it over ramen noodles. A poor man's spaghetti dinner he decided as he sprinkled parmesan cheese on top and settled in front of the television set to eat.

When he'd lived with Sam after they'd moved out of their family home, Sam had been a rather overbearing older brother. Sam nagged him about chores, about keeping the place clean, about where was his half of the rent. He'd criticized his going out with friends to have a couple of beers, to go to a party.

But now as he settled in front of the television for a solitary supper, he found himself missing Sam. He shook his head. Sam would have given him a hard time over what he'd cooked. He'd shaken his head over John's cooking, teased him about his endless variations of ramen noodle dishes.

John plunged his fork into the noodles in front of him. Hey, they were quick and they were cheap. Two important considerations for a bachelor cook.

And since he was living alone, it was even more important to watch the pennies. He finished his supper, tried not to think of what his brothers were having. They were undoubtedly eating much better tonight. He didn't want to think about what they were having for dessert.

Well, he'd never envied anyone, and he wasn't going to start now. If he was going to remain single he was going to have to become a better cook. Maybe he'd ask his

76

friend Joseph Miller for a recipe. He'd become a good cook after living alone for a long time. Many a single Amish woman had brought by meals and baked goods. His mother and sisters had done the same.

Until Joseph had, as he put it, "opened my mouth and put my big foot in it" by saying "how hard could cooking be?" to one of his sisters. She had handed him a salt shaker and invited him to eat his words. Joseph had almost burned his kitchen down the first time he cooked. Now Joseph was often asked for his recipe for macaroni and cheese when the community had a fundraiser potluck supper.

John carried his plate and fork into the kitchen, tossed them into the trash, and popped the top on a can of soft drink. Now it was time to do some work on the place before he showered and went to bed.

Some exciting evening. In the first six months or so after he left the Amish community with Sam, he'd partied hard and enjoyed being out from under the stern eye of his father. He'd had to scramble to find work, of course. His father had used his sons as farm labor and only gave them a small allowance. It hadn't been much preparation for working in the *Englisch* world.

His name was John, but he'd become a

77

Jack-of-all-trades doing all manner of work. He hadn't much liked farming, but he was good with his hands and could fix or build just about anything. Since he'd been driving his brother's hand-me-down truck, he'd even become pretty good at car and truck repair as well. Peter had hired him recently in his now-thriving construction business. Wages weren't much just yet, but as business got better he knew Peter would be able to pay better.

John looked around at the small place he rented and debated what to work on for a few hours. He'd painted the living room and dining room the night before so tonight he decided to cut and nail trim and baseboards. The place was already looking better than it had when he moved in. He and Sam had collected a few items of furniture from thrift stores and discards sitting out for the trash collector. Sam hadn't needed them for his farm. He'd made some furniture for the farm he shared with Mary Elizabeth. So John had inherited a sofa and a battered recliner recently and gotten rid of the lawn furniture he'd used for a time. That was enough for now.

At eleven he quit, swept up sawdust, and hit the shower. He was sore when he went to bed, but it felt good to have accomplished so much in one day.

He might not have much, but he had a skill, a strong body, and a determination to make his own way.

He figured he had a lot after all.

"So what's your question?" Kate asked as she started her car and backed out of the shelter drive later that afternoon.

"How do you get a man to do what you want?"

"I — well," Kate said, and she paused. "I have to think about that for a minute."

Rose Anna twirled the ends of one of the strings to her *kapp* around her finger. "You don't have to answer. I guess it's a silly question."

"I can use a silly question. I had a rough night at work." She stopped at a red light and tapped her fingers on the steering wheel. "I suppose it depends on what you want them to do. But basically, men do what you want if they think it's the right thing to do. If they care about you." She glanced over at Rose Anna. "And, sad to say, if it's what they want to do."

"If it's what they want to do," Rose Anna repeated slowly. "So maybe if you convince them they *want* to do something they will."

Kate pulled into the parking lot behind

79

the Sewn in Hope shop, shut off the car, and turned to her. "Well, yes. You just have to be careful not to be manipulative about it. That would be wrong."

Rose Anna winced inwardly. Mary Elizabeth had once said that she always got what she wanted, and Rose Anna had to admit that she worked hard to get her way when she wanted something.

Or someone. First John. Then Peter. Now John again.

But if you were doing things with the best of intentions it was *allrecht,* right? She loved John, and she just wanted them to be together. She wanted him to come back to her. To come back to his life in their community. To come back to his faith, his church.

She wanted him home.

"Most couples find a way to work together, don't you think?" Kate was saying.

"Yes, if they *get* to be a couple," Rose Anna muttered.

"Ah, so that's the problem. I always thought it was an advantage that the Amish grow up in a community and know each other for years before they date and get married. We don't usually get to know each other for that length of time in my community. Malcolm and I knew each other for

80

about a year before we got married, and that was a long time compared to some of my friends."

She checked her rearview mirror and ran a hand through her short swing of brown hair. "I know people are still wondering how we got together — I mean, who'd have figured, the cop and the con — but it works for us. We have two beautiful kids and a mortgage, and we just celebrated our anniversary last week. We're doing just fine."

Rose Anna knew the story. Kate had been a police officer when Malcolm Kraft came to Paradise looking for Chris Matlock, a former buddy of his in the military. But he wasn't looking to renew their friendship. Chris had testified against him for a crime he'd committed, and Malcolm was out for vengeance.

He'd followed Chris to Paradise where Chris was visiting Jenny Bontrager. Chris and Jenny had met briefly when they'd both been recuperating from injuries suffered overseas and kept in touch. Her stories of her life as a convert to the Amish church and how much she loved Paradise had inspired Chris to come here. Malcolm confronted Chris and, in the confusion of it all, accidentally shot Jenny's sister-in-law, Hannah. Kate had been the first officer on

81

the scene. Hannah had forgiven Malcolm and asked Kate to help make sure he got probation and the rehabilitation and counseling he needed instead of prison. One thing had led to another. Two opposites — a con and a cop — had married and, as Kate said, it was working very well indeed.

Rose Anna and John were such a different story, she thought as she helped Kate carry boxes of crafts to the store.

She and John had known each other all their lives. They'd gone to *schul* together, played and learned and fought and worshipped together. They'd been in and out of each other's homes for years and now shared families as well since their siblings had married each other.

She'd thought John might decide to stay in the Amish community when he'd moved back with his *bruder* Sam, but after Sam married her *schweschder* Mary Elizabeth, and they bought their own farm, that hope was dashed. John had refused their offer to stay with them and moved back to town, and now Rose Anna felt she was back to square one. An Amish *maedel* didn't visit a single man's home without a chaperone, so the only way she could see him was if he visited their mutual relatives.

And she knew with the way he didn't get

along with his *dat* that visits to Lavina and David's *haus* would be infrequent.

Carrie smiled at them as she bagged a purchase for a customer, handed it to her, and told her to come again.

"How nice to see you two," she said, coming out from behind the counter. "New stock! Can't wait to see what you have for us."

The three of them pulled crafts from the boxes, and Carrie got excited about the Christmas tree ornaments made from yo-yo circles. Carrie set aside the pricing guide that was included in the box and said she'd be putting things out that afternoon.

"So did you hear? I'm working full-time here," Carrie told them, bubbling with excitement. "Who'd have thought things would turn around this much since I had to live at the shelter?"

"You're one of their success stories," Kate told her.

"Thanks to you and Pearl. Listen, I'll go tell Leah you're here."

"Don't bother," Kate said quickly. "I haven't been in for two weeks, so I want to look at the new fabric."

As they walked through the entranceway that connected the shop to Stitches in Time, Rose Anna heard Kate sniff. She glanced at her. "Are you okay?"

"Fine. It's just allergies."

But Rose Anna watched her surreptitiously wipe away a tear.

"It makes you feel good, doesn't it?"

She nodded, took a deep breath as they walked down aisles of fabric bolts. "Makes up for all the times you don't make a difference."

It must be like being a *mudder,* Rose Anna thought as she stopped at a table to look at a particularly pretty blue fabric. She remembered how her *schweschder* Mary Elizabeth had bought yards of a similar color and silky texture for her wedding dress and kept it in her closet for a long time when Sam had left her not long before she'd expected to get married. Rose Anna and their *mudder* had been so happy to help her sew it when Mary Elizabeth and Sam had finally gotten married.

She stroked the fabric and thought about buying it for a wedding dress. As it got closer to harvest, other Amish *maedels* would be buying fabric for their weddings and it would get scarce. Many favored blue for their wedding day.

"That would be pretty on you. Are you going to make yourself a new dress?"

Rose Anna glanced up and felt herself

blushing as Leah came to stand next to her. "Oh, hi."

She glanced down at the fabric. Maybe it was early to buy it for a wedding dress, but suddenly she wanted it. She and John would be married. She was convinced of it.

"Why not?"

Leah picked up the bolt and carried it over to the cutting table. Rose Anna gave her the order for the number of yards she'd need and watched her begin cutting the dress length.

She'd take it home and tuck it away on the top shelf of her closet for her wedding day.

Kate brought two bolts over for Leah to cut. "I'm going to have to find a way to sneak this into the house," she told Rose Anna as Leah unfolded the fabric on the table and cut it. "Malcolm bet me I can't go without buying fabric for a month, and there's still another week to go. I'm hoping he's not home yet."

So both of them would be keeping secrets, she thought. There was no way she could show the fabric she'd bought — or at least she wouldn't want to say she bought it for her wedding. She didn't care to have her *schweschders* make comments about that.

"Well, that was a nice end to the morning," Kate said as they walked out to the car. She put her package in the trunk before she got into the driver's seat. "Do you have time for lunch? It'll be my treat."

"I'd love to have lunch, but there's no need to treat me. When Leah rang up my fabric, she gave me more orders for quilts. I'd say I — well, my *mudder* and *schwesch-ders* — had a very nice ending to the morning."

"I insist. I'm in such a good mood. I was so happy to see Brooke in the class even for a short time. It's progress."

Rose Anna nodded, and as they left town she found herself wondering when she would see progress on her own goal.

It was time to take the next step.

5

"You're being quiet today."

Rose Anna glanced up from her quilt and looked at Mary Elizabeth. She shrugged. "Not much to say."

Mary Elizabeth looked at Lavina. "Maybe we should check her for fever. She's never quiet."

She rolled her eyes. "Don't start."

"Seriously, why *are* you so quiet today?" Lavina asked as she stitched on her quilt.

"Just concentrating on my work. Takes concentration to do tiny stitches." She smiled inwardly as she wondered what they'd say if they knew she had been thinking of her plan to win John's heart.

"All Mary Elizabeth is saying is that you love to talk, and today you've barely said a word."

"Just letting you two have a chance to say something," she said, giving them a big smile.

"Very funny," Lavina said. She narrowed her eyes. "Are you coming to our house on Saturday to help me?"

"Schur."

"Mary Elizabeth, you're coming too, right?"

"Ya."

"I'd come, but Waneta and I are helping Mary Troyer with some chores," Linda said. She stood and set her quilt aside. "I'm going to go give the soup a stir. We're having split pea with ham for lunch."

"That'll be *gut* today," Mary Elizabeth said as she glanced at the window. It was a gray, rainy day.

"Rose Anna?"

She looked up as Lavina said her name.

"John will be there on Saturday."

"Really? I thought he was too busy working with Peter on Saturdays."

"Well, not this weekend. So you'd have a chance to see him."

"Allrecht." She resumed sewing.

"I thought you'd be glad to hear it."

Rose Anna shrugged. What could she say? She wasn't going to let herself be teased again about him.

"Kate and I took some crafts to Sewn in Hope after the class yesterday. You should see the shop now. It's doing so well."

"Changing the subject?"

"Just thought you'd be interested."

"If she doesn't want to talk about it, don't fuss at her," Mary Elizabeth said.

Linda walked into the room. "Who's fussing?" she asked as she took her seat and picked up her quilt. She glanced at each of them.

Lavina blushed. "No one."

"I was just saying that Kate and I took some crafts in to the Sewn in Hope shop yesterday," Rose Anna said quickly to ease the awkwardness.

"I'm so glad it's doing well. We should stop in there the next time we go to town. *Danki* for stopping in and seeing Leah. We have a lot of work lined up this month with the new orders you brought from her," their *mudder* said, redirecting them as she often did.

Were mudders *always the peacemakers of the family?* Rose Anna wondered.

She listened as their *mudder* guided the discussion to how Mark was doing.

Lavina was off and running.

An hour later, when Lavina ran down, Linda glanced at the clock. "Anyone ready for a break? Mary Elizabeth, I made your favorite ginger cookies last night."

"I'll go put the teakettle on," she said,

jumping up. "C'mon, Lavina, you know you love them, too."

Linda watched them with a fond smile as they left the room, then she turned to Rose Anna. "You *are* being quiet today, *kind.* Is something troubling you?"

Rose Anna shook her head and continued sewing. "*Danki,* I'm fine."

"Do you want me to speak to your *schweschders*?"

She looked up. "About what?"

"About the way they tease you."

She gave a short laugh. "I guess it's the price of being the baby of the family."

"Well, the three of you are older. I'd think they could stop now."

Rose Anna smiled. "They're not trying to hurt me."

"*Nee.* But I think they are. You have a tender heart."

Surprised, Rose Anna stared at her.

"*Ya,* a tender, easily hurt heart." She studied her. "You know, maybe I'm not the one who should speak to your *schweschders.* Maybe you should think about telling them how they hurt you when they tease. Even if you think they don't mean to hurt you."

She sighed. "I will. Think about it, I mean."

Linda nodded, set aside her quilt, and stood. "We haven't seen Peter around lately."

She held out her hand and clasped Rose Anna's, and they walked down the stairs to the kitchen together.

"Peter's been busy with his business. John — John Stoltzfus — has been helping him."

"I can't remember the last time I saw John. How is he doing?"

Rose Anna shrugged. "I haven't seen him in some time."

"Hope he didn't catch a cold. I heard he met a snowball recently."

She nearly missed a step. "A snowball?"

"*Ya*. But then again, maybe I should worry about you catching a cold instead."

"You know," Rose Anna said finally.

"*Mudders* always know," she said, grinning at her.

The Stoltzfus farmhouse smelled amazing the minute he walked into it on Saturday.

Then again, when didn't it? Something always seemed to be cooking or baking in an Amish home. John made his way to the kitchen, pulling off his jacket as he went and tossing it on a chair in the living room.

He told himself he should have expected to see Rose Anna at her sister's house when he walked into the kitchen. After all, it was supposed to be a family workday, and they *were* part of the same family through marriage.

He stopped in his tracks when he saw her sitting at the table and held up his hands.

She glanced up at him. "What?"

"Just wondering if I need a shield." His gaze focused on the bowl in front of her.

"They're boiled potatoes," she said dryly. "I don't think you need to be worried." She held one up and slid the peel off to demonstrate that it had been cooked.

"Okay," he said slowly. A cooked potato couldn't hurt much, he guessed. "Where is everyone?"

"The men are out in the barn. Lavina and Mary Elizabeth are upstairs doing the tough work. Mark is teething and screaming his head off."

He grinned. "Is that why you're down here?"

"Absolutely. Besides, someone has to fix the food." She jerked her head in the direction of the stove. "I just made coffee if you want some."

He walked over to the stove and poured himself a cup while keeping a wary eye on her. After all, a knife lay on the table within reach.

"Since when do you peel potatoes *after* you cook them?"

"You boil them, let them cool, then the peel slips right off them," she said, demonstrating.

He sat at the table and watched her make quick work of the potatoes in the bowl. Then she used a metal masher to mash them up. She pulled a casserole dish over, and he saw that it had a hamburger mixture in it. After dumping the mashed potatoes on top of it, she spread it like frosting on a cake.

"Shepherd's pie?"

She nodded, got up and slid it into the oven, and set the timer. "It'll be a nice hot supper on such a cold day." She pulled a bowl of Granny Smith apples toward her and began peeling them. "Apple crisp."

"One of my favorites."

She nodded.

"So no snowballs?"

"No snowballs. We might manage some ice cream with the crisp if you want."

"Truce?"

She met his steady gaze. "Truce."

He sipped his coffee and watched her. "So what was it all about anyway?"

She lifted her gaze. "The snowballs?"

"Yeah."

"Maybe I was just having fun."

"You sure?"

Rose Anna nodded. "Just having a little fun at your expense."

"No ulterior motives?"

"Like what?"

"I figured you didn't want me moving back to town."

She rose to check on the shepherd's pie. It seemed to him that she took more time than it usually did to perform the task.

Then she turned. "Why should it matter if you move back to town? You've made it clear that you don't want to stay in the Amish community," she said quietly. "And that you don't want a relationship with me anymore."

The back door opened, and David entered letting in a gust of cold air. He shut the door, turned, and took in the scene. "Did I come in at a bad time?" he asked, sensing the tension.

John shrugged. "It's your house," he said mildly.

"Everything's fine," Rose Anna told David when he looked at her.

David shed his jacket, hung it on a peg by the door, and strode over to the stove to pour a cup of coffee. He leaned against the counter as he took his first sip and studied

John. "So, loafing while the real men work, eh?"

John took a last gulp of coffee. "Just having a cup before I join you."

"Uh-huh. Got a late start on your morning, huh? Partied too hard last night?"

John glanced at Rose Anna, but she acted like she wasn't listening. "Hardly. I had to give Peter a couple of hours before I came here."

"I thought you had today off."

"He had an emergency he needed help with."

"Oh. Sorry."

John just shrugged. He'd been the one who'd let others think he was enjoying his time in town, so he could hardly blame David for coming to such a conclusion.

David tried and failed to hold back a huge yawn. "Where's Lavina?"

"Upstairs trying to get your *sohn* down for a nap," Rose Anna told him. "Looks like you could use one, too."

"He kept us up most of the night. Just started sleeping through the night and now he's decided to get in teeth." He shook his head. "Don't know how our parents lived through having the three of us so close together."

"Why didn't Sam and Amos come in for

coffee?"

"They were busy going over Sam's plans for his farm." He pulled on his jacket. "Guess I'd better get back out there. You know how *Daed* is — he's the only one who knows what should be planted on a farm."

"Wait a minute." Rose Anna went to the cupboard, pulled out a Thermos, and filled it. She put it into a tote bag and added a couple of mugs. Then she took a plastic bag to the cookie jar, tossed in a handful of snickerdoodles, and handed it to David.

She hadn't offered him any cookies, John thought. "I'll be out in a minute," he told David.

"*Allrecht.*" David turned to Rose Anna. "Whatever you're making for lunch smells *wunderbaar.*"

"*Danki.* It's shepherd's pie. We'll eat in forty-five minutes."

John waited until his brother left, then he looked at Rose Anna. "So you're not mad at me and I don't have to worry about a sneak snowball attack any time in the future?"

Rose Anna turned to look at him. "*Nee,* you don't have to worry about that."

She smiled at him, but for some reason he didn't feel reassured.

■ ■ ■ ■

Rose Anna tucked herself into bed early that night. It had been fun helping Lavina paint two second-story bedrooms that day and help soothe her nephew cranky from teething. But staying calm and collected when she was around John had taken a toll.

She didn't dare let him know that she had a plan and she was interested in him. She figured he'd run fast back to town if he knew. So she'd been serene and friendly but not too friendly as she talked to him, as she sat across the table from him and ate and passed him food and especially when she ever-so-casually handed him the tote bag filled with leftovers.

He didn't suspect anything.

But she'd noticed her shoulder muscles were knotted when she drove the buggy home, and she had a slight headache.

She pulled her journal out from her hiding place and wrote about how things had gone that day.

She'd known he was going to be at Lavina and David's house, of course, and so she'd worn her prettiest dress — the forest green one that gave her face a nice, rosy glow. It hadn't been an accident that she'd made one of his favorite desserts, either. She'd brought apples from home just in case Lavina didn't have any.

And when he'd left to go home, she made sure he had a plastic container of shepherd's pie and one of apple crisp to take with him. Maybe it was simplistic to think the way to a man's heart was through his stomach, but she knew a hardworking man who wasn't *gut* at cooking — his repertoire of dishes that revolved around ramen noodles proved that — appreciated a *gut* meal.

Maybe when he ate those leftovers for supper that night or the next he'd think about her.

She chewed on her pencil as she flipped a page and studied the list of people she wanted to talk to about what she'd come to think of as her romantic quest. She'd checked off Jenny — and that unexpected chat she'd been able to have with her that day. Her *schweschders* hadn't been the most encouraging with their advice, but after having watched romance bloom between them and the two older Stoltzfus *bruders* she thought she'd learned something from them.

A bare branch tapped on her window as the wind picked up outside. The wind made a moaning sound. Even though she felt lonely tonight in her narrow bed, she was grateful for it. The pictures on the wall were those she'd chosen — actually, were wildflowers she'd pressed and put in dollar store frames. A quilt her *grossmudder* Miriam had sewn for her covered her bed. Her warm flannel sheets were scented with the lavender her *mudder* liked to tuck into drawers after they came off the clothesline. They brought a scent of summer on a cold night.

But it was no substitute for sharing a double bed . . . she reined in her thoughts and forced her attention on her journal until her eyelids drooped. She tucked the journal under her pillow, turned off the battery-operated bedside lamp, and drifted off to sleep.

She tossed and turned much of the night, dreaming of searching for John and never finding him.

When she woke the next morning she felt listless and not in the best of moods. Fortunately, it was one of her two volunteer mornings at the shelter. She was grateful she didn't have to sit in the sewing room and make conversation with her *schweschders* and *mudder*. Focusing on helping the women at the shelter would help keep her mind off herself.

She took the buggy today since Kate had to do some overtime at work and didn't know when she'd be done. When she pulled into the parking lot behind the shelter she saw Jenny getting out of her buggy.

"What a nice surprise!" she exclaimed and walked over to her.

"I had a free morning and decided to take you up on your invitation to help with a class," Jenny told her. "I ran into Kate the other day, and we talked about Brooke. Malcolm, Kate's husband, counsels ex-military with PTSD, but Kate and I felt Brooke might do better with a woman."

"Pearl told me once that many of the women and children are nervous around men even after they've been here a while."

Jenny nodded. "Can't blame them. Sometimes they've been abused emotionally and physically for years before they come here." She reached into the back of the buggy and pulled out two shopping bags. "I brought some fabric."

Rose Anna grinned as she took one of the bags. "*Wunderbaar.* We can always use fabric."

"So Kate tells me. I had fun picking it out. I don't get time to quilt often around my book deadlines, so I wasn't tempted to take it home from the store."

"How's the latest book going?" Rose Anna asked her as they walked to the back door of the shelter.

"Like usual. Hard to get started," Jenny complained with a wry smile. "It gets to be more fun as I reach the middle. Happens with nearly every book I write. You'd think writing would be getting easier as I get older but it hasn't happened."

She shrugged as Rose Anna knocked on the door. "Sometimes the best things aren't easy."

Rose Anna had to agree with her. She didn't figure getting John to marry her was going to be easy but she didn't care. She hadn't ever wanted anyone but him, so she'd just have to work her hardest to convince him they should marry.

Pearl came to open the door and welcomed them inside. A young woman sat at the table in the kitchen sipping a cup of tea, avoiding their gaze. Rose Anna said hello as they passed and winced inwardly as she saw tears on the woman's cheeks and the bruise on her face. Did the stream of women fleeing their abusers ever end?

She and Jenny climbed the stairs to the quilting room. When she walked in Rose Anna was surprised to find Brooke sitting at the table at the far back of the room.

"Pearl said I could come up here before the class," she said, sounding tentative.

"Absolutely," Rose Anna assured her. She introduced the two women and walked to the front of the room to set her tote bag down and take off her coat. When she turned she saw that Jenny had taken off her coat, set it on a table next to Brooke's, and was pulling fabric from her tote bag.

"I've only been here a couple of times," she told Brooke. "I've never been a very good quilter, but I like to come help and meet new people."

"I thought all Amish women were good quilters."

Jenny laughed and shook her head. "Maybe those who have been born here. I joined the Amish church when I fell in love with an Amish man."

Brooke looked intrigued. "So you were *Englisch*?"

"Very *Englisch*. My father was born here but chose not to join the church. I came here after I was hurt overseas."

"Were you in the military?"

"No, I was covering the war for a TV network."

"Now I recognize you. I saw one of your broadcasts years ago. And Pearl has your books in the library room here."

102

Jenny blushed. "Well, she had to. I gave her some," she said self-deprecatingly.

"They're good books," Rose Anna chimed in. "I think everyone who knows you has bought at least one."

"You got hurt over there," Brooke said quietly. "You know what it was like." She glanced nervously at the window.

"I did. And I do. I'd love to talk to you about it if you want. Any time."

Brooke nodded slowly. "I would."

"I'm going downstairs to get some coffee," Rose Anna told them. "Shall I bring some up for you both?"

"I'd love some," Jenny said. "I brought some cookies I baked."

Rose Anna glanced at Brooke. "Um . . . Jenny's as good at baking cookies as she is at sewing quilts."

"Hey!"

She chuckled as she darted out of the room before Jenny could retaliate.

6

Rose Anna and Jenny walked out to the parking lot together after the class.

"Do you have to go home right away?"

"No, why?"

"Kate and I decided to have lunch. We'd like you to join us. I have some ideas to help Brooke."

"Schur."

Kate came out of the shelter carrying a box that she set in the trunk of her car. "I have to drop another box off at the Sewn in Hope shop after we eat. I can't believe how much our ladies are getting done. We have a real cottage industry here."

Once they were seated in a nearby restaurant and their server had taken their orders, Jenny placed her arms on the table and leaned forward eagerly. "I'm so glad that you invited me to drop by a class, Rose Anna. Kate, you know I've always been a big supporter of what you're doing with it."

She leaned back when the server brought their drinks. "I didn't get to talk to Brooke for very long before she wanted to go back to her room. Both of you know I've had some trouble with PTSD, my brother-in-law, Chris, as well. Kate, he and I were talking just the other day about a friend of his who got a service dog from an organization that supplies them to veterans who are suffering from PTSD, anxiety, panic attacks. The dogs are specially trained to help them with it. Maybe Malcolm could check into that for her."

"How does a dog do that?" Rose Anna asked her, intrigued.

"The dog can sense when a person starts to experience anxiety or panic and helps distract them, makes them feel more secure. I think one could help Brooke."

"I've heard something about this," Kate said as she picked up her cup of coffee.

"What kind of dogs do they use?"

"Mostly German shepherds, some Labrador retrievers and golden retrievers, but sometimes smaller dogs are used. They'll evaluate what's best for Brooke and what's available."

"Are they expensive?"

Jenny shook her head. "The organization covers the cost. They get donations from people."

"I'll have a talk with Malcolm, see if I can take Brooke to him if he needs to see her. As I've told you, Pearl tries to keep men away from the shelter since the women and children have been traumatized by them."

"Sounds good."

Their food came, and the talk turned to talk about jobs and family and children. And in Jenny's case, grandchildren.

Rose Anna fell silent She felt . . . insignificant compared to these two accomplished women who had such dynamic jobs. Husbands. Children.

She frowned. She'd been raised to avoid envy, yet here she sat doing that very thing. And Kate and Jenny were both older than she was. It wasn't like they were her age and had done all that they had.

"Rose Anna? Something wrong with your food?"

She looked up at Kate. "No, why?"

"You're frowning."

She blushed. "I was just thinking of something."

Kate's cell phone rang. She excused herself to answer it, and when she came back she looked harried. "I have to go by the station. Rose Anna, I hate to impose on you. Would you be able to take the box to the shop for me?"

"Of course."

"Great. Thanks." She pulled bills from her purse and laid them on the table, scooped up the uneaten half of her sandwich, and hurried away.

"I hope Brooke can get help," Rose Anna said as they resumed eating. "You know what she said to me one day? She told me she hoped she wouldn't have to stay at the shelter long. Her home had become a prison before she had to leave it. She said she didn't want to feel she'd gone from one prison to another."

" 'Stone walls do not a prison make / Nor iron bars a cage.' "

"What?"

"Sorry. Thinking out loud, remembering something from my college days. I was an English major. It's from 'To Althea from Prison,' a poem by a seventeenth-century man named Richard Lovelace. Reading the poem helped me a lot when I was recovering from my injuries and felt I was trapped in my wheelchair and would never walk again."

She set her fork down. "Brooke has a tough road ahead, but there are people to help her starting with Pearl, you, Kate, and Malcolm."

"I can't help her. All I do is teach a quilting class."

"Brooke said you talked to her that day she climbed under the sewing table and then you got Kate. And you've treated her like a normal person since then, talked with her, really listened to her. It means a lot to her."

She looked up as their server approached. "What do you have for dessert?"

Rose Anna thought about what Jenny said on the way to the shop. She'd never been told she was a good listener. As a matter of fact, her *schweschders* often teased her about talking too much, and it was true that she loved to talk.

She wondered if she'd listened enough to John . . .

When she walked into the Sewn in Hope Shops she was surprised to see Naomi, one of Leah's *grossdochders,* behind the counter.

"Where's Carrie?"

"She had a doctor's appointment, so I'm filling in." She glanced at the wall clock. "She's running a little late. Here, put that box down on the counter, and let's see what you've brought."

They spent the next few minutes pulling out crafts with Naomi exclaiming over them.

"I was just so pleased with *Grossmudder* when she came up with the idea to open this shop to help the ladies at the shelter," she said. "We all know that domestic abuse isn't just an *Englisch* problem. I was lucky that I saw I was engaged to a man who was an abuser," she told Rose Anna quietly.

Shocked, Rose Anna stared at her. "He hurt you?"

"Not with his hands. He never hit me. But I saw how controlling he was, how he could make me feel . . . less than myself. Being around Nick when he drove *Grossmudder* and me to Pinecraft the winter she hurt her ankle gave me a chance to see how a man should treat a woman."

A *kind* came running into the shop through the entranceway from the adjoining Stitches in Time shop. She was the image of Naomi. "*Mamm!* Is it time yet? You said we were going to go to Rachel Ann's for a gingerbread cookie. Is it time?"

Naomi gave her youngest *dochder* a fond smile. "Not yet. Lizzie. We'll go as soon as Carrie gets back."

"But I'm *hungerich*," she said, looking at her *mudder* imploringly.

"Those are my *grossdaadi*'s favorites," Rose Anna said. "*Mamm* and I haven't made them in a long time."

She glanced at the wall clock, then at Naomi. "I could take her and pick some cookies up for my *grossdaadi*. I like to get him a treat now and then."

"Are you *schur*?"

"Of course."

Naomi reached beneath the counter and handed Lizzie a jacket. "*One* cookie, Lizzie. No asking Rose Anna for more, understand?"

Lizzie nodded and looked very serious. She slipped her hand into Rose Anna's and beamed up at her. "Can we go now?"

Rose Anna laughed. Lizzie reminded her of herself as a *kind*. Her *schweschders* always said she had a knack for getting her own way. "Anything we can bring you, Naomi?"

"I wouldn't turn down a snickerdoodle." She pulled a ten-dollar bill out of her pocket and handed it to her *dochder*. "Why don't you get a dozen mixed cookies and we'll share them with *Grossmudder* and your *aentis*?"

"We'll be back in a few minutes," Rose Anna told her, and they walked out of the shop.

John didn't often treat himself to a cup of coffee at a coffee shop, but today had been a really good day.

He had his paycheck in his pocket and work lined up for the next month. And his job had been two doors down from the shop, so he figured he would give himself a treat. Coffee and maybe a piece of pie.

A pretty Amish woman was walking toward him. As she got closer, he realized it was Rose Anna.

She appeared to recognize him at the same time he recognized her. A little girl he knew as one of Leah's great-granddaughters held her hand and skipped beside her. He held the door open for them, and Rose Anna smiled as she preceded him inside.

"I didn't expect to see you in town," she said as they took their place in line.

"Working a job and decided to treat myself to coffee."

"I dropped off some things after the quilting class," Rose Anna told him.

"We get to buy some cookies," Lizzie informed him. She held out the money clutched in her fist. "I'm going to buy a gingerbread man."

Rachel Ann came out of the back carrying a tray of fresh baked cookies. She greeted them, and her gaze fell on Lizzie. "There's my best customer!"

"My *mamm* said Rose Anna could bring

me to get a gingerbread cookie since she has to stay at the shop," Lizzie told her. "And I get to pick out a dozen mixed cookies."

"*Wunderbaar!* Let me set this down, and I'll box up your cookies myself." She turned to her clerk. "Will you put these out for display?"

John watched Lizzie as she moved down the line of glass display cases. She stood with her hands behind her back and leaned closely to study each of the baked selections.

Rachel Ann presented the box of cookies to Lizzie, accepted her money, made change, and invited her to come again.

"I'll be coming to the shop with my *mudder* next week," Lizzie said. "I'll come see you again then."

John happened to glance at Rose Anna just then and caught her smiling at the little girl. Then Rachel Ann was asking Rose Anna what she wanted, and she ordered a dozen gingerbread men to take home.

"Aren't you getting any coffee?" he asked when she accepted the box and turned to leave.

She shook her head. "I just had lunch with Jenny Bontrager. I offered to bring Lizzie here since Naomi was busy."

"Can I have my cookie now?" Lizzie asked.

"May I."

"May I?"

"Schur."

"Aren't we going to sit at a table like when *Mamm* brings me?"

Rose Anna hesitated, then nodded. "We can't stay long. I don't want your *mudder* to worry we got lost."

Lizzie laughed. "We won't get lost. I know how many steps back to the shop."

"I bet you do," Rose Anna murmured.

They walked over to a table by the window and sat down.

"John? What will you have today?"

"Hmm? Oh, coffee and a slice of pumpkin pie."

"Coming right up. Why don't you take a seat and I'll bring it out to you?"

He glanced around the shop. It was always a popular place, and today all the tables were filled.

"John! Come sit with us!" Lizzie called.

He walked over and took a seat. "Thank you, Lizzie."

"I'm thirsty, Rose Anna. May I have a carton of milk? I still have money left from *Mamm.*"

Rose Anna plucked a paper napkin from

the holder on the table and wiped ginger-bread crumbs from the little girl's mouth. " 'If you give a mouse a cookie.' "

Lizzie laughed. "I have that book!"

"I know. I saw it at the shop once. *Ya,* you may have milk."

"Here," John said, handing her two dollar bills. "Use this."

"*Danki,* John."

"Don't worry, I won't bite," Rose Anna told John as they watched Lizzie walk over to the counter.

"I'm not afraid you will."

She fixed him with a steady gaze. "Really? You looked like you'd rather sit anywhere but here."

"Guess I'm still finding it hard to believe we have a truce."

"The only snowballs around here are in the display case," she pointed out.

"Snowballs?" Rachel Ann set John's coffee and pie on the table before him. "Did either of you want a snowball cookie?"

Startled, he glanced up. "Uh, not me, thanks, Rachel Ann."

"*Nee, danki,*" Rose Anna told her. "We were just . . . discussing the bad winter we had."

Lizzie returned with her carton of milk. John watched Rose Anna help her with opening the carton and inserting a straw. She was good with children. He wondered how long it would be before she married and had them. He knew how much she wanted that. She just didn't understand he couldn't give her those things.

"Isn't the pie *gut*?" she asked quietly.

"Hmm? No, it's fine." He didn't realize that he'd stopped eating while he watched her. To prove it he finished the pie in a few big bites and sipped his coffee.

A sucking noise drew her attention away from him. Lizzie grinned showing two missing front teeth. "All gone."

She gathered the carton and the little paper plate her gingerbread man had been served on, took them to the nearby trash bin, and dumped them. Then she looped the handles of the bag that held the box of cookies and looked expectantly at Rose Anna. "I'm ready to go. Unless I can have another cookie."

Rose Anna stood. "You remember what your *mudder* said."

Lizzie sighed. *"Ya."* She turned to John. *"Danki* for the milk."

He smiled at her. Such a polite little girl. "You're welcome." His gaze lifted to Rose Anna. "Good to see you again."

She nodded. "You, too."

John sat there watching them leave the shop and walk past the window. Rose Anna glanced in as they passed, and their gazes locked. Then Lizzie must have said something for she turned her attention to her.

The shop bustled with people all around him, but strangely John felt lonely. He finished his coffee, disposed of his trash in the bin and left, grateful that he turned in the opposite direction from Rose Anna and Lizzie so he didn't have to see them again.

"Hope you weren't worried," Rose Anna told Naomi when they walked into Sewn in Hope a few minutes later.

"*Nee.* I figured Lizzie talked you into eating her gingerbread man at the coffee shop. She loves going there on the days she comes to work with me."

She glanced at the clock on the wall and frowned. "I am getting worried about Carrie, though. I hope nothing's wrong. She didn't think she'd be long." She bit her lip. "I have a quilting class to teach in a half hour, but I suppose Leah or one of my *schweschders* could teach the class if I have to stay here."

"I can help if you need me," Rose Anna found herself offering impulsively. "I don't have to rush home."

116

Naomi's frown cleared. "That would be *wunderbaar.*"

She shrugged. "I've loved helping with the quilting classes at the shelter." She gestured at the shop. "And it's the least I can do after Leah and all of you have done so much for the women there. This shop has given them a purpose, a way to make some money to help themselves." She paused. "Hope."

"We're so happy at how people are responding to it," Naomi told her. "This is the first lull since I came over today."

"We got the cookies," Lizzie told her *mudder.* "Here's your change. I got milk, but John gave me the money for it."

"John?"

"John Stoltzfus." His name came out with a little lisp because of her missing front teeth.

"You didn't ask him for it did you?"

Lizzie shook her head. "Promise."

"He offered," Rose Anna told Naomi.

"Lizzie, go put the cookies on the table in the back room next door. And don't help yourself to any."

Naomi waited until Lizzie raced off through the entranceway to Stitches in Time then turned to Rose Anna. "So how is John? I haven't seen him since he helped Peter and Sam some with renovating this shop."

"He's fine."

"Fine? That's all you can say?"

She shrugged. "We didn't talk much."

"Probably not with Miss Chatterbox along." She tilted her head and studied Rose Anna until she wanted to fidget. "I always thought the two of you would end up together."

The shop door opened, and the bell atop it jingled.

Naomi turned her attention to the customer who'd entered. "Welcome."

"Saved by the bell," Rose Anna murmured.

She glanced over at Stitches in Time. How could she be so close and not see if they had any new fabric? She hurried over knowing she was using it as an excuse to avoid Naomi's curiosity about John.

Her emotions were swirling inside her. She hadn't expected to see him in town and was more surprised than she'd expected.

So surprised, in fact, that she hadn't even been able to figure out how to use the opportunity to further her plan. And even more than the surprise had been seeing his reaction to her with Lizzie. It had been obvious in the first seconds after he'd spotted her approaching the coffee shop even though he'd quickly schooled his expression.

Why had he been thrown off by seeing her with the *kind*? The Amish believed in helping each other, and the women were always minding each other's *kinner* when needed.

And why had he seemed to watch her so intently as she helped Lizzie while they sat at the table? Was it possible — *nee,* it wasn't possible that he thought about having *kinner* of his own. The Amish grapevine carried news faster than the *Englisch* Internet. Some said he was enjoying his single life.

She knew he was *gut* with *kinner.* She'd seen how he was with his nephew Mark. And Lizzie was an especially charming *kind.*

It was one of the reasons she wanted him to be her *mann* — after all, being a good *dat* was an important quality for a *mann.* She wanted *kinner,* lots of them.

She walked into Stitches in Time and felt at home like she always did. She'd been coming here since she was younger than Lizzie. Her *mudder* had given her a shopping basket and let her choose fabric for her first quilt.

Leah had designed the shop to look like a room in an Amish home. The weather might still be cool and dismal, but inside, a fire crackled merrily in the little fireplace, and it was cozy and warm. Coffee and the cookies Lizzie had chosen were set out for all to enjoy. Baskets of scissors and sewing supplies were arranged on a big wooden table for classes in quilting and knitting that were offered several times a week.

Bolts of colorful fabric were set on tables arranged around the room with one wall filled with cubbies overflowing with yarn in every color and texture. Shelves held all kinds of kits for shoppers to take home and make sewing, quilting, and knitting projects.

Mary Katherine, Leah's oldest *grossdochder,* sat at her loom weaving something in spring colors. She glanced up and waved, so Rose Anna walked over.

"That's lovely," she said, watching as she wove the warp through the pink, lavender, and robin's egg blue fibers.

"I'm enjoying working with these colors," Mary Katherine said. "I'm hoping we'll have a nice spring. We're setting up the display window with things to make for spring and summer."

"Spring is always too short in Lancaster County. We go from a long winter to a few weeks of spring, and then suddenly it's a long, hot summer."

"I agree."

Leah walked over. Well, she seemed to

bounce over, thought Rose Anna. She didn't know anyone with the energy Leah had.

"*Gut* to see you," she told Rose Anna. "We have some new fabric."

"You get new fabric too often for my budget," Rose Anna said with a groan. But she walked over to check it out. Several of the bolts of fabrics were bright and cheerful spring and summer colors that would work well for some baby quilts. She carried them over to the cutting table where Leah cheerfully cut the required lengths.

Naomi appeared in the entranceway between the two shops. "Carrie just called. She's not going to make it back in time. Are you *schur* you wouldn't mind teaching the lesson?"

"Not at all." She followed Leah to the counter to pay for her fabric, but when she got out her wallet the older woman refused her money.

"It's on the shop since you're helping us out."

They had a good-spirited tug of war over that and finally compromised on Rose Anna paying for half of the fabric.

Rose Anna slipped into the back room and called her *mudder* to let her know she'd be home later than she'd expected. The call went to the answering machine in the phone

121

shanty, so she left a message. When she came out of the back room, she saw that several women had arrived and were getting their projects out of tote bags and serving themselves coffee.

These women were strangers to her, but they had one thing in common: quilting. It was Rose Anna's vocation and avocation, a joy and sometimes a pain when she had to rush to fill an order. A quilt was a labor of love whether for someone she knew or someone she didn't. A comfort above all. Sewing one took imagination, creativity, and hours and hours of work.

As the women spread their work out before them, she saw apprehension, doubt, frowns, and sometimes smiles. And as they looked up at her as she approached the table, introduced herself, and said she'd be helping with the class, she saw a real eagerness to learn that warmed her heart.

Quilting had already become something they aspired to do, wanted to do better, and were investing their time and money in.

They were *Englisch,* young and old and obviously from different backgrounds. She could see from a quick glance that they were at many different levels of skill.

But today, for one hour, they were sisters enjoying an activity that had been born as much from a woman's natural need to be creative as well as one to provide warmth and decoration for her home.

When the class was over, she pulled on her coat and gathered up her purse and the shopping bag of new fabric. Leah and Naomi thanked her. She shook her head and told them that it had been fun and thanks wasn't necessary and meant it.

She paused at the door and looked back. She'd come here as a *kind* to find fabric to make her first quilt, and now she stood here as a woman to help others discover what she'd come to love doing for a living. God had had a plan for her, had set her on this path, and she realized that she had never thanked Him enough for it. Sending up a silent prayer of thanks, she started for home and a few hours enjoying sewing her own quilt.

7

Rose Anna found her *dat* sitting at the kitchen table drinking coffee when she went downstairs early the next morning.

He blinked in surprise as she walked into the room. "You're up early. Very early."

She yawned, got a mug, and poured herself coffee. "I spent extra time in town yesterday, so I need to catch up on my work." She frowned. "Where's *Mamm*?"

"She has a cold coming on. I told her to stay in bed."

"And she listened? She really must not be feeling *gut*. I'll go up and check on her in a minute." She looked at the gas stove. "So no breakfast?"

"I'll cook you something if you want."

"*Daed!* I meant *you* haven't had any breakfast yet. I don't expect my parents to make me breakfast at my age."

He grinned. "I know. I'll get something after I'm finished with my chores."

"You'll have something now." She rose. "What would you like?"

He shrugged. "Cereal's fine."

"Daed!"

"Well, maybe some burned toast."

"I haven't done that in ages. I'm a *gut* cook. You love my fried chicken," she reminded him.

Chuckling, he rose and hugged her. "I'm just teasing you. Some eggs will be fine. However you want to cook them."

Rose Anna poked around in the refrigerator. "There's some ham left from supper last night. I'll fry it and make you some scrambled eggs. Oh, there's some leftover boiled potatoes, too." She carried the plastic containers over to the counter near the stove.

She poured him another cup of coffee before setting a cast-iron skillet on the stove and placing two slices of ham in it. In minutes, the scent of sizzling meat filled the kitchen. Cubes of potatoes went into another skillet with some butter. She broke eggs into a big bowl, whisked them, and set them aside to cook when the potatoes and ham were done.

Her *dat* loved biscuits, but she figured he'd want to get back out to the barn and finish his chores on such a cool morning.

125

So she sliced some bread and placed it on a pan under the broiler to toast, watching it closely while she cooked. She had a tendency to burn toast because she didn't pay attention and it browned so quickly.

Rose Anna found her appetite waking up as she forked up the ham, set it on a platter, then piled the fried potatoes next to it. She was pleased to catch the toast at just the right color of golden brown and set it on another plate. The eggs went into the skillet where the ham had cooked. A few minutes later she set a bowl of them nicely scrambled on the table.

"*Gut* job," her *dat* proclaimed. He said a prayer of thanks and then dug in.

Her *mudder* wandered in a few minutes later in her winter bathrobe looking a little flushed. "I thought I must be dreaming when I smelled food cooking," she told them.

"Rose Anna cooked me a fine breakfast," Jacob told her. "You go back to bed and rest. I'll bring you up some breakfast."

"It's just a cold, Jacob," she told him.

Rose Anna touched the back of her hand to her *mudder*'s forehead the way she had done to her *kinner*. "You're warm. Sit while I find the thermometer."

"Such a fuss. I'm going to get dressed so I

can help your *dat* with the chores. Luke called him last night and said he couldn't come today."

"You will not," Rose Anna said firmly. "*Daed,* make her sit while I find the thermometer."

When she returned her *dat* had done as she'd asked. Her *mudder* sat talking with him at the table and looked even more flushed than she had minutes before.

"I knew it!" Rose Anna said when she took the thermometer from her *mudder*'s mouth. "It's 102 degrees."

"I'll take some aspirin, and I'll be fine."

Rose Anna fetched aspirin, a glass of water, and one of juice, then fixed a plate of food for her *mudder* before she made one for herself and sat down to eat.

It felt *gut* to take care of her parents when they'd always been the ones to do that for her. She knew she sometimes took them for granted. What *kind* didn't — little or grown? But as she ate, then made tea for her *mudder* and herself, she couldn't help noting that there were more strands of silver in their hair and lines on their faces.

Her *dat* cleaned his plate and rose to put it in the sink. He bent to kiss her cheek. "*Danki* for breakfast."

She rose and hugged him. "*Danki* for being my *dat*."

His eyebrows went up.

"Well, well, you're very *wilkum*." He turned to Linda. "Try to eat a little more and then go back to bed."

"But —"

"I'll be out in a few minutes to help after I see that *Mamm* is doing as you say," Rose Anna told him. She turned to her *mudder*. "No arguing with us. If you don't get rid of your cold, you can't babysit Mark this Saturday for Lavina."

She smiled when she saw her *mudder* hesitate then nod. "You're right."

Her *dat* pulled on his coat and black felt hat, then went out the back door.

Rose Anna piled the dishes in the sink, filling it with dishwashing liquid and warm water, then pulled on her own coat, bonnet, boots, and gloves. The wind was a cold slap in the face as she ventured outdoors. She shivered as she marched toward the barn.

Inside it was warm and filled with the sounds and scents of their horses. She hurried to help him clean the stalls and feed them, pulling out an apple she'd quartered and tucked into her pocket as a treat.

"You do that and they'll want you to help me every morning," her *dat* told her with a grin.

"They deserve it. They work hard to help you farm. More than I do."

"You have your own work," he said as he opened a new bag of feed. "And you help me when I need it like today."

"It would have been easier for you if I'd been a sohn not a *dochder.*"

"Maybe easier," he said. "But not better." He studied her. "What is this, Rose Anna? Why are you thinking I wished you were a *sohn*?"

"Days like today when one of the men who helps you can't come, it would be easier for you if I'd been born a man."

"*Kind, kinner* is a gift from God, and He gives us what — who — He feels is best. I'm grateful for you, for all of my *dochders.* And I don't want you to ever doubt that."

He gave her a gentle smile. "Now, no more of that thinking."

She bit her lip and nodded. "We'll see if you feel that way if I turn into an old maid."

Jacob chuckled. "That's not going to happen. When God sends the right man, I'll be watching you take your vows just as I did your *schweschders.*" He tilted his head and studied her. "I'm thinking it's been a long time since Peter visited."

"He's just a friend. And I don't think he's happy about it." She shrugged. "He's not

129

the one God's supposed to have set aside for me. I'm beginning to think he's not coming."

"You've always been impatient," he told her, his eyes twinkling. "My most impatient *dochder.*"

She sighed gustily. "I know."

"Be patient, *kind.* God has a plan for you, a wonderful plan."

"And you're always right."

He grinned as he picked up the handles of the wheelbarrow. "That I am, that I am."

John had sometimes called himself a Jack-of-all-trades . . . well, a John-of-all-trades might be more accurate.

He did a little carpentry, a little farming, a little fixing buggies, and since he'd been driving a pickup, even a little minor car repair. He'd gone down this path in the beginning as a way to survive when he left his home. After all, when you grew up on a farm, you learned how to do a little of everything. And it suited his temperament. His *dat* had often berated him for not being able to stick to doing one thing at a time.

Well, it was a good thing that he wasn't a stuck-in-a-rut sort of person, that he'd been restless enough to want to learn how to do many things. Because when he wasn't quickly able to find a permanent, full-time job, he'd been able to pick up a lot of part-time jobs.

And then Nick, Naomi's *mann,* happened to run into him one day as he built some shelves at Saul Miller's shop, and he got what he felt was his best part-time position ever.

"I saw your truck outside as I was returning home after my last tour," Nick said.

"I heard the business is working out well for you."

"I love it. I was a driver and tour operator before I became Amish as you know, so doing Amish buggy rides seemed a natural transition when I converted. Anyway, can you take a break for a few minutes and get some coffee with me? I have something you might be interested in."

They went to the coffee shop, and over coffee and pie Nick told him how he'd been approached by an *Englisch* man who needed help with his horses.

"He came to me about my business," Nick said with a chuckle. "I think he thought all Amish know about horses. Well, they do, but little did he know I only became Amish and bought the buggy tour business when I wanted to marry Naomi."

He sipped his coffee. "I'm still learning

about horses myself. Had to when I traded driving people around in buggies instead of automobiles for a living."

"The *Englisch* man isn't far wrong," John said. "Most Amish families have to own at least one horse to pull their buggy. We had more, of course, since *Daed* had a farm before he turned it over to David."

"Well, this Neil Zimmerman needs someone part-time to help and the money's good," Nick said. "Here's his business card. Why don't you give him a call? You can use my name as a reference."

John fingered the card. "Thanks for thinking of me. And the reference." He paused. "Can I ask you something personal?"

"Sure."

"Few people — those who were *Englisch* — convert to the Amish faith. I only know a couple who have. Usually it's the other way around."

"True."

"So . . . are you happy that you did?"

Nick grinned. "Best thing I ever did. Well, second best thing. Marrying Naomi was the best." Looking thoughtful, he stared off into the distance for a long moment. "I knew more about the Amish than many before I made my decision. I'd lived near them, driven them, for years before I fell in love

132

with Naomi. I might not have converted if I hadn't fallen in love with her, but it was certainly what I wanted to do after knowing her better."

He hesitated. "Are you thinking of not coming back, John?" he finally asked.

"Back?"

"Back home."

"It's David and Lavina's now."

"You know what I mean."

John sighed. "What is there for me there now, Nick?"

"Everything," he said simply. "Everything."

Now, as John picked up a pitchfork and prepared to muck out a stall, he found himself thinking about what Nick had said. What had he meant by "everything"?

He pondered that now as he worked at the horse farm and still had no answer.

The only thing he knew for sure right now was that he needed to thank Nick for telling him about the job.

He spent three or four hours a day, five days a week, and it had become one of his favorite jobs. John understood horses — probably liked them better than people most days — and they seemed to like him.

David and Sam were the ones who loved to farm. John had helped on the family farm growing up, and he still did what he could for them, but he loved feeding and taking care of the horses.

What must it be like owning horses such as these? he wondered as he brushed the glossy black coat of the horse aptly named Midnight.

Willow, a pretty brown mare, batted her long eyelashes at him and butted his arm with her head.

At least one female liked him.

That made him think about how he'd run into Rose Anna at the coffee shop that day. He chuckled as he thought about what she'd think if she knew his thoughts turned to her right after his equine flirt tried to get his attention. But Willow reminded him of the way Rose Anna used to look at him when they were first dating what felt like many years before. Now she puzzled him with her changing moods.

Well, she'd always been a woman of changing moods. Impulsive. Fun-loving. Passionate about everything she did.

It was an easy job mucking out stalls, feeding, and exercising the horses. And it was something he could do around his other work. The trouble was that he had a lot of time to think about things. Like Rose Anna. Like his life.

And the more time he spent with the horses the more he wanted to.

If Neil only knew that he'd have paid *him* to exercise one of the horses. He saddled Midnight and took him for a ride — something they seldom did with one of the buggy horses back home. He sat astride the beautiful, powerful stallion, drew in the needle-sharp air of early morning, and imagined what a joy it would be to take the horse for a run in the pasture soon.

He'd thought nothing could be better than driving the pickup truck that had been passed down by the Stoltzfus men.

He'd been so wrong.

Late spring snow crunched beneath the horse's hooves, the only sound in the early morning. The workout — though short — sent puffs of white into the cold air.

Reluctantly, he slowed the horse. Midnight snorted and shook his head, but when John tightened his legs around him and pulled on the reins he followed the command and started back toward the barn.

"I know, fella," he said as he dismounted and patted the horse's neck. "It'll warm up soon. Then we'll go for a run for as long as you like. I promise."

He unsaddled the horse, slipped off the bridle, and picked up a grooming brush.

Could it be that he — the restless Jack-of-all-trades guy and maverick of the family — had finally found what he wanted to do with his life?

And how ironic was it that it was something he'd never be able to do full time, for himself? Neil was obviously a very prosperous *Englisch* man and horses cost a lot of money. It wasn't just the initial purchase price which was hefty in itself. He'd been to horse auctions with his *dat* so he knew what they cost. They always seemed to need big bags of food and expensive supplements and visits from the veterinarian and blacksmith.

Not much different from having children in a way.

He wouldn't be having those in the near future either. But he liked being on his own. He did. He told himself that as he left the barn and drove to his next job.

Rose Anna sewed a Mariner's Compass quilt one of Leah's customers had commissioned.

It was quiet in the sewing room today. Her two *schweschders* were working at their homes, and her *mudder* was helping clean a friend's home since the friend had been laid up with a sprained ankle.

So Rose Anna could sit and think about

her plan in peace and not be asked why she was being so quiet. Or teased by her *schweschders* for something. She loved them, but they could be so annoying. She supposed that was what *schweschders* did.

Running into John unexpectedly had made her realize she had not only not made the most of the opportunity, but she needed to plan for such an unexpected opportunity in the future.

After all, who knew how long it might take to convince him that she was the one for him. Marriages only took place after harvest in the fall, and while that seemed like a long time from now, time had a habit of passing quickly.

She was *gut* at planning. Making a quilt was an exercise in planning. Once she had an order for one she'd choose fabric, spend a lot of time cutting it into many, many small pieces and sewing them together. Planning and patience had become part of her daily life, and while she had used them well in her work, she had to use them more to achieve her goal of marrying John this year.

Footsteps ascended the stairs, and a moment later her *dat* appeared in the doorway. "Got time for a break?"

"*Schur.*" She set her quilt down and fol-

137

lowed him downstairs to the kitchen.

"House is too quiet these days," he complained as he poured himself a cup of coffee.

"I'd think you'd enjoy it," she told him as she put the kettle on. "The three of us made a lot of noise through the years. When we weren't racing around the house we were arguing."

He chuckled. "I loved every minute of it."

"Soon Mark will be walking, and then he'll be running around." She dug cookies out of the cookie jar, spread them on a plate, and set it before him.

Jacob reached for a butterscotch cookie and bit in. "Can't wait. He's growing like a weed."

Before she sat down, Rose Anna gave the big pot of soup simmering on the back of the stove a good stir. It was her *dat*'s favorite — potato with chunks of ham. She saw him glance at it. "It isn't quite ready yet. If you're *hungerich,* I could fix you a sandwich."

"*Nee,* it's just that it smells so *gut* cooking. The cookies'll do me until lunch."

She poured herself a mug of hot water and sat to dunk a teabag in it. How different he was from John, she couldn't help thinking. So many women her age seemed to look for a *mann* like their *dats.*

Hers was sweet, caring, steady.

John was the opposite: headstrong. Some-times broody. Worked at any number of jobs but didn't seem certain about a career — or life path.

He was nothing like her *dat.*

But maybe that's what she liked. John was exciting to her — not quite a bad boy but one who had always stood out from the other boys even from a young age. Amish *kinner* were taught to conform for the good of the community, not the individual. But he didn't believe in . . . conforming as much as his two *bruders* had. When he was young he was always up for a dare, always willing to test the limits. As an adult he spoke up more, seemed to care less that their *dat* didn't approve of him. And while his *bruders* had reconciled with their *dat* and returned to the family, to the church, he'd refused.

That gave her pause. She wondered if he was enjoying his time in the *Englisch* world a little too much. What if he wasn't just do-ing *rumschpringe* but making the transition to staying in the *Englisch* community?

"Where did you go?" her *daed* asked, giv-ing her an amused grin.

She frowned. "Sorry. Just thinking."

"Must have been serious stuff."

She shrugged. "Not really." She glanced over at the door to the *dawdi haus.* "You know, it's quiet around here not just because Lavina and Mary Elizabeth are married but because *Grossdaadi* is away."

"*Ya.* I miss my checkers buddy, too. But it was *gut* for him to get away from the weather for a bit, and maybe it'll cheer him up a little being with his friends in Pinecraft."

"It's hard not to see him and *Grossmudder* every day."

He patted her hand. "She loved you dearly. But she's with God now, and we have to be happy for her." He perked up. "That's your *mudder* home already. I'm going out to put the buggy up."

The kitchen door opened a few minutes later, and her *mudder* came in, bringing with her a chill breeze.

"I thought you wouldn't be back for another couple of hours."

"*Ya,* I got everything done that was needed, and Fannie is lying down for a nap." She took off her bonnet and coat and hung them on the pegs by the back door.

Rose Anna got up, poured a cup of coffee for her *mudder,* and set it on the table for her. "*Daed* and I were just talking about how quiet the house is these days."

"True."

She propped her elbow on the table and rested her chin on her hand. "Well, who knows, the two of you may have your old maid *dochder* on your hands for years to come."

Linda gave her a fond smile. "Seems like another of my *dochders* said the same and she's now married."

"Mary Elizabeth," Rose Anna said with a nod. "I remember her telling me she was going to sew an Old Maid's Puzzle quilt, but she didn't end up doing it."

"*Nee,* she got too busy making plans to marry Sam a short time later."

Rose Anna sighed. "I get your point."

"You'll never guess who I saw on my way home."

"Who?"

"John."

She sat up, alert. "Where?"

"At the Zimmerman farm. You know, the *Englischer*'s horse farm."

"What was he doing there?"

"Exercising a horse. He's beautiful."

"He is." Then Rose Anna realized her *mudder* meant the horse. She reddened.

Linda laughed. "It was a beautiful black stallion that was taking every bit of his rider's wits to control."

"John loves horses so much." She sipped her tea thoughtfully. "I didn't know he was working there."

"I thought you might be interested."

Rose Anna smiled inwardly. *Ya,* she was interested. She'd have to check it out soon. Very soon. It would be another likely place she could run into him.

Deliberately this time.

The clink of spoon against cup made her look over at her *mudder.* "What's the smile for?" Rose Anna asked suspiciously.

"I can almost hear the wheels turning in your head," she said with a grin. She finished her coffee. "Well, I'm ready to sit and put my feet up and get some sewing done. How about you?"

8

The *gut* thing about driving a buggy was that they looked alike. At least they did in one Amish community.

So Rose Anna was able to drive past the horse farm a number of times over the next two weeks. She didn't know how else to figure out when John worked without raising questions from whoever she asked.

But it was hard to find reasons to be leaving the *haus* early in the morning, which is when she figured he was most likely working. Her *dat* mucked out stalls and fed their horses early in the morning and again before supper. She left early for her quilting class twice the first week and didn't see him exercising any horses outside. And there was no sign of his truck.

She was beginning to wonder if her *mudder* had really seen him but then, at the end of the second week, she happened to be out driving with Mary Elizabeth, and there was the pickup truck parked by the farm's barn.

"What are you looking at?" her *schweschder* asked her as she gave the farm a long look.

She thought she managed a careless shrug. "The horse farm."

Mary Elizabeth leaned out the window. "Isn't that John's pickup truck?"

"Is it? Why would he be there?" she asked innocently.

Her *schweschder* gave her a suspicious look. "Gee, maybe because he's working there."

"Really?"

"*Ya,* Sam told me."

"Well, Sam didn't tell me."

"*Nee,* but maybe someone else did. The Amish grapevine is alive and well, after all."

Rose Anna lifted her chin and stared straight ahead. "I wouldn't know. I don't gossip."

Mary Elizabeth just laughed. "Oh, you love nothing better."

"I do not."

"Do, too."

"Do not."

They looked at each other and dissolved into giggles. "By the way, *Daed* says the house is too quiet lately. Maybe you and Lavina could come over and we could run up and down the stairs and argue and such."

"I'll see if Lavina and I can come over and do that. But I'd have thought he'd enjoy the peace and quiet." She tilted her head and studied her. "Aren't you annoying enough on your own?"

"I'm his favorite."

Again Mary Elizabeth erupted into laughter. "Keep it up. I'm not arguing with you."

"*Ya*, you are."

"*Nee*, I'm not."

"*Ya*, you are."

They looked at each other and once again began giggling. "I've missed you."

"Me, too. Maybe since you're not a newlywed anymore we could see each other a little more. If you can tear yourself away from your *mann*."

"It's tough. He's kinda cute," Mary Elizabeth said, her eyes twinkling. "It's taken a lot of time to get the farm in order. It sat for a long time without anyone taking care of it." She frowned. "You remember what it looked like when Sam and I bought it and started fixing it up."

Rose Anna nodded. "Mice in the kitchen. Snakes in the basement. Bats in the attic." She shuddered. "The bats were the worst."

"I agree."

"Sam never minded that David got the

145

family farm because he was the *bruder* who came back when their *dat* got the cancer, but I knew Sam wanted to own a farm so much. We were so blessed to be able to buy it from Sarah Fisher with the bishop's help. Land is so expensive in Lancaster County these days." She paused and glanced at Rose Anna. "I wonder what John will do if he ever decides to come home."

"I don't know. I haven't seen John in ages."

"I thought you said you had a plan —"

"I don't think John enjoys farming as much as David and Sam," she said quickly.

"Did he say that to you?"

"*Nee,* it's just my impression."

"Well, he's coming on Saturday to help Sam." She cast Rose Anna a sidelong look. "Maybe you'd like to come help me clean and paint an upstairs room."

Rose Anna studied her. "I guess I could do that."

She pulled into the driveway of Sam and Mary Elizabeth's farmhouse.

"Coming in?"

"*Nee,* I need to get home. *Mamm*'s still a little under the weather with her cold, so I'm cooking supper."

"It's hanging on, isn't it?"

"Seems to be. Same thing is happening to

others who caught it. Quilting class tomorrow?"

"*Schur.* Pick me up?"

Rose Anna nodded.

"We can drive by the horse farm, and you can act like you're not looking for John."

"Very funny."

Mary Elizabeth smirked. "I thought so."

She escaped, laughing, before Rose Anna could smack her arm.

The front door opened and Sam came out. He waved to her. Rose Anna waved back. She watched the way he waited for Mary Elizabeth with such love written on his face. Rose Anna wasn't jealous . . . but oh, she wished that John looked at her that way . . .

Thinking of him, she found herself retracing her route. Maybe he was still at the farm. Maybe he'd be outside as she passed, and she could figure out some way to talk to him.

But when she passed by, his truck was gone. Sighing with disappointment she found a driveway further down the road so she could make a U-turn and head home.

Her *dat* was in the barn when she arrived. Winter was slower, quieter for farmers so they caught up on equipment repair, planned for spring planting, made furniture, or worked some other job.

"Is it wishful thinking that I smell spring in the air?" she asked.

"*Nee,* you're right. I smelled it, too. I saw crocus peeking up in your *mudder*'s flower garden in the front yard."

"She'll love that. I'm going inside and starting supper."

"What are we having?"

"It's a surprise."

"That's your favorite thing to cook, *ya*? Or the result?" he teased.

"I think it's liver and onions, come to think of it."

He made a face. "Tell me you're joking."

She laughed. "You'll just have to wait and see."

When she entered the kitchen she wasn't surprised to see her *mudder* already there. She turned from putting a pan in the oven. "Did you have a *gut* day?"

"I did. But I guess you forgot I promised to cook supper?"

"I'm feeling *gut.*"

"What are you making?"

"Meatloaf."

"I just told *Daed* I was making liver and onions."

Linda chuckled. "You didn't."

She grinned. "I did. How long do you

think it will be before he comes in to see what's cooking?"

Linda thought about it. "He should have been in here by now."

The back door opened, and Jacob walked in.

They burst out laughing.

"What?" he asked them, looking from one to the other. "What?"

John was getting a soft drink in a convenience store when he heard his name called. He turned and saw one of his *Englisch* friends. "Hey, Simon."

"Haven't seen you in a while."

"Been busy working. You know how it is."

"No, actually I don't. Just got laid off again." He shoved his hands in his pockets and leaned against the refrigerated cases in front of them. "Say, there's a party at Adam's tonight. You going?"

"I don't know. I'm pretty tired after work. Running two part-time jobs right now."

"Aw, you turning into an old man?" Simon asked, elbowing him and chortling.

Sometimes he felt like one. It was so ironic. When they'd first left home and moved into an apartment together, his *bruder* Sam had done nothing but nag him about using his newfound freedom to go to

149

parties and drink beer. Now he was so tired when he came home he ate supper, did a little repair on the place as part of getting the rent break, showered, and went to bed.

John paid for his soft drink and moved aside. Simon put his suitcase of beer on the counter and pulled out his wallet. It was stuffed with bills. Simon's parents must still be helping him out.

They walked outside.

"You remember Adam's address?"

"Yes."

"Some chicks will be there. You remember Becky? She's been asking about you. Anyway, think about it. And bring your own beer."

"I'll think about it."

He drove home, showered, and pulled on old jeans and a t-shirt and went into the kitchen to rummage in the refrigerator. He pulled some leftover spaghetti and meat sauce from the refrigerator and nuked it in the tiny microwave that had come with the apartment. Every night he ate alone, and usually it didn't bother him. Sure, he missed Sam. The three brothers had maybe grown even closer than those from other Amish families because they'd had such a difficult father.

He forked up a bite of spaghetti and

thought about how he even missed the time he'd lived back home. He had moved back briefly when he couldn't afford a place of his own after Sam got married.

Not that he missed his father and his endless criticism.

There just had to be more to life than work and sleep, didn't there?

So he finished up his supper, tossed the paper plate in the trash, and contemplated the offerings on the tiny television that night.

And found himself changing into his one good shirt and pair of jeans and heading out to buy a six-pack of beer.

Adam opened the door to his apartment, one arm around his girlfriend. "Hey, John, long time no see," he shouted over the hard rock blasting from a nearby speaker.

The small apartment was crowded with about a dozen people. John recognized a few of them and stopped to say hello on the way to putting the beer in the refrigerator. There was nothing in the refrigerator but beer and a couple of Chinese takeout containers. Before he put his beer in it, he detached a can, popped the top, then made his way back into the crowded living room.

"How's it going?" seemed to be the most popular question. John sipped the only beer he intended to have since he was driving and hoped he sounded reasonably intelligent discussing sports. After all, he'd only been following *Englisch* sports for a short time on television.

Simon had promised there would be women. Well, he referred to them as chicks, but John wasn't calling them that. But Adam's girlfriend was the only woman in the place so far.

Then the front door opened, and three women walked in giggling. One of them was Becky. She looked over, and their gazes met as she set a grocery bag on a table and took off her coat with a provocative shrug. After tossing it on a chair and picking up the grocery bag, she made her way over to him

She wasn't like any Amish women he knew. Her hair was a short, spiky, scarlet color and she wore more makeup than any *Englisch* girl he'd ever seen. Tonight she wore a low cut black top with a tiny skirt and shiny boots.

"Hey there, Gorgeous," she said, leaning in so he could hear above the music. Her lips brushed his ear. "I was wondering if I'd see you again."

He felt a blush creep up his face and hoped it didn't show. "I've been working."

"You know what they say about all work

and no play." She ran her fingers up and down his sleeve. "Well, maybe you Amish guys never heard that." She pulled a bottle of vodka from the grocery bag. "I'm going to go fix myself a drink. Want one?"

"No, thanks. I've got my beer."

She returned with a plastic cup and took some deep gulps, then reached for his beer and took a sip of it. "Shooters," she said with a giggle.

"Let's find someplace quiet to talk." She grabbed his hand and led him into the kitchen. Later he wondered if it had been a good idea to go there. It was close to her bottle of vodka — too close. She filled her glass again and took more sips from his can of beer.

"How is your job going?" he asked her.

"Okay. Boring. I hate retail. Customers can be so rude."

"I'm sorry."

"Sure you don't want some?" She held out her cup.

"No, I'm driving."

"I came with Yolanda so I can have a few, enjoy myself." She frowned as she glanced over his shoulder. "Uh-oh."

"What?"

"I think she just left with someone. Oh well, you'll give me a ride, won'tcha?" She gave him a tipsy smile.

"Sure."

They tried to talk, but the noise level kept rising as more people arrived. And then John thought he smelled something funny. Becky noticed it, too.

"Someone's got some weed. They should share," she said with a pout.

He tossed his beer in the wastepaper basket. "That's it. I'm leaving. If you want a ride, you need to come now."

"But I just got here."

"I'm not staying."

"Oh, you're a party poop. Usually Amish guys like to cut loose when they get away from home." She frowned. "Come to think of it, you've never been much fun. Come on, loosen up." She stood on tiptoes to kiss him and wobbled so that she had to grab at the counter to steady herself.

He stared at her. Why had he thought he'd like to see her? He suddenly had an image of Rose Anna. Determinedly he shook it away.

"I'm going. Do you want a ride or not?"

"Not. I can get a ride easy." She turned her back on him and refilled her cup.

John grabbed his jacket and started out. He didn't see Simon anywhere or he would have thanked him for inviting him.

Outside the air was cold but welcome. The apartment had been stuffy with so many people jammed in the small space and some of them smoking who knew what.

He got into his truck and rolled down the window to let in some fresh air. Just as he stuck his key in the ignition, he saw two police cruisers pull into the lot. He waited, letting the engine warm, curious to see where the officers — one male, one female — were headed.

They went straight up to Adam's apartment, and one of them knocked on the door. Someone opened it, and loud music poured out, then stopped abruptly.

John couldn't help breathing a sigh of relief that he'd left when he did. The officers didn't go inside, but there was an extended conversation going on with whoever answered the door. He presumed it was Adam. One of the officers stepped aside as several people left. A few minutes later the officers returned to their car.

He pulled out and headed home.

A block later, he caught a glimpse of flashing lights in his rearview mirror. With a sinking heart, he pulled over and shut off the engine.

Officer Kate appeared at his window. Relieved, he smiled and greeted her. She took the driver's license and registration from him then to his utter shock told him to get out.

"I wasn't speeding."

"I know. You were just at the party?"

He nodded. "I just had one beer. And not even the whole can," he said, remembering how Becky had helped herself to it.

"Get out of the vehicle, please."

And there, beside the road he'd traveled all his life, he learned what a Breathalyzer test was and how humiliating it was to follow the directions to show he wasn't driving under the influence.

Something seemed different when Rose Anna walked into the quilting classroom early one morning.

Two women were already sewing at the front of the classroom.

Lannie stood by the table at the rear of the room where Brooke sat sewing. She sucked at her thumb and stared wide-eyed, then turned to Rose Anna.

She pulled her thumb from her mouth. "Doggie!"

Doggie? Had she learned a new word? The *kind*'s *mudder* had confided she'd been slow to talk.

Then the head of a German shepherd

156

emerged from behind the table. Rose Anna jumped.

"King. Sit." Brooke looked up and gave her a tentative smile. "Rose Anna, meet my new buddy. Kate had me talk to her husband, and he hooked me up with an organization that pairs veterans who have PTSD with service dogs. It's a new experience having a dog like this."

"I thought such dogs were only for blind people." Rose Anna set her tote bag on a nearby table.

"So did I."

Rose Anna couldn't help thinking how magnificent he was. He had big, expressive brown eyes and the typical Shepherd markings. His tongue lolled as he watched her.

"He's supposed to help me deal with my anxiety. We're only here until noon, and then we're being picked up to go for more training."

She frowned and glanced nervously at the window. "I dunno. I think I might go back to my room and wait there."

Rose Anna watched, concerned, as Brooke's breathing became jerky and perspiration beaded her forehead. She clutched her fabric with shaking hands.

Oh my, Rose Anna thought, her heart sinking. Brooke was having an anxiety attack like she'd done the first week she'd attended class.

And then before she could say anything King moved closer, put one of his paws on Brooke's knee, and whined. They gazed at each other, and then Brooke began petting his head. Long moments passed. Her breathing eased as she focused on the dog, and she seemed to become calmer. She hugged the dog, eased back, and began to sew again.

Relieved, Rose Anna took her things to the front of the room.

Kate came in a few minutes later. Rose Anna quietly told her what had happened.

"Looks like it's going pretty well," Kate said.

She walked over to the bin where the week's quilt blocks were stored. As women filtered into the room, she and Rose Anna greeted them and passed the blocks out.

Soon the room was a hive of activity with women talking cheerfully as they sewed. Some worked on their quilt blocks. Others sewed projects for the consignment shop. Children worked on their own crafts or colored at the little table in the corner.

Rose Anna sighed. This was her second favorite place in her world. The first, of course, was the sewing room at home.

"Everything okay?" Kate asked her.

"Fine, why?"

"You sighed."

"It was a happy sigh. Like a happy cry. I am so glad my sisters got me to come here."

Kate grinned. "Me, too." She covered a yawn. "Sorry, I had to work some overtime last night." She paused. "You might have heard something about it."

Rose Anna frowned. "No, why? Did something bad happen near my area?"

"No. It's just you know how word gets around in a small town about what the police do."

"Didn't hear about anything." She watched Kate yawn again. "You should have slept in this morning. I could have taught the class."

"And miss this? No way." She stood. "I think I'll go downstairs and get some coffee from Pearl. You want some?"

"No, thanks."

That was odd, Rose Anna thought. What was Kate saying — or not saying? She hadn't heard of anything happening.

She shrugged and decided to walk around the room again.

Edna came rushing in. "Sorry I'm late. But I got the best news. I got a job! I start Monday!"

She was instantly surrounded by the other women who wanted to hug her and hear all the details. Edna had been at the shelter for some time, and she'd had trouble finding a job.

"Just think. I can move into my own place in a month or two." She turned to Rose Anna. "Where's Kate? I wanted to tell her. She let me know she heard about an opening and had a friend give me a ride to the interview."

"She'll be back in a minute. She just went for a cup of coffee."

Edna glanced around the room. "It's strange, but I'm going to miss this place. It's been my home. And the classes. I'm going to miss them so much." She teared up, pulled a tissue from her pocket, and wiped her eyes.

Kate walked in and when she saw Edna crying hurried forward. "Oh no, you didn't get the job?"

"I got the job!"

"Happy tears," Rose Anna told her with a grin. "She's crying happy tears." She felt her own eyes tear up as Kate embraced Edna.

"I have a friend who teaches," Rose Anna told Kate when everyone settled back into sewing and Edna went to tell Pearl the good news. "She told me she always feels a mix of emotions when her students graduate. She's happy for them but sad to see them go. Now I know how she feels."

Kate nodded, blinking hard as she sipped her coffee.

"It's important what you and Pearl do here," she told Kate.

"You, too," Kate said. "And I couldn't have started the classes without Lavina, and later, Mary Elizabeth and you."

"You'd have done it all on your own. You're a strong woman." She tilted her head and studied Kate.

"I doubt that."

"Doggie! I want hug doggie!" Lannie cried.

"He's a working dog, sweetie," her mother told her. "We don't pet them when they're helping their owner."

But the request was moot — they watched as Brooke left the room, King at her side. It was eleven a.m., Rose Anna noted.

"She stayed longer than usual," Kate noted quietly. "Maybe King is going to help her." She sighed. "It's been a good morning. A good morning indeed." She turned to Rose Anna. "I'm glad I came. I can go home and sleep. I don't work again until Saturday."

Saturday. Rose Anna remembered she'd be seeing John at Mary Elizabeth and Sam's house on Saturday.

She nodded. "Yes, a very good morning," she agreed and picked up her quilt to sew.

9

Saturday had finally come.

Rose Anna woke just as weak dawn light crept into her bedroom window. John would be at Mary Elizabeth and Sam's house today. It was perfect timing — he'd be there for several hours and witness his *bruders* and their *fraas*. Surely all that marital bliss would influence him to think about going down that path with her.

Wouldn't it?

She lay in bed for a few minutes and enjoyed a little fantasy of what that would be like.

And woke an hour later. Shocked at what she'd done, she jumped from bed and dressed quickly.

Her *mudder* looked up in surprise when she clattered down the stairs and rushed into the kitchen. "In a hurry?"

"I overslept."

Linda raised her eyebrows. "You're not

often up this early."

She walked over to the stove and poured herself a cup of coffee. "I promised Mary Elizabeth I'd help her today."

"I know. I'm going, remember? I would have gotten you up if you didn't come down soon."

She took a sip of coffee and winced when she burned her tongue.

"Slow down. We'll get there soon enough." Linda rose and pulled a tray from the oven. She transferred pancakes from it to a plate and set it before Rose Anna.

"Where's *Daed*?" She asked as she spread butter over her pancakes then doused them with maple syrup.

"He ate already and went out in the barn." She glanced at the kitchen window. "Looks like we'll have a pretty day. It's warming up."

The back door opened and her *dat* came in. He strolled over to her *mudder* and handed her a clutch of wild violets. "Found these in the yard."

Rose Anna watched them exchange a tender look. She couldn't help wondering if John would be more in favor of marriage if he'd experienced such scenes with his parents. She knew from talking to him and Lavina and Mary Elizabeth how harsh

Amos Stoltzfus had been with their *mudder* as well as with his *sohns*. It was so sad. Amos had changed after he had the cancer and went into remission, but he and John still couldn't seem to get along the way his *bruders* did with their *dat*.

"Rose Anna? Something wrong with the pancakes?"

"Hmm?" She dragged herself back from depressing thoughts. "*Nee*. They're *gut* like always. I was just thinking about something."

Linda rose to find a little vase for the violets. "I packed some food if you want to put it in the buggy, Jacob."

"*Schur*." He picked up the wicker basket and headed out again.

Her *mudder* turned to her. "I put the brownies you baked last night in the basket. I'm so surprised your *dat* didn't find them."

Rose Anna finished the pancakes quickly and walked over to the kitchen window. She laughed and shook her head. "He's out there poking through the basket."

Linda marched over to the door, opened it, and yelled her *mann*'s name. When she shut the door and turned back she was chuckling. "He almost dropped the basket."

She snatched up her jacket and purse. "Ready, *Mamm*?"

165

"I'm beginning to wonder why you're so eager to go clean and paint."

"It's fun seeing how they're bringing the old farmhouse back to life, isn't it?" Rose Anna responded pertly.

"If you think I don't know when you're up to something, you have another think coming," her *mudder* murmured as they drew on their coats and picked up their purses.

A few minutes later Jacob pulled the buggy into the drive of Mary Elizabeth and Sam's farmhouse. John's red pickup was parked by the barn.

Linda slanted a knowing look at Rose Anna. "Well, well, look who's here."

Rose Anna gave her *mudder* her most innocent look.

She could tell by her expression that she hadn't fooled her.

Everyone was gathered in the kitchen enjoying coffee and cinnamon rolls. Standing together she thought how alike the *bruders* looked.

Her gaze immediately landed on John — far and away the handsomest of the three to her — as he picked up a hand-sized roll. He looked up and nodded at her as he bit into the roll.

"I'm so glad you could come!" Mary Elizabeth greeted them.

"Where are Lavina and Mark?" Linda asked as she shed her coat.

"She'll be here soon," David assured her. "Mark was fussy last night, so he's having a nap."

Mary Elizabeth took her coat and held out a hand for Rose Anna's. "Have some coffee and be sure to try Waneta's rolls. They just came out of the oven." She went to put the coats in another room.

Rose Anna had just eaten breakfast, but she walked over and poured herself a cup of coffee so that she could get closer to John.

"Glad you could come to help today," she told him as she added cream to her cup.

He shrugged. "I try to help where I can."

"He helps himself to any food he can find for free," Sam teased, elbowing him so he could get closer to the platter of rolls on the table. "Have you figured out how to cook anything other than ramen noodles?"

"I've always known how to cook more than ramen noodles," John said defensively. "And tell me what you know how to cook. I'd say you're a lucky man to have gotten married to such a good cook as Mary Elizabeth."

David chuckled. "Got you there, Sam."

John turned to his older brother. "And

you got lucky as well."

Linda gave Rose Anna a knowing look.

John licked icing from his fingers. "And it sure doesn't hurt that Mom is living in the *dawdi haus* at your farm and bakes rolls such as these, does it?"

She sipped her coffee thoughtfully. So was John saying that the way to a man's heart was through his stomach? She'd make sure some of the double fudge brownies she'd baked and brought today made their way home with him when he left.

Providing her *dat* hadn't sneaked too many of them before her *mudder* had caught him rifling through the wicker basket.

The men finished their coffee and rolls and headed upstairs. Mary Elizabeth had said that they'd be sanding the floors in two upstairs bedrooms. The women would be scrubbing walls in two other rooms in preparation for painting them on another workday.

"I'll clean up the kitchen and then be right up," Rose Anna told Mary Elizabeth and her *mudder.*

Once they were upstairs she found a box of plastic baggies in a cupboard, slipped a couple of brownies into one, and tucked it into her purse. She wanted to make sure that they weren't all eaten up so she could send some home with John.

She heard footsteps on the stairs and spun away, walking quickly to the sink.

John walked into the kitchen and was surprised to see Rose Anna there.

He scooped up a box of sandpaper that had been left on the kitchen table. "Each of us thought the other one took this upstairs," he said with a grin.

"How is work going?" she asked him before he had a chance to leave the room. "I heard you got a new job taking care of horses."

"Word sure gets around."

She nodded.

"It's part-time. I'm helping at the Zimmerman horse farm."

"Probably doesn't seem like work, does it, since you love horses so much? I remember how you used to go out and sleep in the barn with your family's horses." She frowned. "Of course, that was often because of your *dat* being so hard to get along with."

Touched that she'd remembered, he shrugged and tossed the box from hand to hand. "Sometimes it was nice being out there with them instead of him. It's no fun mucking stalls at the horse farm, but the other day when I exercised Midnight I was

169

thinking I'd pay the owner to ride that horse. But don't tell him I said that."

She returned his grin. "He won't hear it from me."

"Hey, John, did you get lost on the way to the kitchen? Or are you down there eating all the rolls?" they heard Sam call down from upstairs.

"I'm coming!" he shouted back. He cast a glance at the rolls.

"I brought double fudge brownies for dessert," she told him.

"Those are worth waiting for. See you later."

He met Mary Elizabeth on the stairs as he went up.

"What's taking you so long?" he heard her ask Rose Anna when she got downstairs. But he didn't hear her answer.

John spent several hours helping Sam and David sand then stain the floors in two rooms. Every so often he could hear the women laughing and talking as they worked in the next room.

Then he heard the women descend the stairs, and a short time later delicious smells drifted up.

Mary Elizabeth appeared in the doorway. "Ready to eat?"

"Always," he told her and he was the first

one to make it downstairs and wash up. He couldn't wait to get his hands on one of Rose Anna's double fudge brownies. She'd made them many times for him after she'd offered him one from her school lunch years ago.

Lunch was a hearty chicken and noodle casserole and dishes of stewed tomatoes and green beans canned after the fall harvest. He ate hungrily. The work had been hard, and since he didn't often get home cooking like this, he ate his fill and more.

Rose Anna sat opposite him eating far less than he did. She'd always been delicate, he mused, and ate little. Her mother was a wonderful cook, so she certainly didn't lack for delicious meals. And he knew from eating often at their house that Rose Anna and her sisters were good cooks as well. She had been small as a young girl and stayed slender as she got older.

"Who's ready for dessert?" she asked when empty plates were pushed aside. She produced a platter laden with big squares of brownies, and it was passed around.

John bit into chocolate heaven. Man, if the woman went into business selling these she'd make a fortune, he thought.

"Want another?" she asked him.

He nodded vigorously and was sad to see

the remaining brownies taken by the others.

Rose Anna smiled at him mysteriously.

The percolator bubbled cheerfully on the stove. As soon as it finished perking, they each had a cup and talked about returning the following week to paint the newly scrubbed walls in the upstairs bedrooms.

David excused himself to go outside to the phone shanty to call Lavina. When he returned, he was frowning.

"Lavina said Mark is running a little fever, so she's going to stay home," he told them.

"Oh, *nee,* I was so looking forward to seeing him today," Linda said, sounding disappointed.

"We could stop by on the way home," Jacob pointed out.

A big smile spread over her face. "That would be *wunderbaar!*"

Sam stood and put his dishes in the sink. "I'll help you hitch your buggy, Jacob."

"Oh, but I should help with the dishes," Linda said.

"I'll do that," Rose Anna told her. "You two go on."

"But how will you get home?"

Rose Anna looked at John. "Would you mind giving me a ride so I can stay and help Mary Elizabeth?"

"Sure."

"John, maybe you could look at Nellie's right foreleg before you take off. She's favored it the last day or two," Sam said.

"Be glad to."

He pulled on his jacket and followed Sam out to the barn. After they hitched up the Zook buggy, he looked over Nellie's foreleg and sure enough, he detected a mild strain. He wrapped it up and, as he did, showed Sam how to do it.

"If it's not better Monday give the vet a call."

Sam nodded. "So how's the job going at Zimmerman's?"

"Great. Pay is good, and I get to work with horses." He stroked Nellie's neck. "I was missing the horses most of all since I left home."

"I bet. I heard you talking to Nellie in your sleep one night when we lived at the apartment."

"I don't talk in my sleep."

"Do, too."

"You're full of it."

But as he turned to walk out of the barn, he wasn't so sure about that. When they'd shared a bedroom as kids, David had told him he was talking in his sleep.

Sam clapped him on the shoulder. "Anyway, *danki* for the help today."

173

"Anytime."

They walked back into the house. Mary Elizabeth and Rose Anna had cleared the table, and Rose Anna was finishing up washing the dishes and putting them away.

"John, I packed some of the leftover chicken casserole for you," Mary Elizabeth told him. She handed him a loaded tote bag.

"Great. Thank you so much."

"You know you're welcome to come to supper anytime. You don't have to do work to earn a meal here."

"You're sweet," he told her, touched.

Rose Anna dried the last dish and put it in the cabinet. "I'm ready to go when you are."

John said goodbye to Mary Elizabeth and walked to the truck with Rose Anna. He held her door open for her and then rounded the hood to climb into the driver's side.

He glanced at the loaded tote bag sitting between them. "Your sister was sweet, but I hope she doesn't think I starve since I'm a bachelor."

"I imagine there are plenty of women who bring you food."

"Not where I live."

"The *Englisch* women don't drop by with a sample of their cooking the way the *mae-*

dels do in our Amish community?"

"No. They don't cook as much as Amish women. At least from what I've heard." He wondered if Becky even knew what a kitchen was other than a place for a refrigerator to store booze.

"Well, I have a surprise for you." She pulled a plastic baggie from her purse and handed it to him.

"Brownies? You saved me some?"

"I remembered you always liked them. You seemed disappointed they went quickly today."

"I was. Thank you. I might save one to go with my lowly cold cut sandwich for lunch tomorrow."

"John?"

"Hmm?" He glanced over as he drove.

"You seem happier lately."

"Dad wasn't there today."

"I don't think that was all of it. You just seem happier."

He wasn't surprised it showed. She'd always been able to read his moods, understand them, more than anyone he knew. That was a pleasure — and a pain since he could no longer be with her.

"It's the new job. Just part-time, but it's working with horses."

"You've always loved them."

He nodded. "Nick, Naomi's husband, let me know Neil Zimmerman was looking for someone to help him. So I'm there around my other jobs."

"It looks like a beautiful place. I've only seen it from the road, of course," she said quickly when he looked at her curiously.

"The stables are nicer than the homes of some people," he told her. Actually, the stables were nicer than his current place, but she didn't need to know that. It made him feel like less than a success that it was so small and in such bad shape. But it wouldn't be long before he had it fixed up.

"I always like helping *Daed* with our horses," she told him.

"I remember how much you like horses, too." It was one of the things they had in common.

John told her about Midnight and about Willow. He decided it wasn't a good idea to tell her how Willow reminded him of her and her flirtatious looks.

"Sounds like Willow has you charmed."

He chuckled. "I think she likes me for the apples I bring her."

It was nice talking to her this way. She was the only person who'd ever truly understood him. He'd missed this closeness with her, deliberately blocked it because it was something he couldn't have anymore.

It took him by surprise how much he'd missed her. Suddenly he didn't want to drop her off and go to his place.

The Zimmerman farm was up the road. What if . . .

He turned to her. Tried to sound casual when he didn't feel that way. "Do you have to get home right away?"

Rose Anna stared at him, puzzled at the question. "*Nee,* why?" she asked slowly.

"Want to take a look?"

"Are you *schur* it's *allrecht*?"

He nodded. "I stop by sometimes when I'm not working."

"It's nice when work's fun. That's how I feel about quilting. When I'm not quilting, I'm helping Kate teach it."

"Kate Kraft?"

"*Ya,* she's the one who started the classes at the shelter. I told you that once."

"Right, I just forgot for a minute. I guess you two are friends, huh?"

She nodded. "I love helping with the class. I do it two mornings a week now since some of the women are making crafts for the shop."

"Here we are," he said as he pulled into

the drive of the farm and parked near the stables.

"Wow, you're right," she said, looking awed as they got out of the truck. "The place is so big."

He keyed in the code to enter the barn and they walked inside.

Rose Anna jumped when a big black horse stuck his head over the stall door.

John stopped in front of it and stroked the horse's nose. "This is Midnight. Sometimes I wonder if he thinks his middle name is Magnificent."

She laughed. "He'd be right." She reached out to touch him but jumped when he snorted and shook his head.

"You know you want the pretty girl to pet you," John told him.

He took her hand in his and brought it to Midnight's head. "There, doesn't that feel good, boy? Her hands are softer than mine."

Rose Anna felt a tingle race up her arm at John's touch. She jerked her head to stare at him and saw him staring at her. So he felt it too, she thought, breathless.

She started to pull her hand away but his tightened over it, drew it to his face so that she touched his cheek.

"I missed you," he whispered, his eyes darkening.

"I —"

Willow shook her head in the next stall and moved restlessly.

Startled, Rose Anna stepped back, her eyes wide as she stared at him. They drew apart.

A moment later, the barn door was pushed open and bright sunlight poured inside.

"John! Couldn't stay away, huh?" a male voice called.

John stepped back and turned as a man strode toward him.

"No, I wanted to check on Midnight since he's feeling a little off the last few days. Neil, this is Rose Anna Zook, a friend of mine."

"I saw your truck pull in." He turned to Rose Anna. "How you doin', little lady?" He stuck out his hand and shook hers vigorously.

"Good, thank you. You have some beautiful horses."

He stood there, hands on hips, feet wide apart, a portly man who looked to be in his late sixties and who wore the air of a satisfied, prosperous landowner.

"The place is my own little piece of heaven," he said, nodding. "It's my hobby." He looked at John. "So what do you think? Should we call the vet?"

He shook his head. "I think he's feeling

much better. But it's your call."

Neil patted Midnight's neck. "No, I agree. His eyes are brighter, and Bob told me he ate well this morning when he fed him."

"Well, I need to take Rose Anna home, so I'll be going unless you need me to do anything."

"Naw, it's your day off. Go enjoy with your young lady." Neil slapped him on his shoulder. "Nice to meet you, Rose Anna," he told her. "You come back any time."

"Thank you."

They followed him out of the barn. Neil waved to them as they got in the truck before he headed toward the big farmhouse.

"Neil seems nice."

"He is." He helped her into the truck. "He told me he spent thirty years working in the legal field, and when he retired, he finally got to do what he'd always wanted to — raise horses. Says finding what you love to do means you don't feel like you're working at all."

"Sounds like a wise man."

She got to do that. She loved to quilt, did it for her living, and then did even more by working on teaching quilting to the women at the shelter.

"So you're getting to do something you love in this job. How about the others?"

180

He hesitated as he put the key in the ignition. "I took whatever I could find when I left the farm," he said finally. "I was grateful for it. I needed — need — the money. But it wasn't easy. We Amish are known as hard workers, but some of the *Englisch* think we don't get enough education only going to school through the eighth grade. So there are some things I won't ever get to do."

It was on the tip of her tongue to tell him he could go to school, get a high school degree. She'd heard there was something called a GED test that was accepted as a substitute for a high school diploma.

But she wanted him to come back to the community he'd been born and raised in so she resisted doing that. If he went to school, then he'd be staying in the *Englisch* world.

If you really love him you should want him to be happy, she told herself. And that might not be with you, with the Amish.

"What would you do if you could do anything you want?" she asked him.

"Do this full time," he said with a wave of his hand toward the barn. "Work with horses."

He sighed and turned his attention to putting the truck in gear and backing out of the driveway, then headed toward her home.

They passed farms with fields that lay

dormant. Here and there she glimpsed a sign of spring — a few green buds on a bare-limbed tree, a few hardy crocus and daffodils poking their heads up. It wouldn't be that long before Amish farmers brought out their plows and workhorses and the land would be planted.

Silence stretched between them. She searched for words. It was easy to say that God had a plan for him and everything would work out all right, but right now she was having trouble believing that about her own life so how could she speak the words?

"I think it's *wunderbaar* that you're getting to do what you love," she began. "Even if it's part-time. Who knows where that'll lead?"

He merely grunted.

"David didn't think he had a future when he left home," she reminded him. "But when your *dat* got sick and he returned, he ended up taking over the farm. Sam wanted a farm and didn't think he could afford one. But he was able to buy one after all, and we were there today helping to work at it."

She let the words hang there in the space between them.

John said nothing — didn't even grunt this time. But she knew he heard her.

"I believe in you. God does, too. He's got

a plan for all of us even when we can't see it." She stopped, stared at her hands clasped in her lap. "I do believe that even on days when it's hard."

He pulled into the driveway of her home and stopped the truck. She gathered her purse and the tote bag she'd carried packed with brownies earlier that day. "*Danki* for the ride. And for taking me to see the horses."

She turned to open the door and felt his hand on her arm. Turning, she stared at him.

"Thank you for the brownies. And I'm glad you enjoyed visiting the horses." His gaze dropped to his hand. "Rose Anna? Do you want to go for a drive maybe tomorrow after church?"

Her heart leaped into her throat. "Does this mean you want to go to church?"

"No, sorry. But I'll pick you up after."

It was a step. She nodded slowly. "I'd like that."

And when she climbed the steps to her house she felt her spirits soar.

10

Rose Anna felt like a teenager again waiting for John to show up on Sunday after church.

Her plan was coming true.

Since it was a church day, she spent three hours in a service at the Miller house, then helped serve and clean up the light meal afterward.

John waited for her a block from the home that hosted the service. He'd suggested it out of consideration for church members who might be offended by his driving a truck so close to the services.

When she climbed inside, she set her purse down on the seat between them, buckled her seatbelt, then withdrew a waxed paper package and handed it to him.

"What's this?"

"I thought you might like a sandwich made with church spread."

He shot her a quick grin. "One of my favorites."

"I know."

"I have peanut butter on hand most of the time. I should get the marshmallow crème next time I'm at the store and make it at home."

When he had to stop at a traffic light, he unwrapped it and took a big bite. "Good stuff." He slanted a look at her. "Thank you."

She just smiled at him, thinking the way to a man's heart . . . and it was such a pleasure to feed those you loved. "It was no trouble. So where are we going?"

"No place special. I thought we could take a drive in the country."

"Sounds *gut.*"

A Sunday drive was one of the favored activities of Amish couples. Not that they were a couple, she reminded herself. A buggy ride was an inexpensive way for a couple to spend time together, be private, and get to know each other. If there was a covered bridge it was also a way for them to sneak a very private kiss away from the eyes of passersby.

She felt heat rise in her cheeks at the thought of them kissing and had to shove the image away. Instead, she cast a surreptitious glance over at him and watched him enjoying his sandwich as he drove.

"So do you like driving the truck more than a buggy?"

"Yeah. I just have to be careful to watch the speedometer."

He gave her an odd look but didn't say more.

"It's nice to go fast, I suppose," she allowed as she watched the scenery speed by. "But there's something about taking time and enjoying the ride."

"You can't go as far in a buggy," he pointed out. "That's how the church keeps its sheep close at hand."

"Sheep?" She'd never heard him be so critical of church.

He shrugged. "Let's face it. A buggy limits how far from home a person can roam."

"But why would anyone want to leave here?" She half-turned in her seat. "You've seemed happier since you've been working with horses. But are you really happy living away from the community?"

"It's okay."

"Tell me about the place you live now. I know you gave up the apartment you shared with Sam."

"It's not much, just a little caretaker's cabin on a nearby farm. I'm fixing it up as part of my rent."

"You don't ever get lonely?"

186

He jerked his head to look at her and looked surprised. "No. Why would you think that?"

"I'm so used to having family around." She paused and wished she could take back her words. Family had never been a comfort to him the way it had for her.

"It does get quiet sometimes without Sam to nag me," he acknowledged. "Big brothers do love to nag."

"And big *schweschders.*"

"Funny how we each had two siblings to nag us, huh?"

She nodded. She'd always thought it was one of the things they had in common. They'd shared many a complaint about being treated like the less smart, less mature member of the family.

"Would you like to stop for some hot chocolate?"

"Schur." Had he remembered it was one of her favorites, or was he only asking because it was cold out?

He stopped at a diner, left the truck running so she'd stay warm with the heater on, and ran in to get their drinks. When he returned, he had a drink carrier and a brown paper bag.

The chocolate was hot and topped with whipped cream. And in the bag she found the little cinnamon sugar-dusted homemade doughnut holes the diner was famous for, warm and crusty and sweet.

She held out the bag to him. He took one and popped it into his mouth. She laughed. "You look like a chipmunk."

He plucked one out of the bag, put it in the other side of his mouth, and mugged at her.

"Definitely a chipmunk."

He snorted a laugh and then choked. She thumped him on the back, biting her lip and struggling to contain her mirth.

"I'm fine!" he gasped. "You can stop beating me now."

She sat back and smiled at him. "I wasn't beating you."

"You were being pretty enthusiastic." He took a sip, then another of his hot chocolate.

"Just trying to save you from death by doughnut."

"I'd forgotten what a smart mouth you have," he told her as he started the truck.

"I'm just smart," she said pertly. It felt so good to be with him. She wondered if he felt the same way. She glimpsed a hint of smile lurking at the corner of his mouth as she gave him a covert glance.

"My *schweschders* act like I talk outrageously," she said. Then, horrified at what she'd blurted out, she put another doughnut hole in her mouth to shut herself up.

"They still giving you a hard time?"

She jerked her head to stare at him.

"They always did. Thought they'd have stopped by now."

"I'll always be the *boppli* of the family," she complained.

"Yeah, me, too."

She thought about it. "That's true. You're the youngest in your family, too. I think that was the first thing we discovered we had in common. Then came horses. The interest in them, I mean."

"True."

"Do you miss them?"

"Miss them? My brothers? I just saw them yesterday, remember?"

"*Ya,* but it's not the same now that they're married and not living at home." She fell silent. "Even when my *schweschders* were driving me crazy treating me like a *boppli* and everything, they were my best friends."

"I know. I feel the same way about my brothers. We got closer than most because Dad was so rough on us. We were a real unit when we decided we had to leave."

"They've both come back," she said quietly. Oh, how she wanted to ask him if he still thought it wasn't for him. But she

189

didn't want to disturb this . . . ease between them that she'd longed for these past months.

"I'm glad I started going to the quilting class at the shelter," she said, staring ahead at the road. "I became friends with Kate and a lot of women I'd never have met if I hadn't gone there. Of course, there's a downside. The women go on to their own lives and get jobs and their own places." She looked at him. "What about you?"

"What about me?"

"Have you made any friends away from our community?"

He frowned. "Not a lot. Not much time."

"That's too bad." But she didn't really mean it. If he wasn't making friends, maybe that meant that he wasn't putting down roots in the *Englisch* community.

And as much as she wanted him to be happy, she really wanted him to be happy in her community — *their* community. If that made her a bad person, well then, she guessed she was a bad person.

John gave Rose Anna a wary glance. She hadn't talked for miles.

Rose Anna had never been a quiet person. Sure, sometimes in the past she talked too much, and it wore him a little. But she'd gone silent after he said he hadn't made friends in the *Englisch* community.

Why had that made her stop talking? Did she feel sorry for him? That didn't sit well. He didn't want her pity.

"I went to a party the other night," he found himself telling her.

"Was it fun?"

He shrugged. "It was okay." That nagging worry came back again. What if Kate had told her that she'd pulled him over for a sobriety test after it? But once again her expression didn't change, and she didn't say anything to indicate Kate had spoken about it.

"I'm doing some work on the place I live to get a break on the rent. That's taking up a lot of my evenings when I come home."

"All work and no play . . ."

"Yeah. Well, I'm used to working hard. I watch TV sometimes to relax." He tapped his fingers on the steering wheel as he slowed down behind a buggy. "I can see why the bishops want to keep it out of Amish homes. There's so much to watch — sports and movies and music shows. It can be addictive. Sam couldn't tear me away from it when we first moved into an apartment together and we had a small set." He chuckled. "I got better about not watching it so much."

He caught a glimpse of movement to the right off the road. A deer bounded into the path of the truck. He jerked the wheel to the left and tried to swerve out of the way but felt the impact of it hit.

Rose Anna threw her arms up in front of her face and screamed.

John pulled the truck over to the side of the road, shut off the engine, and turned to her. "Are you all right?"

She lowered her arms and nodded. "I think so."

He unbuckled his seat belt and got out to check on the deer. When he heard her door open, he waved her back. He didn't want her to see it if it was bloody — or dead. "Don't get out. It might hurt you."

"Not if it's hurt."

To his shock, the deer struggled to its feet and ran off.

"Well, guess it's not hurt too bad."

"Gut," she said, slipping out of the truck and holding onto the door handle as if she needed its support. "I'm not *schur* if I could have handled seeing it killed." She took a deep breath. "That doesn't happen often when you ride in a buggy."

"Nope. Only heard of it happening once."

He opened the passenger-side door for her and waited until she tucked her skirts inside before he shut it. Then he thought to check for damage to the truck. There was only a small dent to the bumper to show anything had happened.

Relieved, he walked around to his side. "Well, that was some excitement I can do without." He rested his hands on the steering wheel. Thank goodness it had been daylight and he'd been able to see the deer and swerve. Too often drivers weren't as lucky at night in these parts.

He glanced at her and saw she was clenching her hands in her lap. "You're sure you're okay?"

"Schur." But her smile was shaky.

A car sped past, and the gust of wind shook the truck a little. He started the engine. "We need to get off the side of the road so there's not another accident."

"You're right."

He saw a sign for a restaurant that featured "Amish home cooking" ahead. Locals and tourists alike favored it. "Listen, why don't we get something to eat before I take you home? I wouldn't want to drop you off so upset. Your parents might think I did something to you."

"They wouldn't do that," she told him.

"Well, you can save me from going home to ramen noodles."

She laughed, and her hands relaxed in her lap. "You know you love them." She saw the sign for the restaurant and sighed. "But it would be nice. *Danki.*"

When they had settled into a booth and gotten their menus, John began wondering if he'd been rash to suggest having a meal together. They'd come here several times before he left home. And it seemed like there were so many couples seated around them. A server was walking around lighting little lanterns on each table as the supper hour drew near. She lit the one on their table and walked on. The flickering light from it seemed to make the atmosphere cozier, more intimate.

John watched the way Rose Anna's skin glowed in the light as she studied her menu, her eyes downcast. Sometimes he forgot just how lovely she was, her complexion so pure, her lips a natural tint like her first name.

"They haven't changed the menu since we've been here," she said and looked up. Her eyes sparkled. "No ramen noodles."

He chuckled. "Not exactly an Amish specialty."

They ordered, and as they enjoyed their supper, he watched the last of her nerves vanish and the bubbly Rose Anna emerge.

She told him a story about the first day she'd taught quilting at the shelter after Kate had called her a master quilter and how she kept showing how to do it wrong. He told her one about being careless and approaching Midnight from the wrong end and being embarrassed about his horse-tending skills in front of his new boss.

"Lucky for me Neil understood I hadn't been around horses in a while," he said as he pushed his empty plate aside. "He told me nearly being kicked wasn't a lesson I'd forget anytime soon."

"Kate told me I showed the ladies that no one is perfect and we're supposed to be having fun," she told him. "I don't know how many times I've told them that a seam ripper will be their favorite tool."

He knew the one she meant. After all, his mother was a quilter and a seamstress. Too bad people couldn't go back, rip out the part of their life that hadn't gone as planned, and redo it, he couldn't help thinking.

Their server wheeled a wooden dessert cart over. "Hope you saved room for dessert," she said cheerfully. "No one can resist our homemade pies — especially the shoofly pie and the Dutch apple pie."

John chose the Dutch apple. He'd never

195

been able to resist pie.

And as he watched Rose Anna lean over and study the cart with wide eyes, he felt something turn over in his heart and realized he'd never be able to resist her again either.

Rose Anna watched John drive away.

They'd had a wonderful afternoon. At least she had. *Nee,* she could tell he'd enjoyed himself, too. But then, as they drove home he'd been so quiet. And he'd given her a long, serious look when she thanked him, her hand on the door handle.

She sat down in a rocking chair on the front porch and watched the taillights of his truck until they vanished from view.

The front door opened. Her mother peered out. "I thought I heard someone in the drive. Are you coming in? It's chilly out."

Rose Anna rose and followed her inside. They stopped when they saw Jacob snoozing in his recliner, a book open on his chest. Her *mudder* grinned at her and put a finger to her lips, silently telling her to be quiet. They tiptoed past.

"Why were you sitting on the porch?" Linda asked when they got to the kitchen. "Is anything wrong?"

She shook her head as she unbuttoned her

coat. "*Nee*. We went for a drive and stopped for supper."

"How's John?"

"*Gut*. He likes his part-time job helping at the horse farm."

"I see. Tea?"

"That would be nice." She hung up her coat then sat at the table and watched her *mudder* put the teakettle on to heat. "He likes it a lot."

Linda sat at the table. "I see."

"I'm worried about John. He said he's found what he really wants to do with his life." She rested her chin in her hand, her elbow on the table. "How's he going to do that when he hasn't got any money?"

"God works in mysterious ways."

The teakettle whistled. Linda rose, poured hot water into two mugs, and set them on the table.

Rose Anna chose a tea bag from the bowl on the table, unwrapped it, and dunked it into the water. "His ways are certainly a mystery to me sometimes."

"Think about David and Sam."

"What about them?"

"Neither of them thought they would ever own farms."

Rose Anna brightened. "And now they both do." She sat there stirring her tea, thinking about that.

"Ya." Linda sipped her tea. "I always loved what Phoebe used to say about worry."

" 'Worry is arrogant. God knows what He's doing.' "

She smiled. "Exactly." She sighed. "I miss her."

"We all do. *Mamm,* when is *Grossdaadi* coming home?"

"Next week."

"I miss him."

"I do, too. But he's having such fun in Pinecraft. I'm glad his friends talked him into going."

Friends. She and John had talked about friends.

Linda covered a yawn with her hand. "I think I'm ready for bed." She rose, washed her mug, and set it in the drainer. "Guess I'll go wake up your *dat* so he can go to bed."

"He'll say he wasn't sleeping — that he was just resting his eyes."

She laughed. "I know. And that he's not really tired."

"Men are so silly sometimes."

"True." She bent and kissed Rose Anna's cheek. "See you in the morning."

Rose Anna was washing her own mug when her *dat* walked into the kitchen a few minutes later. He looked rumpled and sleepy as he kissed her cheek and said good night.

She watched them walk, arm in arm, toward the stairs to the bedrooms. Her romantic heart yearned for that closeness with a *mann* one day. Sighing, she checked to see if anything else needed to be done in the kitchen, but it was spotless. She turned off the gas lamp and climbed the stairs to her room.

The next morning, Rose Anna walked into the quilting class at the shelter and found Kate and several women gathered around a weeping Brooke.

"Why do men have to be such jerks?" she demanded, taking a tissue from one of them and wiping tears from her face.

Shocked at the unexpected storm of emotion, Rose Anna's steps faltered. She saw Kate sitting next to Brooke quietly talking to her, so she continued on to the front of the class to set her things down and take off her coat.

Brooke's outburst was such a surprise. She didn't say much in class — to the other women or to Kate.

"Why does everything have to change for me, and Robert gets to live in our house and have his life go on like nothing happened?" she heard Brooke wail. "That house is mine, too! All the time I was putting my life in danger in Afghanistan he was sitting there not working, living on my pay."

"It's not right that all of us had to leave to be safe," Salina, one of the newer shelter residents, said.

"My counselor says it's the victim that always has to be the one who changes," Millie chimed in.

"You need to give your lawyer another call and see what he's doing to boot the guy out," Jane told her.

"I know it seems really unfair," Kate said. "But every one of you took a very big, very brave step when you left. You could have stayed, continued to take the abuse. But you said enough. That doesn't make you victims in my eyes."

Rose Anna could see that Kate's words were sinking in. Several of the women got quiet, looked thoughtful. They began drifting back to their seats at tables and picking up their sewing. Kate continued to talk quietly to Brooke who appeared to be calming. She didn't see King today and wondered why the dog wasn't with Brooke. Maybe he could have calmed her.

She walked over and greeted each of the women and those who began filtering into the room.

"What block are we working on this week?" Salina asked, her face alive with enthusiasm.

Rose Anna had almost forgotten in all the excitement. "I'll get it," she said and quickly retrieved the plastic bin from the shelves on the wall. She passed them out to those who wanted to work on them and went back to the front of the room to explain how to sew them.

Soon the room became its usual hive of activity, alive with happy voices and whirring sounds from the many sewing machines.

Kate joined her at the front table and sat to take out her own work in progress.

"Is Brooke feeling better?" she asked quietly.

"Much. Thanks for getting everyone back on track."

"All I did was get out this week's block. Salina asked me about it, and I realized it was time to start the class."

"Staying with the routine is important." Kate threaded a needle. "These women have had nothing but disruption for months, sometimes years, trying to cope with their situations. They've lived with men whose mood changed from one moment to the next, lived with insecurity and instability. This place and this class gives them a chance not just for safety but for getting centered again."

Rose Anna had heard that term before. She supposed she'd always taken being centered for granted having been taught that her faith was her center, the foundation for her life. And not for the first time she said a silent prayer of gratitude that she had grown up loved and made to feel secure not just by her family but by her community.

"You're quiet this morning," Kate noted.

"I was just thinking how lucky I've been to grow up without what some women have had to experience. But lucky's not the right word." She searched for the right one.

Kate smiled. "I know what you mean."

"What about you?" she ventured cautiously. They'd become friends through the class, but she really didn't know much about Kate. "What kind of family did you have?"

"My dad was a police officer and my mother was a stay-at-home mom who went to college when my older brother and I started school. We were pretty average. My parents are coming up on their fortieth anniversary soon. I have to say he did a good job not bringing the stress of the job home.

I hope I do half as good." She paused in her stitching. "Some cops don't handle it well, and they become abusers."

She looked up and smiled. Rose Anna followed the direction of her glance and saw that Brooke was still sitting at her machine and, even better, had a much happier expression on her face.

Salina stood and looked anxiously around the room.

Kate got up and walked over. "Problem?"

"Where's Lannie? Have you seen Lannie? She was just here by my side a minute ago."

Every woman in the room immediately began looking around them. Rose Anna did the same, and then out of the corner of her eye caught the twitch of movement in the curtains on the window at her side. Tiny bare toes peeked out from beneath them.

Rose Anna motioned to Kate who caught her signal and immediately walked over.

"I wonder where Lannie could be," Kate said loudly. "I'll have to use my superior detective skills to find her."

She bent down and tickled the toes, and Lannie giggled and thrust the curtains aside to reveal herself. She threw herself into Kate's arms and got a big hug before wiggling down to run to her mother.

What a morning, thought Rose Anna, joining the other women in laughter. It had started with tears and high emotion and was ending in shared laughter.

Quilting was the thread that bound them together just as it did the women in her community. It gave them a reason to gather, to share their joy and their pain and their hopes and fostered their creativity. Rose Anna looked at the sign Pearl had bought at Leah's shop and hung in the room.

"When life gives you scraps, make a quilt," it read. She smiled.

11

Sometimes Rose Anna thought she should pinch herself. Maybe she was dreaming, but she felt as though something changed after that day she and John went out.

He was stopping by to take her for drives, for the occasional supper, a workday at David and Lavina's or Sam and Mary Elizabeth's farm.

Neither of them used the word dating.

She was cautious and stepped around the term. Somehow it would make things too serious. She sensed he was wary of being pulled back into the community, and there was no way she wanted to scare him away.

But how she longed to ask him to come to church. Or to a singing. They had always enjoyed attending a singing.

So they acted like good friends — which they were, really — and not a couple dating.

One afternoon he took her to see a movie.

It wasn't the first time she'd seen a movie, of course. She and her *schweschders* had gone to see several that friends had called "chick flicks" and enjoyed them. John took her to see the latest *Star Wars* movie. She'd been wide-eyed at the fantastical action on the screen, and oh my, the noise was something else. It wasn't exactly the type of movie she would have chosen, but she enjoyed watching John's fascination with it.

Afterward they indulged in pizza.

"Do you go to the movies often?" she asked him as she chose a second slice.

"This is only the second one since I moved to town. I've been too busy working. Then there's the money. Movies aren't cheap. That's probably why people watch so much television." He helped himself to a third slice.

She glanced at the door and her eyes widened. "Look who's here."

"*Gut-n-owed,* Rose Anna. John, how are you doing?" Isaac Stoltzfus asked as he came to stand next to their table.

"Fine. You?"

"Doing well."

"Join us?"

He nodded and slid into the booth next to John. Their server walked over. "I came in for a takeout order. Stoltzfus."

"I'll see if it's ready yet."

"Thank you." He turned back to them. "So how are things in the *Englisch* world, cousin?"

"Good. Rose Anna and I just went to a movie."

"Ah, one of the few things I miss about my *rumschpringe*." He smiled reminiscently. "Movies. Hard rock. And pizza from this place. Emma and I came here often when we were dating. I'm taking some home. She said she has a taste for some."

Rose Anna knew that was his way of saying his *fraa* had a craving for something because she was expecting a *boppli*. At last week's church service there had been no doubt that Emma was not only expecting — she was due very soon.

As the two men discussed the movie she and John had just seen, she found herself remembering how Emma had despaired of Isaac enjoying the *Englisch* world during his *rumschpringe*. He'd cut his hair into an *Englisch* style, dressed in jeans, and looked to be the latest to leave the Amish community.

But somehow he'd changed his mind, and Emma had been credited with bringing him back to the fold.

Rose Anna wasn't a close friend of

Emma's, but Lavina was close to Emma's *schweschder,* and she'd said Emma had seriously considered leaving the church to be with Isaac.

She'd worried for a long time that John might decide to stay in the *Englisch* community. Even though they were seeing each other, he hadn't said anything about returning. Both his *bruders* had begun taking small steps back toward the community by attending a church service. A fun activity like a singing.

Something.

But John hadn't. He enjoyed *Englisch* things like the movie they'd just seen. And oh, how he loved his truck.

Could he give those things up?

She realized they'd stopped talking and were staring at her. "I'm sorry, what were you saying?"

"We're boring you by talking about movies," Isaac said with a grin.

"I'll take you to a chick flick next time," John promised her. He glanced at Isaac. "I think she fell asleep for a few minutes."

"I did not."

"I heard snoring," he said, his eyes twinkling.

"John! I did not fall asleep, and I definitely did not snore!"

She glared at him, but that just resulted in the two men laughing harder. It was really tempting to reach over and smack John on the arm, but she was saved from unladylike behavior when the server came to the table with Isaac's pizza.

Rose Anna glanced up at Isaac as he stood, handed the server the money, and took the large square box from her. "Tell Emma I said hello."

"I will."

"Are you okay?" John asked her as Isaac left.

"*Schur.* Why?"

"You barely said a word while Isaac was sitting here."

"I don't talk every minute," she responded with a touch of tartness.

"No?" he teased.

"*Nee,*" she said firmly.

"I know we were talking a lot about the movie." He nodded when the server came to ask if they wanted refills on their soft drinks.

"I figured you hadn't seen him in a while."

"I haven't." John fell silent.

Rose Anna sipped at her soft drink and wondered if it was the right time to ask him if he'd come to a church service . . .

"You know, Isaac mentioned some things

he missed about the *Englisch* world," she began carefully. "But he obviously missed many more about our community."

"Why do you say that?"

"Because he returned."

"So?"

"What do you mean 'so'?"

"What are you trying to say, Rose Anna?" He sat back, ignoring the pizza on his plate.

"I'm not saying anything." Frustrated, she found herself shredding the paper napkin in her lap.

"I was wondering when you'd start trying to talk me back. That's what you were thinking while Isaac and I were talking."

"I'm not trying to talk you back!" She balled up the napkin and set it beside her plate.

"No?"

"No!" The pizza she'd eaten was churning in her stomach. "I haven't said anything about that to you." She wanted to. Oh, how she wanted to. But she was afraid to bring it up.

The server came with their check and offered a takeout box for the remaining pizza. After casting a wary glance at their tense faces, she moved on to another table of diners.

Rose Anna gathered up her things as John

tucked bills into the leather folder. They walked out to the truck without speaking. Miserable, she stared straight ahead as he drove her home.

"Danki," she said when he pulled into the drive in front of her house. "I had a *gut* time." Well, she had up until they had their first fight.

"Rose Anna, I'm sorry for snapping at you. It's just that I feel . . . pressured when I'm with you."

She turned to him. "I don't pressure you."

He touched her hand. "You pressure me just by being you."

"What is that supposed to mean?"

"From the day she's born, an Amish *mae- del* thinks about getting married."

"That's not true!"

"No?"

But there was some truth to his words. Marriage and family was highly valued.

"I'm not like that," she insisted. But her conscience jeered. She'd set out to win him hadn't she? But she didn't want to marry him just to be married!

She jerked open the door and slid out of the truck. And when she went inside and threw herself onto her bed in a fit of self-pity, she told herself she'd been a silly *mae- del* to think things had been going so well.

■ ■ ■ ■

John muttered most of the way to the Zimmerman farm. He didn't think he'd said anything so bad, but Rose Anna had given him the silent treatment all the way home.

Then when they got to her house, she hadn't asked when she'd see him again. No, she'd thanked him politely — oh, *so* politely — and gotten out of the truck and went inside.

Well, everyone in the Amish community knew great emphasis was placed on their young people marrying and settling down to have families. Most of their friends were married and had already started their families. Her own sisters certainly hadn't exactly been old maids when they'd married. And David and Lavina already had a beautiful little son.

He'd once teased Rose Anna for being a romantic when she was a teen and she dropped her purse and a romance novel had fallen out.

Don't tell him she wasn't interested in getting married. He might not be the smartest man on the planet but he knew better than that.

He was so wound up thinking about it,

feeling defensive, he worked off his mad by mucking out a stall.

"Whoa there, I don't care to wear horse doo-doo today!" Neil said with a chuckle.

John lowered the shovel. "Sorry. Didn't hear you come in."

"No problem." Neil glanced down at his boots. "Can't own horses without getting a little manure on you."

He didn't know what to say to that, so he went back to shoveling.

"Something bothering you?"

Setting down the shovel, he looked at Neil. "No sir. Did you need me for something?"

"Nope. But you sure are putting your back into it."

He shrugged and went back to his work.

"Seems like when a man's upset, it's usually got to do with a woman. You have a fuss with that pretty little lady you brought here one day? Rose Anna was her name, right?"

He nodded. "I guess."

"You mean she didn't tell you so?" He sat himself down on a nearby bale of hay. "Never knew a woman who didn't let you know for sure if you upset her. My Doris sure did, bless her heart. Wonderful woman, but she could get a mad on and keep it for days until you apologized."

213

John felt his mouth twitch. His boss had such a colorful way of talking.

"What did you do?" Neil asked.

"What makes you think it was my fault?" John demanded.

"It's always our fault."

Now he did grin. "Well, I sort of implied Amish women were only interested in getting married, and she got offended."

"Well it's true women are more interested in the institution than we men are. That's because they're smarter than we are."

"Oh really?"

Neil laughed and slapped his knee. "Once you let her convince you she's right, you'll find out you've never been happier, son." He sighed and stared off into the distance. "I miss Doris every day."

The older man reminded John of Rose Anna's grandfather the last time he'd sat and played checkers with him. What did you say to someone like that? He didn't have much experience with saying the right words when they had lived life more than he did.

Something about the way Neil looked a little lonely as he sat there, staring off into the distance, made him take a seat on another bale of hay. No, he didn't have the fancy words, but he could listen.

214

"Tell me about Doris."

Neil dug in his back pocket, pulled out his wallet, and withdrew a photo. He showed it to John. "Most beautiful woman in the world. Took this the day our son got married. She died a year later."

John studied the photo. Doris was an attractive woman with silver hair and a nice smile. Nice looking, but the most beautiful looking woman in the world? Hardly. And then he looked at her eyes and saw the love shining in them. They told a story without words about the relationship the two had enjoyed.

"Doris was there for me through some lean times when I was setting up my practice," Neil said. "She helped in the office until I could afford to hire a secretary and paralegal. Smartest woman I ever knew. A true partner in every sense of the word. Just a wonderful wife and mother."

Neil tucked the photo back in his wallet. "So how are you going to apologize?"

"I don't think I have anything to apologize for."

"Do you want to be right or do you want to be happy?"

John stood and picked the shovel up again. "A man can't be both?"

"Oh, you have a lot to learn, son."

Willow snorted as if in agreement and moved restlessly in her stall.

"Vet stopped by earlier," Neil said, getting to his feet to wander over and stroke Willow's nose. "Said she's doing well, everything looks like the foal is getting in position for delivery. Could be any time now."

He looked at John. "How many foals have you seen born?"

"Probably half a dozen."

"It's awesome. Only thing better is watching your child born."

The mare backed away from him, switching her tail, moving restlessly around her stall.

"Acts like it's my fault she's uncomfortable," Neil told him. "Seems like Doris went through a phase like that when she was about to deliver our son."

"My oldest brother said his wife yelled at him when she was in labor. Lavina is one of the sweetest women I know." *Unlike her tart sister Rose Anna,* he thought but didn't say.

"You never said why you're living in town. Are you doing that running around time? What's it called?"

"*Rumschpringe.*" John shrugged and finished shoveling manure and used straw into the wheelbarrow. "No, when I left home it was with my brothers. Our father just got impossible to live with."

"Sorry to hear it. My father was a mean old guy. Got mad at my younger sister once for sassing him like kids will. Threw a big can of peaches at her. It was the closest thing at hand as they stood in the kitchen. Anyway, if she hadn't ducked in time, no telling what could have happened."

He sighed. "Well, I think I'll go eat my supper. You feel like beef stew just come on up to the house. There's plenty."

"Thanks."

John spread fresh hay in the stall and turned to Willow. "All nice and clean for you, Little Mama. Time for you to have that baby."

He hadn't said anything to Neil, in case he was wrong, but Willow was going to foal tonight.

Sure enough, he'd just finished cleaning stalls and feeding the other horses when Willow kicked at her stall and uttered a high-pitched neigh.

When he looked into her stall, he saw she was sweating and dripping a little milk.

He wasn't going anywhere tonight. "I'll be right back," he told Willow, and he headed up to the house to tell Neil he was going to spend the night.

"Hey, decided to have some supper?" He

held the door open.

John shook his head. "Thanks, but I'm going to spend the night in the barn if that's okay with you. I think Willow's going to foal tonight."

"Okay. Should I call the vet?"

"You said he thought she was doing well when he was here earlier. So he doesn't think she'll have any problems?"

Neil shook his head.

"Then it's up to you."

"Okay. I'll finish my supper and check in with you in a while."

John was glad he'd had something to eat earlier in the day. That stew had smelled good.

When he returned to the barn, Willow was acting more agitated. He talked to her in a soothing voice as he got a blanket and settled down next to her stall.

Neil came out a while later and surprised John with a container of stew and a Thermos of coffee. "Thought you could use this."

Touched, John took them from him. "Thanks. You didn't have to do this."

"What, you tell me you're staying for my horse and you think I'm going to let you sit out here hungry? Anyway, I phoned the vet, and he's tied up on a call on the other side of the county. Said he'd get here soon as he can."

John made quick work of the stew as he watched Willow. He'd barely finished when Willow lay down in her stall, and he could see contractions rippling across her abdomen.

"Showtime," Neil said.

He leaned on the stall and watched as John entered the small space, careful to stay to the far side. "My father always said most animals give birth without any help from us."

They didn't have long to wait. The birth was quick and uncomplicated, and before long the foal slid out onto the hay.

John sat there watching, awed as he always was at the miracle of birth. He wondered what it must be like to witness the birth of your own child.

The vet walked in just as the foal struggled to its feet.

"Well, well, good job," he announced.

"We didn't do anything," John told him.

"I was talking to Willow," the vet said, chuckling.

Rose Anna was helping wash dishes in Fannie Mae Miller's kitchen after church service when Emma Stoltzfus, Isaac's *fraa,* walked up and joined her at the sink.

"Is there enough room for me?" she asked, giggling as she maneuvered her sizeable abdomen up beside Rose Anna.

Rose Anna laughed. "Barely! Ouch, your *boppli* kicked me!"

"I think it's a boy," Emma confided, placing a hand on her abdomen. "Doesn't want to help doing dishes." She sobered. "Are you *allrecht*?"

"*Schur.* Why?"

"Isaac said he ran into you and John the other day at the pizza place in town and you looked unhappy after he joined the two of you. He was afraid he might have said something to upset you."

"It was nothing."

"*Allrecht.*" Emma picked up a dishtowel and held out a hand for the plate Rose Anna was rinsing.

Rose Anna hesitated, then glanced around. There were too many women in the room to say anything.

Picking up on her unspoken signal, Emma worked quickly helping dry the dishes Rose Anna handed her. Their work done, they walked out to the porch where they could have some privacy.

"Something Isaac said did upset me, but it wasn't his fault."

Emma studied her. "I don't understand."

Rose Anna looked over at the door, then back at Emma. "Can we talk without you saying anything to him?"

"Allrecht."

"John was talking about the movie we'd just seen, and Isaac said he missed them." She twisted her fingers in her lap. "It made me think about how John doesn't seem interested in coming home."

"I see."

"Do you?"

"I know you're . . . fond of John. I could see that before he left the community." She paused and pulled her sweater closer as a cool breeze swept across the porch. "So you're hoping he'll come back the way his *bruders* did."

"Ya."

Emma patted her hand. "I know it's hard to watch. It *schur* was when Isaac seemed so enamored of *Englisch* ways. But most of the Amish return. You know that."

"But not all."

"*Nee*, not all." Emma sighed and rubbed her abdomen. She looked at Rose Anna. "What else did Isaac say he missed? Besides movies?"

"Hard rock. And pizza from that restaurant. He said it's where the two of you went

221

a lot after a movie."

Emma smiled. "We did. I seem to be craving pizza a lot in this pregnancy. I'm not *schur* how much of my craving is for that food or a reminder of a time when I was thinner."

The front door burst open and two *kinner,* a little girl and a little boy, ran laughing to their *mudder.* Emma leaned down and wrapped them in an embrace. "Of course, times like this I don't miss those days."

Rose Anna glanced over at the door and saw Isaac watching them, his expression full of love for his family.

He didn't look like he missed anything at that moment.

Emma kissed each of her *kinner.* "Tell your *dat* that I'll be ready to go in a few minutes. I need to talk to Rose Anna."

"Maybe on the way home we can stop for ice cream?" her son asked hopefully.

"Maybe."

"With sprinkles?"

"Maybe."

They watched as the *kinner* raced back to their *dat,* and then the three walked to get the family buggy.

"So tell me how you convinced Isaac to return to the community."

Emma leaned back in her rocking chair

and seemed to look inward. "All I can say is it has to be his idea." She stopped and bit her lip. "I'm sorry, that probably doesn't seem helpful. But it has to be something he wants to do. Back when Isaac went through his period of not knowing which world he wanted to live in, he was a bit of a bad boy. Like John is. I tried to change him. Then I tried to change myself to win him."

She sighed and shook her head. "Please promise me you won't try to become someone you aren't to win John's love. Don't change to be what you think he wants. Don't . . . become intimate or anything like that. You won't end up happy." She stopped as if she'd said too much.

A few minutes later Isaac pulled up in front of the house in the buggy. Emma shot Rose Anna a grin. "He may have to come hoist me up out of this chair."

Rose Anna stood and held out her hand. Together they got Emma up, and then they stood there laughing at the absurdity of it. They walked to the stairs, their arms companionably twined.

"So are you going to stop for that ice cream? Your *kinner* look like little angels."

Almost immediately there was an indignant cry from her *dochder*. "*Daed!* He pinched me! *Daed!* Make him stop!"

223

That sent Emma into a fit of giggles. "Oh, *ya,* they are little angels *allrecht*!"

Rose Anna watched her walk to the buggy and couldn't hold back her own giggles as she saw the pained look Isaac gave his *kinner.*

12

Rose Anna tried not to obsess about the first fight she'd had with John.

But it was tough.

She felt he'd accused her of being overly interested in getting married. She was indignant at the accusation. Then her conscience chastised her that she *had* decided to pursue John with marriage as her goal.

But that hadn't been the only reason she wanted him. She truly loved him and wanted to see him return to the community for his own salvation. If he returned, and it was to marry someone else, she hoped she could be happy for him. She could do that, couldn't she?

Couldn't she?

She didn't even know if they were friends anymore. She hadn't heard from him for two days.

So she concentrated hard on her work and hoped she looked serene and unconcerned because she didn't want her *schweschders* teasing her.

The effort proved too much. When everyone went downstairs for a break she decided to take a walk. "Going to get some fresh air. Back in a while."

The family knew she liked to walk so they left her alone. So maybe she'd done a *gut* job of covering up how upset she was feeling.

Rose Anna lifted her face to the warm rays of the sun. It was a perfect spring day in Paradise . . . one of those rare days when the breeze was warm but not too warm. Birds were singing and the scents of flowers blooming almost — almost — drowned out the scent of the freshly applied manure and fertilizer on the fields on each side of the road.

She found herself singing a hymn as she strolled. Such a *gut* God to provide so *wunderbaar* a day. Spring was short in Lancaster County and so each day must be appreciated, she told herself.

But her spirit still felt dull and depressed. Even the sight of sunny yellow daffodils bursting in bloom weren't perking her up.

When she came to the point she knew was a mile from her *haus,* she turned around. She was just two farms away when she saw a van *Englisch* drivers used to transport passengers. The side door slid open, and an elderly, white-haired man stepped out.

"Grossdaadi!" she cried and began running toward him.

His head came up and he grinned. "Rose Anna!"

He held his arms open, and they hugged.

"Oh, *Grossdaadi,* I missed you so!" She clung to him, blinking back tears until she heard the driver clear his throat. She stood back so *Grossdaadi* could hand the driver some bills, and then he took the handle of his rolling suitcase.

"Let me do that," Rose Anna insisted.

"What's this?" he asked her, flicking his finger at the tears on her cheek.

"It feels like you've been gone forever." She'd been so self-absorbed and so miserable since the fight with John she'd forgotten *Grossdaadi* was due home today. He'd brightened up her day like her walk hadn't been able to.

"Look who I found on my walk!" she called as they went in the front door.

Her *mudder* came out of the kitchen wiping her hands on a dish towel. "Abraham!" She rushed forward to hug him. "It's *gut* to see you! Did you have a nice time in Pinecraft?"

227

"I did, but it's *gut* to be back. Nothing like home. Where's Jacob?"

"In the barn, of course. You're just in time for lunch. Are you *hungerich*?"

"Always. You know me." He chuckled.

They walked into the kitchen just as Jacob came in the back door.

"I made your favorites since I knew you were coming," Linda told him.

"Food's his favorite," Jacob said. He embraced his *dat*. "So you finally remembered where home is."

Grossdaadi sat at his usual place at the table, and Rose Anna sat beside him.

"Figured you needed some help planting."

"Your timing's as *gut* as usual," Jacob said with a grin as he washed his hands at the sink. "It's pretty much done."

He winked at Rose Anna. "So, what's new with you, *kind*?"

"The usual. Quilting and teaching quilting at the shelter."

He raised his eyebrows. "That's all?"

She shrugged and nodded.

"I was hoping for a game of checkers with John."

"*Daed* will be happy to play with you."

"But —"

Linda set a bowl down in front of him. "Chicken and noodles. Your favorite."

His eyes lit up. "*Schur* missed your cooking."

Her *mudder* took her seat and looked at her *mann.*

Jacob said the blessing, and *Grossdaadi* dug into the bowl of chicken and noodles. He took a bite and smacked his lips. "Nobody makes this better than you, Linda."

"That's because your Miriam taught me how to make it the way you like it." She smiled. "I think of her every time I use one of her recipes."

"Or quilt," Rose Anna spoke up. "*Grossmudder* taught me how to quilt. *Mamm,* too," she said quickly.

"But your *grossmudder* taught you the most," her *mudder* said without taking offense.

Grossdaadi glanced around, then looked at Rose Anna. "Don't you tell your *schweschders,* but you were her favorite. She said Lavina and Mary Elizabeth teased you too much because you were the youngest."

Linda set a slice of pie in front of him. "More coffee?"

He grinned. "*Ya, danki.*" He dug into the pie.

"Tell us about Pinecraft, *Grossdaadi.*"

"It's just like you've heard," he said

229

between bites of pie. "You really can walk outside your rental and pick an orange off a tree. I did a lot of playing shuffleboard. Took some nice walks. And caught some fish. They have this fish there in Phillippi Creek. Never saw anything like it. Greenish-brown fish with a long snout. Looked like something from the dinosaur age. Got these big teeth."

He leaned over and made chomping noises at Rose Anna.

"Stop!" she said, giggling.

"My friend told me they can get to be three, maybe four feet long. Up to two hundred pounds. Not *gut* eating, though."

He finished his pie and looked hopefully at Linda who nodded finally and served him another small slice. "Saw my first alligator, too, I did."

Grossdaadi leaned over again and made snapping noises with his teeth at Rose Anna. "Had even bigger teeth than the garfish."

She giggled and gently smacked his arm. "If you chomp me, I won't be able to bake your favorite cookies."

He drew back and tilted his head as he studied her. "Well, *kind,* when will you bake me some?"

"This afternoon."

"Guess I won't bite you then." He turned

back to his pie.

"Let's not go overindulging him again," her *mudder* warned. "I distinctly remember the doctor wanted him to take off a few pounds last time I took him for a checkup."

"Maybe you'd like to work off those two pieces of pie helping me in the barn," Jacob suggested.

"Kinda tired from traveling," he said. "Maybe after I take a little nap."

Rose Anna heard a knock on the front door. "I'll get it."

She couldn't have been more shocked when she opened the door and found John standing on the porch.

"Hi," he said. "Can we talk?"

She hesitated.

"Please?"

She wanted to hold her heart safe from him. He'd hurt her so. But finally she relented. "I can't stay long. *Grossdaadi* just got back from Pinecraft. I want to spend some time with him."

"Do you mind if I say hello to him?"

She shook her head and walked back to the kitchen. "*Mamm, Daed,* I'm going for a short drive with John."

"John! When are you coming to play checkers with me?"

"I hope to soon," John told him as he slid

a wary glance at Rose Anna.

"Gut, gut," Amos said. "Well, I'm going to take that nap. Linda, wake me for supper if I'm not up before then."

"I'll be *schur* to." She appeared to be trying to keep a straight face. But a smile won.

"Leave the dishes and I'll do them when I come back."

"Allrecht. I'll do that."

Rose Anna grabbed her light sweater from the peg and followed John out to his truck.

She wondered just what he had to say.

John stared at the steering wheel, but he didn't start the truck. "I want to apologize."

She gave him a wary glance. "You do?"

He nodded. "I shouldn't have said such a thing to you."

"You hurt my feelings." She heard the petulance in her voice but couldn't seem to help it.

"I know. I'm sorry."

"Why did it take you so long to tell me that?"

"Want to see?"

Rose Anna frowned. "See?"

John glanced in the rearview mirror and then pulled out onto the road, heading toward town.

"Where are we going?"

"You'll see," he said mysteriously.

"Remember I said I didn't want to be away long."

"I know."

13

"We have a special guest today," Kate told Rose Anna when she walked into the quilting class.

"Who?" She set her things down on the front table and wondered at Kate's barely suppressed excitement.

"It's a surprise."

It had been an interesting week so far, she thought. First, *Grossdaadi* had returned. Then she'd been introduced to Willow's lovely little foal.

Women filed in and nearly every seat was filled at the tables. Still no special guest had appeared.

And then someone vaguely familiar walked in and set a cardboard box down on an empty table. She wore a black mini-dress and hair tinted pink at the ends. It took Rose Anna a moment to recognize her.

"Jamie! I haven't seen you in years!"

They hugged.

"Steve and I were in town for a quick visit with family, and I stopped by to say hello to Leah." Jamie explained. "She told me what Kate had started here and said Kate would like me to talk about quilting." She turned and offered her hand to Kate. "It's wonderful what you've done."

"It's been such fun," Kate said simply. "And the shop wouldn't have been possible without Leah's help."

"And neither would my career."

"You'd made a success of yourself without my help." Leah said. "You had the talent — and the drive."

Jamie spun around. "Oh, I didn't think you were going to be able to come!"

"I'm sure my granddaughters can handle things just fine without me for an hour or two." She gazed around the room. "So wonderful to see how the class is doing. Everyone looks so happy!"

"Sewing's good for the soul!" a woman sitting near them said.

"True, true," Leah said, smiling. "Well, I'm going to find a seat so you can get started."

Kate introduced Jamie and explained that she was a former resident of Paradise who'd earned her art education degree here and now had her art quilts displayed in galleries in New York City.

Jamie was the same sweet and humble woman she'd been when she worked part-time at Stitches in Time around her college studies. She talked about how she'd started out fascinated by the quilts sewn by Leah and her granddaughters at Stitches in Time. She'd found herself wanting to do something different and slowly evolved into doing the art quilts.

She and Kate held one up and showed it to the women.

"It's kind of like doing a picture or a painting in fabric," Jamie explained. "I sketch out my idea and then cut the fabric and lay it out on a big table or the floor, see if it looks the way I want it to. Then I do a lot of appliqué work basting and then stitching the pieces on the background. Sometimes these quilts go together quickly because I'm working with big pieces."

They set that quilt down and picked up another. "And then there are the quilts like this one that took weeks to finish."

Jamie paused and smiled. "The point I want to make is there's no wrong way to design and make a quilt. You should be creative and do what you love. Where would we be if so many years ago women had not sat down with pieces of leftover fabric and made something useful and beautiful with them?"

She glanced at the window.

After displaying a few more quilts, she opened the floor to questions, and there were many. Kate had to finally call for a last question a half hour later, and Jamie beamed at the enthusiastic reception the women gave her as they thanked her for coming to speak.

The four of them went out to lunch afterward. Jamie shared photos of her husband and two children.

"So I guess you're not sorry you left Paradise," Rose Anna said as she gazed at the photos of the tall buildings of New York City.

Jamie shook her head. "You know, Jenny Bontrager once told me that from the air the fields in this area look like a quilt. I looked out the window of the plane and saw what she meant. It was hard to leave the place I'd been born in. But Steve and I both knew New York City was where we needed to work." She smiled as she tucked the photos back into her purse. "We couldn't be happier."

Rose Anna had made a dozen or more Around the World quilts and daydreamed over them as she stitched, but she'd never wanted to explore beyond the Lancaster County line.

"I've missed this," Jamie said as she dug into her shoofly pie for dessert. "I can't buy it in New York City."

"I'll give you the recipe," Rose Anna told her. "It's really easy to make."

"I think living here with two cultures that are so different — *Englisch* and Amish — made it easy to adjust to how diverse the Big Apple is."

"I always wondered why they call it the Big Apple," Leah said.

"I have no idea," Jamie told her, laughing.

On the way home, Rose Anna thought about what Jamie said about having to move to where she could do the work she loved.

John had been forced to find whatever work he could do in town when he and his *bruders* left the farm. She knew he didn't love farming as much as David and Sam did, and he wasn't the type to complain. But he'd had to work two and three jobs to support himself.

Now that he'd added working at the horse farm, he was even busier but she'd never seen him happier.

If a person had to live in a certain place to do the work he loved, then did that mean he'd have to stay in town and never rejoin their Amish community?

She didn't want to think about that. She wanted him back in their community. Besides, the Zimmerman farm had once belonged to an Amish family who'd sold it to Neil before they moved away. So really, it was right on the border of the Amish community . . .

John was right on time for supper that evening.

Rose Anna made supper since he was her guest. It gave her the chance to make his favorites. He'd always claimed she made the best fried chicken — what was it with men and fried chicken? — so she'd made not one but two batches of it as well as mashed potatoes and gravy and spring peas and biscuits.

Grossdaadi had come out of the *dawdi haus* and offered to taste test for her, so she'd given him two biscuits hot from the oven with some butter and honey. Now he sat in the kitchen and kept her company.

She indulged him further by listening to him tell her not once but several times how happy he was that John — not some other young man — was stopping by.

He hinted she was being "courted," and she insisted John was just a friend.

When there was a knock on the front

door, he beat her there to welcome John.

John soaked up the attention from the older man. His own *grossdaadi* on his *dat*'s side had died when he was just a *kind,* and his *mudder*'s side lived hours away, so he hadn't had a close relationship with any male relatives.

She knew God had a reason why He did things, but she didn't know why John couldn't have had a more loving family. If he had, things would have been so different with the two of them . . .

"Rose Anna?"

She jerked to attention. *"Ya?"*

"Danki for such a *wunderbaar* supper."

She glowed not just from the praise but from the way he was speaking in their language more and more.

He turned to her parents. "And Linda and Jacob, *danki* for having me in your home."

"You're *wilkum,"* Linda told him and Jacob nodded.

A few minutes later they excused themselves. Rose Anna suspected it was so that she and John could spend some time together.

Grossdaadi got out the checkerboard and challenged John to a game.

Rose Anna just laughed, shook her head, and began clearing the table.

■ ■ ■ ■

It felt like another world.

John sat in the Zook kitchen playing checkers while Rose Anna cleared the table.

She'd refused his help, insisting that she'd let him help dry the dishes when the game was over.

Of course, one game wasn't enough for *Grossdaadi.* They played three before John insisted he had to help Rose Anna dry the dishes. Abraham grinned, folded up the checkerboard, and took it and a piece of pie into the *dawdi haus.* He paused at the door, caught his eye, and winked at him.

Hmm, thought John. Was the old man playing matchmaker? He picked up a clean dish towel and waited for Rose Anna to hand him a dish to dry.

"He looks happier."

She nodded. "I think it was *gut* for him to get away for a bit. But I missed him so."

"I did, too," he admitted.

She handed him a dish, but he didn't take it until she looked at him. "I missed you."

"Did you?"

John saw the doubt in her eyes and hated that he'd put it there. "I did. I really am sorry." He remembered his conversation

241

with Neil.

He stood there drying dishes with her in the quiet room and thought about how if things had been different this chore might have been something they did of an evening like couples did. Or if he had chores in the barn she might do the dishes alone and they'd have a cup of coffee and some conversation before they headed off to bed.

He nearly dropped the dish he was drying and forced his thoughts away from such a dangerous direction.

"John? Are you *allrecht*?"

"Uh, yeah, of course." He cleared his throat. "I just remembered something I need to do tomorrow."

She handed him another dish and smiled. "How is Willow's foal?"

"Doing well. Neil said you can drop by any time and see her again."

"He seems like a nice man."

"He's been a good man to work for."

"You're frowning."

"I'm worried about him. He's got a heart condition. I'm thinking of calling his son."

She touched his hand. "He's that bad?"

"I'm not sure. But what if his son doesn't know about it?" He stared down at her hand. It felt so good, so right to have the contact. Made him think of how it was just

242

the two of them, alone.

"Rose Anna? Is there any coffee left?" her mother called.

Startled, he stepped back, dropping Rose Anna's hand as if it burned.

Linda walked into the room and glanced around. "So Abraham went to bed?"

"Just a few minutes ago."

She poured two mugs of coffee and then turned to John. "So did he cheat?"

John laughed. "Of course. It's okay. I'm on to him."

She picked up the mugs and started out of the room then turned. "Rose Anna, don't go giving him more pie, hear?"

"Oh, I won't," she said quickly.

The door to the *dawdi haus* opened, and Abraham walked out with the empty plate in his hand. Linda's head swiveled in his direction, then back to Rose Anna. All Linda had to do was raise her eyebrows, and Rose Anna bit her lip and looked apologetic.

Linda shook her head as she left the room.

"Guess I came out at the wrong time," he said as he put the plate and fork in the sink. "Sorry."

But he stuck his hand in the cookie jar and grabbed one before heading back into his quarters. "Gonna make me some snickerdoodles tomorrow?" he asked Rose Anna.

She rolled her eyes. "You have such a sweet tooth, *Grossdaadi*." She waited until he closed the door. "*Mamm* gets after him if he eats too many sweets, but I like to indulge him."

"What about me?" he asked, taking her hand again.

"Are you asking for snickerdoodles?" She gave him a flirtatious smile.

He nipped at her fingers. "These are fine for a nibble."

She tried to pull her hand back. "They must taste like lemon dish detergent, silly." But he wouldn't release her hand, and she felt unnerved by the intensity in his eyes.

Out of the corner of his eye he saw movement. It took a moment to react, but then when he saw it was Jacob he dropped her hand again.

John waited for Jacob to say something, but the older man just moved past him with his coffee cup and refilled it from the percolator on the stove.

He let out the breath he hadn't realized he'd been holding as Jacob grabbed a cookie from the jar and left the room without comment.

Giggling. John heard giggling and turned to see Rose Anna unsuccessfully trying to stifle her mirth behind her hand.

"That wasn't funny," he growled.

"I'm sorry," she finally managed. "What did you think he was going to do? Challenge you to a duel or find a shotgun to make you marry me?"

"Of course not!" he said, frowning as she continued to take the whole thing lightly. "But it was a little . . . unnerving."

"I'm sorry," she said, struggling to put on a serious expression. But her eyes danced with humor.

He rolled his eyes. "You're incorrigible."

"That's her middle name," Linda said as she walked up behind him. "Just thought I'd put these in the sink," she said as she set down the two mugs she carried.

John muttered under his breath as his heart jumped up into his throat. Honestly, did her parents practice sneaking up on their daughter's male friends?

Then he realized what he was thinking. Did she have male friends? He knew she'd seen Peter for a time.

He suddenly craved some time with her.

"Rose Anna, make *schur* you pack some leftovers up for John."

"Thanks," he told her.

Linda nodded and left as quietly as she'd come in.

"John?"

"Hmm?" He realized she was holding out a mug to him to dry.

He made swift work of drying it and setting it and the second one into the cupboard. Then he threw the dish towel down on the counter top and grabbed her hand.

"Come on, let's get out of here."

"Where are we going?" she asked as he pulled her out the back door.

"Anywhere," he said. "Nowhere."

She laughed. "My favorite place."

What had happened in the kitchen?

It was the first time since she and John had started seeing each other again that he had reacted in such a way.

She wasn't complaining. She just didn't know what to make of it.

Rose Anna began having second thoughts even before they reached John's truck.

"John?"

"What?" He opened the truck door and looked at her expectantly.

"Maybe it's not such a *gut* idea to go for a ride."

"Why? It's not late."

What a dilemma. She wanted them to be more than friends, but this was the first move he'd made toward that, and only days

246

after their disagreement. As much as she wanted to go for a quiet drive with him where they wouldn't be interrupted she wondered if he'd want more. Their last kiss was a long time ago but she still remembered it . . .

Something Emma had said to her that day they talked came to her. Emma had said to be careful not to change for John and had seemed to hint to be careful about intimacy.

She hesitated, and then she got into the truck. John had never pressured her about anything. There was no need for her to worry about that.

She wasn't naive. He was a man, and Amish men wanted the same things from women that *Englisch* men did even if they weren't as obvious about it. Most waited until after marriage. But she'd heard of marriages in her community that produced *boppli* less than nine months after the wedding day. People were people wherever they lived, whatever religion they practiced.

He drove out into the country, and they rode with the windows down to catch the scents and the breeze of a warm spring evening in Pennsylvania.

Rose Anna couldn't imagine a more wonderful place.

She told him about Jamie's visit and her

life in New York City. "She said she and Steve love it there. They can do the work they studied for. I can't imagine seeing skyscrapers instead of mountains. Busy streets instead of country roads like this. And so many people. Can you?"

John shook his head. "I've never wanted to live anywhere else."

"Except in town."

He shrugged. "Where else could we go when we left the farm? But I'm still not far from the community."

He was farther than he thought, she wanted to say. But she didn't dare. It would ruin the mood, and she wasn't going to do that.

As if he read her thoughts he reached over with one hand and linked his fingers with hers. He let their hands rest on the seat between them.

Buggies passed them on the other side of the road. Amish couples were out for a ride enjoying the spring evening.

Things weren't really as different as they might seem, she thought. Only they were in an *Englisch* truck.

Rose Anna recognized friends and church members but didn't wave since they didn't look in their direction.

She'd shared what had happened in her

day, so he told her about his. He joked that Willow's foal was becoming as much a flirt as her mother.

"Why doesn't she have a name?"

"Neil hasn't gotten around to it yet. Willow was already named when he bought her as most of his horses were. He says it's hard to pick the right one."

John glanced at her. "Maybe you'd like to come visit and help suggest a name."

"I guess you don't remember I wanted *Daed* to let me call one of our horses Button."

"No, I never heard that story. Why did you want to call him Button?"

"Because the silly thing tried to eat the buttons off my jacket. That was before I convinced him apples were better."

"So then you named him Apple?"

She laughed. "*Nee.* We called him Brownie because he was such a rich, dark brown color. It was a simple name, but it fit him." She glanced at him. "I heard that sometimes the *Englisch* name their cars and trucks. Does this one have a name?"

"I think that's something the *Englisch* women do, not the men."

"But if it had a name it might be Second Hand Rose, don't you think? After the *Englisch* song?"

"Where would you have heard that song?"

"A woman was singing it to herself as she sewed a quilt in class one day. She was using material from a couple of old dresses her daughter had outgrown." She tilted her head and studied him. "You inherited the truck from your *bruder* Sam and he from David."

"True. But I'm not calling it Second Hand Rose." He grimaced at the thought.

She giggled. "Not manly enough, huh?"

"No!"

They fell silent as dusk fell. It was a comfortable, companionable silence.

"*Danki* for supper," he said when he took her home.

It always did something to her heart when he slipped into using his old language. She wondered as she had in the past if he realized it. "You're *wilkum. Grossdaadi* was *schur* glad to see you. I hope it didn't make you feel uncomfortable."

"Not at all."

"But my parents did."

He started to shake his head and then he sighed. "Only at the end."

"I'm *schur* it wasn't their intention."

He was silent, tapping his fingertips on the steering wheel. "No," he said at last. "Your mother announced herself before she came into the room."

"To be fair, my *dat* didn't." She had trouble repressing her grin.

He chuckled. "No, he didn't. But a man shouldn't have to in his own house. A woman shouldn't have to, either," he said quickly. "If I had a daughter, I might behave the same way."

Rose Anna couldn't help it. She giggled. "With your background, I'm sure you'll see every man who comes to see your *dochder* as bad."

"Hey, where did that come from?"

"Even before you left home you enjoyed being a little bit of a bad boy."

He grinned at her. "And you liked that."

She folded her hands in her lap and tried to look prim. "That's not true." But she had. She did.

And he could never know that.

His grin faded. "Look, Rose Anna, I'm not spending my time in town running around, all right?"

"I didn't say you were."

"That might have been true in the past. But it's not anymore."

"Allrecht."

He released her hand and muttered something under his breath. After checking his rearview mirror, he pulled over and then

251

turned to look at her.

"There isn't anyone but you, Rose Anna. I don't expect you to believe that but it's true."

14

Rose Anna studied him. This was the man she'd known all her life — loved most of her life. He'd teased her unmercifully, charmed her, and then devastated her by leaving her.

But he'd never lied to her.

"I believe you."

John leaned back in his seat. "You do. Just like that."

She nodded.

He reached for her hand, and she let him take it. "No one's ever believed in me like you."

"That's not true. Your *mudder* does."

"I wish I believed that. She needed to stand up to my *dot*. She never did."

She squeezed his hand. "I know. And I'm sorry about that. But I'm not *schur* she could, John."

"*Schur* she could! We were her *kinner*!"

Once again, he lapsed into their language.

She just knew it was the language of his heart. Maybe it was foolish of her, but she still believed he hadn't left the Amish community. He'd left it temporarily but not for forever.

"It must have been so hard for her, caught between her *mann* and her *kinner* —"

"Are you going to make excuses for her?" he demanded, trying to pull his hand from hers.

She grasped his hand in both of hers and refused to let go. "*Nee.* But it's not my job to judge her, John." She waited until he looked at her. "Or yours. Look, I heard that the bishop came and talked to your parents years ago."

"You heard that?"

She nodded.

"Nothing's secret in our community, is it?" He turned to stare out at the road. "*Ya,* he came and talked to them. And things got worse for me and my *bruders.*"

He slammed his hand on the steering wheel, then he checked traffic and pulled out onto the road making a U-turn so fast the tires squealed.

Rose Anna didn't know what to say. She hadn't seen him this upset in a long time.

Before she could speak he slowed, shook his head. "I'm sorry."

"It's *allrecht*."

"*Nee,* it's not. I'm no better than my *dat* if I talk to the woman I care about that way."

Care about. Not love.

She stared at him. It wasn't what she'd always dreamed of hearing him say. But it was more than he'd ever said.

The ride back was silent. She could barely see his face now that dusk had faded into night. There were few street lights out here in the country, but when they passed under one his face looked set and unhappy.

He pulled into the driveway and sat for a long moment. "Sorry."

"I'm sorry, too."

His head whipped around. "For what?"

"That you had such a hard time with your *dat.* Maybe one day you can forgive him."

He made a short noise of disgust.

"John, you can't keep your heart closed to him."

"Bet?"

"It's not our way. It didn't used to be yours." She reached for her door handle. "And I don't believe it is now."

"You've seen how he behaves with me. He might have changed with David and with Sam, but he *schur* hasn't with me." He glanced at her. "He still argues with me, still has a problem with me. He thinks I'm

255

a failure since I left. And since I work three part-time jobs and have no future, he's not far wrong."

"He's wrong, and you're wrong to even say such a thing!" She sighed and leaned back in her seat. "I don't know why the two of you still rub up against each other the wrong way. Maybe the next time he starts you could find a way not to respond."

"You're blaming me?"

"*Nee*, of course not. But just don't let him get to you."

"I try."

"I know." She opened the door and slid out of the truck.

"Rose Anna?"

She turned. *"Ya?"*

"I —" he stopped. "See you tomorrow?"

"I'll be at Sam and Mary Elizabeth's, helping."

It was easy to see his grimace in the harsh overhead light in the truck cab. "Is my *dat* going to be there?"

"I don't know."

"With my luck he probably will be. He likes telling my *bruders* how to run their farms." His words came out as a growl.

She bit back a smile. "Maybe I'll see you there."

"Allrecht."

She climbed the stairs and went into the house, and only then did she hear him leave. But this time it wasn't with a squeal of tires. She supposed that was some progress.

The next day dawned bright and beautiful. She woke to a warm spring breeze coming in the open window. She could smell the lilacs blooming in the garden and hear birdsong.

She'd gone to bed alternately happy he'd said he cared about her and sad that he was still hurting about his relationship with his *dat*.

Even though John seemed happier working part of the week for Neil, what he'd said last night troubled her: *He still argues with me, still has a problem with me. He thinks I'm a failure since I left. And since I work three part-time jobs and have no future, he's not far wrong.*

It was all so sad. How could either of them think a man who worked as hard as John was a failure?

She rose and dressed for the day. And if she wore a nicer dress than she normally would have for a family workday what of it?

John told himself he wouldn't do this for anyone but Rose Anna.

He loved his *bruder* Sam and his *fraa*

257

Mary Elizabeth, but he couldn't help feeling some dread at the thought of encountering his *dat.*

When he arrived at Sam and Mary Elizabeth's farmhouse, he was relieved to see only one buggy parked in the drive.

He put the truck in park and shut off the engine. His stomach growled. He hadn't taken time for breakfast. There had been the morning chores at the horse farm before coming here. He knew Mary Elizabeth would feed him and feed him so much better than he could himself. Her cinnamon rolls weren't as legendary as Leah's, but they were *schur gut.*

He walked in the back door and his heart sank. There was his *dat* sitting at the kitchen table drinking coffee. Even the sight of his *mudder* sitting beside him didn't cheer him up. He bent and gave her a kiss on the cheek.

Mary Elizabeth turned from the stove. "John! So glad you could come today!" She beamed at him, her smile so like Rose Anna's. "Have you eaten? I saved you some breakfast."

"*Nee,* I haven't."

Sam handed him a mug of coffee. "Why don't you get married so my *fraa* doesn't have to feed you?"

258

"I'm still waiting for her to realize she married the wrong *bruder* and leave you for me," he returned, taking a seat at the table as far from his *dat* as he could.

Their *dat* muttered something John pretended not to hear.

"Sorry, John, you're going to have to settle for someone else," Mary Elizabeth told him as she served him a plate. She smiled at Sam. "I'll be staying with my *mann.*"

Was it his imagination that they shared a smile that held some meaning he didn't understand?

He shrugged and dug into the bacon and *dippy eggs.* Mary Elizabeth set a basket of fragrant cinnamon rolls in front of him.

When he reached for one, his hand collided with his *dat*'s. Amos glared at him. "You first," John said, determined to avoid being drawn into any disagreements with him today. He picked up another roll and bit into it. "This is *gut,* Mary Elizabeth."

"Danki."

The back door opened, and Rose Anna walked in carrying a basket.

John's heart lifted. The day had suddenly gotten better. When she smiled at him, he was glad he'd come.

She set the basket down on the nearby counter. "Brownies," she mouthed at him before walking over to hang up her sweater.

"*Mamm, Daed,* so glad you could come!" Mary Elizabeth cried as they walked in.

"David and Lavina are right behind us." Linda took Mark's hand and helped him wave at everyone. Jacob leaned over her shoulder and made silly faces at him.

"She barely said hello to us before she took Mark," Lavina said dryly as she walked in. "And I'd swear I saw her elbow *Daed* to get to him first."

Jacob nodded and feigned a grimace of pain. "She got me in the ribs with her sharp elbow."

"I'm surprised Lavina didn't try to sell him to a tourist on the way here," David said as he entered with Lavina. He yawned. "Mark kept us up last night. Teething again."

He slumped into a chair. "Just how many teeth does a *kind* get, anyway?"

"Count yours," Sam told him as he set coffee before his *bruder.* "That's how many."

"Maybe we should just loan him to you to practice on," David said, narrowing his eyes at him. "Then you won't think it's a joke."

"Sounds like a *gut* idea," Mary Elizabeth said. "What do you think, Sam? We're going to need the practice."

She walked over and held out her arms to

Mark. He gurgled at her and lunged into them.

John's fork stopped midway to his mouth. Something was going on. There was a shift in the atmosphere in the kitchen . . . an undercurrent . . . all eyes were on Mary Elizabeth and Sam.

"Mary Elizabeth, what are you saying?" Rose Anna demanded.

She laughed. "Sam and I are going to have a *boppli.* I'm due in December."

Amos made a noise that caused John's attention to shift from Mary Elizabeth's glowing face to his *dat*'s. He was crying. Actually crying — this stern man who had been so hard to get along with was actually crying. When he realized John was staring, he sent him a glare and then got to his feet and awkwardly hugged Mary Elizabeth, then Sam.

David and Lavina were next, and Mark had evidently decided he didn't want to be practice anymore. He reached for his *dat,* and David took him from Mary Elizabeth.

John waited his turn to offer congratulations. Misty-eyed, Mary Elizabeth accepted his hug. Then John turned to Sam and slapped him on the shoulder, his version of a brotherly hug. "So, another *bruder* not just married but settling down with a *bop-pli.*"

"God is *gut,*" Sam said fervently. His glance slid to Rose Anna talking to his *fraa.* "When are you going to wise up, *Bruder*?"

Once, John would have insisted he was happy being a bachelor, and since his *bruders* had gone and settled down, he was the last of the Stoltzfus men and had to live it up in his *rumschpringe.*

Was he getting older or wiser?

Rose Anna broke away from Mary Elizabeth and walked toward him.

Or was it that he was seeing her clearly for the first time?

Amos cleared his throat. "So, what are we going to do today?"

John went off to the fields with the men while Rose Anna followed the women upstairs to convert one of the bedrooms into a nursery.

The crops they'd planted were doing nicely.

Well, not as nicely as they would have if he'd been listened to, according to Amos. He clomped around the fields in his boots, telling Sam he shouldn't have planted this next to that; he should have done this, not that.

Sam listened and nodded and stayed

good-natured. So did David who'd had to listen to the same thing about his own farm.

John opened his mouth to say something, but Sam caught his eye and shook his head. So he subsided and watched their *dat* walk off for a break.

He hadn't done any actual work except his own form of unwanted supervision, but John did what Sam asked with the crops and about staying silent.

Once Amos was out of hearing range, he turned to Sam. "Why did you signal for me to not say anything?"

"You're just wasting your breath," Sam said, taking a break to wipe the sweat from his forehead with his bandanna. "And he means well."

"He just loves to tell others what to do."

Sam shrugged. "He does have a lot of experience."

John snorted.

David walked over. "He wasn't the best of *dats,* but it's not the easiest job in the world, you know."

"What do you mean?"

"All these nights either Lavina or I have spent walking the floor with Mark, I've found myself worrying about what kind of *dat* I'll be."

"We can't be worse than our *dat* was,"

John told him.

"*Schur* we could. He isn't the worst one in the community, and you know it. And it's not something that only happens in our community."

"Of course it isn't. But I don't believe you'll make the same mistakes he did."

Sam laid his hand on David's shoulder. "You care about being different. So you will be."

David sighed. "I hope you're right."

"You're just tired. I appreciate your help, but we've done all we can today. Why don't you see if you can take a nap with your *sohn*?"

David nodded. "*Gut* idea, but Lavina and I have decided we're keeping him up today so he'll sleep tonight."

"I'm off to the horse farm," John said as he checked the cell phone Neil had gotten him. "Neil texted me that he wants to see me."

"Hope everything's *allrecht.*"

"Me, too." He'd been hoping to do something with Rose Anna — a drive, supper, something — but that would have to wait.

He let Rose Anna know he had to go see Neil. "Maybe I can stop by later if it's not too late."

"*Schur.* Hope nothing's wrong."

264

John found himself worrying on the drive over. When he got to the horse farm, he saw a vehicle he didn't recognize. It wasn't the vet's. He went into the barn first and saw Neil talking with someone whose back was turned to him.

Neil brightened when he saw him. "Here's John now."

The man turned, and John saw he was a younger version of Neil with his sandy hair and gray eyes. John walked toward him, his hand outstretched. "Hello, you must be Brad. Neil's told me a lot about you."

"He's told me a lot about you, too," Brad said. But he wasn't smiling, and his eyes were cool and assessing.

"Brad's here for a quick visit," Neil told him. "I talked him into taking a look at the new foal."

"And now that we've seen her, maybe we can go back to the house."

Neil clapped him on his shoulder. "Now don't be in such a hurry."

Willow chose that moment to lean over her stall to greet John with a whinny.

Brad jumped a foot.

"Did you make her do that?" he demanded in an accusing tone.

Surprised, John shook his head and moved closer to stroke her nose. "She's just friendly."

Brad moved farther away from the stall. "My dad tells me you've been a lot of help to him. You're not too busy with your own farm?"

"I don't have one."

"I told you, John's older brother inherited the family farm. John does other work. I couldn't manage without him here."

John didn't think he was overly sensitive, but he was picking up the feeling that Brad didn't like him for some reason.

"Brad and I are going out for dinner. Care to join us?" Neil said as John walked over to start portioning out the horse feed.

Brad didn't second the invitation.

"Thanks, but I've been helping my brother on his farm all day, and I'm dirty."

"We can wait for you to shower and change."

Neil stood behind his son, so he didn't see how coolly Brad was eyeing John. "Thanks. Maybe next time."

"Sure," Brad said. "I stop in every so often to keep an eye on Pop."

"Ha! I have to drag you here. You never have liked horses."

"You got that right. See you, John."

"Nice to meet you," John said politely. And wasn't surprised when Brad didn't return the sentiment, choosing to turn his back and walk away with his father.

As soon as the two men left the barn John turned to Willow. "Sure isn't like his *daed*, is he, girl?"

Willow shook her head as if in agreement.

John was glad Neil hadn't picked up on his son's reaction to him. It was evident at least to him that Neil had wanted them to meet, maybe even like each other.

John shrugged and continued the work of the evening feeding. He didn't figure it mattered much. He'd been working for a few months now for Neil, and this was the first time he'd seen Brad. Neil had told him his son had taken over his law practice in Philadelphia and was quite busy and successful. He didn't figure he had to worry about Brad deciding to leave it and take over his job.

Whistling, he fed the horses. He thought later maybe he'd head to Rose Anna's house. With luck he'd be invited for supper.

He breathed in the warm fresh air through the open truck window. So far today he'd heard that Mary Elizabeth and Sam were expecting a *boppli*, he hadn't had a blow-up with his *dat*, being asked here hadn't been for any bad news, and it was a beautiful spring evening. It was turning out to be a pretty *gut* day.

Rose Anna swiped at the perspiration on her forehead with the back of one hand. It was hot work weeding the kitchen garden. "Where did spring go? It lasted the blink of an eye."

"That's Lancaster County for you," her *mudder* said looking cool and unruffled like she always did.

Normally Rose Anna enjoyed working in the garden. But she didn't like being hot. Especially this early in the year. And it was barely eleven in the morning.

"Looks like we'll have some lettuce for a salad in a few days," Linda said with satisfaction. "Nothing better than early lettuce."

"Yes, there is. Spring peas," Rose Anna told her, gesturing at them.

"Well, I think that's enough for a morning. I say we take a break and get cooled off."

They brushed dirt from their hands and skirts and went into the *haus*. The cool interior felt like a blessing. After washing their hands, they fixed a glass of iced tea and sat at the kitchen table.

"I asked Mary Elizabeth if she needed help in her kitchen garden, but she said she's not having any morning sickness."

268

Linda sipped her tea. "*Gut.* It plagued Lavina. I know she was so grateful for your help when she was carrying. I was sick so much when I was carrying," she said with a rueful shake of her head.

"I'm sorry. I've seen how much *mudders* go through watching Lavina since she became a *mudder.*" Rose Anna took some cookies from the jar and placed them on a plate. She was hungry for a snack after the hard work weeding. And she'd never been able to resist cookies.

"But how could I mind when I had three lovely *dochders*?" Linda fanned her face with her hand. "It's like . . . a rainbow. You can't have the beauty and joy of a rainbow without rain or a thunderstorm. But a rainbow, Rose Anna."

Her mature face glowed and seemed to become younger, reminding Rose Anna of what she'd seen on the faces of her *schweschders.*

"Just think, *Mamm,* it won't be that long before you have two *grosskinner.*"

"The months will pass quickly. They always do."

"It doesn't feel that way to me." Her appetite fled. Time was passing, and she was no closer really to her plan to wed John. She set the cookie on her plate.

Linda reached across the table to pat her hand. "That's because you've always been impatient. My most impatient *kind.*"

Her lips quirked into a rueful grin. "You mean immature."

"*Nee.* Everyone grows at their own rate. And some never mature."

Now Rose Anna couldn't repress a giggle. "You're thinking of your *Onkel* Naiman."

She grinned. "*Aenti* Barbie says every day she remembers that 'a happy heart makes the face cheerful'."

Rose Anna remembered the rest of the quote from Proverbs. *But heartache crushes the spirit.* Sometimes she felt it nearly had crushed John's.

"Anyway, *Aenti* Barbie *schur* has the patience of a saint with his antics, doesn't she? But who can stay angry with such a sweet, cheerful man like him?"

"No one I know."

"Well, what do you say we get cleaned up and go into town for some shopping? We haven't done that in ages."

Rose Anna studied her *mudder*'s face. "Are you suggesting this to cheer me up?"

"Do you need cheering up?"

She leaned back in her chair and sighed. "Maybe a little. We've talked about this before, *Mamm.* I'm not envious of my *schweschders.* Truly I'm not. But sometimes I wonder when I'm going to get married."

"I know, *Lieb.* I know. It's so hard waiting on God's timing sometimes."

She wondered what her *mudder* would think if she knew her *dochder* had said God needed her help. Her *schweschders* had reacted with shock and laughter when she'd said it months ago. Obviously they hadn't told their *mudder.*

Cheered by her understanding, she put her chin in her hand and rested her elbow on the table. "Just where do you have in mind? This trip into town?"

Linda glanced around. "Promise you won't tell your *dat*? He'd tease me."

She nodded.

"Stitches in Time. We need fabric."

"He always says we have enough."

They looked at each other and laughed.

"Quilters never have enough fabric."

"Men never have enough tools."

Rose Anna thought about it. A trip to town to buy fabric. And maybe John would stop by later. It was turning into a pretty *gut* day.

"Bet I can be ready in fifteen minutes," Rose Anna said.

"I can make it ten," her *mudder* told her.

271

They scrambled up from the table and headed for the stairs to the bedrooms.

15

It felt like Christmas when Rose Anna walked into the quilting class later that week.

She and her *mudder* had found some wonderful new fabric for themselves in Stitches in Time, and even better, they spotted some inexpensive holiday fabric for the class.

Then Leah had added a shopping bag full of fabric she'd saved to donate to the class. So Rose Anna had a full bag in each hand as well as her tote bag and purse. She barely made it up the stairs to the sewing room.

The minute she placed the bags on the front table and announced what she'd brought, the women pounced on it.

The women oohed and aahed over the fabric, and when two reached for the same piece at once, it was so nice to see how quickly each tried to make the other take it.

"Nothing like new fabric," Betty, one of

the new shelter residents said as she admired a fat quarter of fabric printed with spring flowers. "Now wouldn't this make a nice quilted table runner for our shop?"

"I knew you'd love it," Rose Anna said with a smile.

Her smile grew wider when Brooke walked in with King and took a seat at the table she liked at the back of the room.

Kate rushed in a few minutes later, apologizing for running a little late.

"Look who's here," Rose Anna murmured, tilting her head toward the back of the room.

"It's good to see Brooke back," Kate said with a nod. "I think I'll give her some time to settle in before I go back and talk to her." She set her tote bag with her quilt project down. "Ah, I see you brought more fabric."

"*Mamm* and I took a trip into town the other day. Sort of a mother/daughter day, just the two of us. So, of course, you know what shops we had to visit first."

"Those days are the best," Kate said, looking thoughtful. "I love the days my daughter and I can do something together. The last mother/daughter day we had she and I went to a Disney movie and had a fancy lunch out. The guys — Malcolm and our son — had a guy's day. They went fishing and had

274

hamburgers."

She pulled out her cell phone and pulled up a calendar. "That was a whole month ago. I need to find the time to plan another. But first, Malcolm and I get to have a date night."

"A date night? But the two of you are already married."

Kate grinned. "It's our way of spending time with each other, of not taking each other for granted. And parents need to get away from their kids sometimes and remember that they're a couple, too, not just parents. Lots of people are doing it these days. *Englisch,* I mean."

Oh, how different the *Englisch* were from the Amish, Rose Anna couldn't help thinking. She'd never heard of any couple in her community having a date night, but Amish couples did so much together. Married couples plowed and planted the fields together, often shared child-rearing, attended church services and work frolics, and were seldom apart.

"We're going to dinner and a movie tonight," Kate was saying. "I'm hoping I don't get called into work like last time."

She turned to Rose Anna. "I've seen a certain red truck parked outside your house a lot lately. When I'm on patrol," she added.

Rose Anna felt herself blush. "John's a friend"

"Hmm."

She couldn't help laughing. "Hmm?"

"If you say so." She threaded her needle, glanced up at the class happily chatting and sewing, then focused again on her quilt. "Isn't there a saying about how 'in the spring a young man's fancy lightly turns to thoughts of love'?"

"Who said that?"

"Some British poet. Tennyson, I think. I read it in Freshman English in college."

"John's a friend," she repeated.

Chatter stopped. Brooke stopped at the table where Kate and Rose Anna sat. King stood patiently by her side. "I thought I'd show you my block. I only had to rip the seams out twice this morning."

"A seam ripper was my best friend when I was learning quilting," Kate told her. She put her own work down and took Brooke's block in her hands. "Nice job. Very straight seams." She showed it to Rose Anna who nodded her approval.

"I'm enjoying the class," Brooke said. "I didn't see the point of quilting." She bit her lip. "Sorry, I don't mean to offend."

"You're not," Kate assured her. "We've

heard that more than once, haven't we, Rose Anna?"

"It was the first thing Carrie, the manager at the shop, said."

"Well, what I've discovered is it relaxes me," Brooke told them. "I don't find myself anxiously watching the windows." She reached down to scratch between King's ears. "This guy helps, too. And you know, he's a service dog, but he sure does let me know he's happy to be with me."

Indeed Rose Anna could see the adoration in the dog's eyes as he gazed up at Brooke.

"A friend told me to do like she did and get a dog when my kids become teenagers," Kate said. "She said we need to have someone happy to see us when we get home."

"Well, you'll still have Malcolm," Rose Anna pointed out.

"But dogs love us so much. I'm not sure there's a man who loves us as unconditionally." With a final pat on his head, Brooke turned and walked away.

"She's probably right," Kate muttered.

They both watched to see if she'd continue walking on out the door — she'd already stayed far longer than she ever did — but she resumed her seat, and King sprawled under the table.

As Rose Anna sat and sewed, she told herself she was so lucky to have grown up seeing how happy her parents were. Otherwise, she might have wondered if happy relationships only happened in the romance novels she read.

She knew that there were happy marriages in her community, but after hearing about how it had been so different in John's *haus*, she knew not to trust the image others showed. It might be just as much of a sham. Well, Amos and Waneta had healed their relationship after he recovered from his cancer but living in that *haus*, seeing that unhappy relationship, and Amos treating his sons so badly had affected all three men.

David and Sam had managed to recover from it and had happy marriages with her *schweschders* who had loved them and brought them back to the Amish community.

But John?

"Rose Anna?"

"Hmm?"

"Are you okay? You seem sad."

"Sometimes it is, here," she said slowly, quietly. "Why do people have to be so mean?"

"You mean men."

She sighed. "I suppose I do."

"It's hard to understand." Kate set her quilt down. "I see people victimized all the time."

"Yet you seem to still believe people can be good."

"I do. If we don't, we might as well just give up, don't you think?"

"I guess so." She set her quilt down. "I'm going to walk around and see if anyone needs help."

And shake off this strange mood she seemed to have slipped into.

"I want to apologize for my son."

John turned and saw that Neil had come into the barn.

"Why would you do that?"

"Because he could have been a lot friendlier when the two of you met."

John shrugged. "Don't worry about it."

Neil sat down on a bale of hay and watched John feed a carrot to Midnight. Willow whinnied and stomped her feet and tried to get his attention.

"I suspect he was a little jealous."

"Midnight?"

"Brad. He's always been afraid of horses, so we don't share my interest. But he comes here and sees that you and I do."

"I work for you."

"I told him you'd been a big help to me. More than just someone working for me."

John looked at him. "I hope he doesn't think I'd try to take advantage of you."

"You mean seeing as how I'm an old man?" Neil grinned.

Appalled, John shook his head. "I don't think of you as old. You do more than men half your age."

"Well, that's a nice thing to say, but fact is, I'm old enough to be your father."

"Brad's lucky to have you as his father."

"How so?"

When John hesitated, Neil waved a hand at him. "Come on, explain."

"Not everyone has a father who loves his son, encourages him, is proud of him." Appalled at saying so much, John turned to Willow and fed her a carrot. She took it but turned away from him as if miffed.

"I'm sorry. Rough childhood, huh? Well, I never did think that everyone did. I told you I didn't. My dad was a mean, unhappy man. Some say it's a pattern, that a kid who's abused becomes an abuser. But I think it can be different. I was determined I was going to be different with my son. And I have been."

He paused. "Did you make up with that sweet girl of yours?"

"I did."

"I'm glad to hear it."

Neil fell silent. It was so quiet they could hear the foal suckling her mother.

"Is she the one?"

"Pardon?"

"You know, is Rose Anna the one you feel is meant for you? Like my Doris was for me."

John stared at him, not knowing what to say. He wasn't used to personal questions from those who weren't family or friends.

But the truth was, he'd become a friend, maybe more. He was the father John would have liked to have had. Maybe that's why Brad had resented him. He'd sensed the two were more than employer/employee. He wondered what Neil had told Brad . . .

"And don't say 'it's complicated' the way young people do these days," Neil said. "You know when a woman's the one for you, and there shouldn't be any shilly-shallying around about it."

"Shilly-shallying?"

"Oh, you know what I mean. Some men aren't sincere with women. They play the field. That's not you, is it?"

He shook his head and wanted to change the subject, look away from Neil's direct gaze. But he couldn't.

281

"No, I'm not. But no matter what I feel, I don't have anything to offer her."

"What nonsense is that? You're a nice, steady guy. Decent. Hard-working. You have a lot to offer her."

"I don't have a farm or a business. I work for other people. Several other people." Neil knew he had other part-time jobs.

"You think that bothers her?"

John shrugged. "Most Amish men don't offer marriage unless they can support their wives."

"That's what men of my generation used to feel. I'd say you're old-fashioned, but that's the way the Amish are about it, huh?"

John nodded.

"How's your young woman feel about that?"

"I — we haven't talked about it."

"But I bet you know how she'd feel about it."

Rose Anna would say it wasn't important if he owned a farm. Or a home. Or had his own business.

"Yeah, I see you know," Neil said with a nod. He pulled out an unlit cigar, put it in his mouth, and looked thoughtful. Then he pulled it out and pointed it at John. "She's Amish, but what are you, John? Are you Amish or *Englisch*?"

"I — I haven't joined the church."

"So can you get married if you're not both members of the church?"

"No."

Neil stood. "Seems I remember weddings only take place here in the fall, after the harvest. So I guess if you have something permanent in mind with that sweet young woman, you need to get a move on. I'm going on up to the house. Ready to have some supper. If you have a mind to join me, I'd enjoy the company."

He started toward the barn door then turned back, a twinkle in his eyes. "Interrogation's over."

John couldn't help chuckling. He quickly finished up the evening chores and walked up to the house. Neil's housekeeper always fixed him a nice supper before she left. They ate on tray tables in the living room so Neil could watch a basketball game and get entirely too worked up over his favorite team.

"My alma mater," he confessed. "They contacted me for a donation. I told them they'd get one when they fired the basketball coach."

The meal and game over, Neil and John loaded the dishwasher. And then Neil was politely kicking John out.

"Go take Rose Anna for a drive," he said, opening the back door. "You're only young once. Don't waste it."

John wanted to object, but Neil claimed all he wanted was a book and an early night.

He got into his truck and started for Rose Anna's and then realized his mood was too uncertain. Neil had made some good points, but things were more complicated than the older man realized. The *Englisch* didn't understand the way the Amish thought. Rose Anna had been angry with him for saying Amish *maedels* sought marriage, but marriage — family — was the cornerstone of the community. She could say what she wished, but if they didn't marry in the church she'd have only two choices: marry someone else or leave the community to be with him and be shunned.

Rose Anna was too good at reading his moods, so he worried about going to her house. He even got as far as slowing in front of it and then he shook his head, went on with the intention of making a U-turn and heading to his place.

It was just his bad luck to pass his old home and see his *mudder* sitting out on the porch in a rocking chair.

And even worse luck when she recognized his truck and waved at him.

He wanted to drive on. Oh, how he wanted to drive on. But what could he do? How did you ignore your own *mudder* and drive on?

So he slowed, pulled into the drive, and parked. He sat there for a long moment trying to figure out what to do and then realized he had no choice. He had to get out and talk to her.

With any luck, his *dat* wouldn't come out and get into a discussion with him that would undoubtedly turn into something unpleasant. He shut off the engine, got out, and climbed the steps to the porch.

She pulled a chair closer to hers. "Sit, sit! I wasn't expecting you."

"I was heading home after work."

"You live in the opposite direction."

He nodded. "Just out for a drive."

"You were going by Rose Anna's, weren't you?" Waneta smiled, looking satisfied. "I've seen the way the two of you look at each other when you come here to help David or go to Sam's to help him."

"Don't go matchmaking," he said with more heat than he intended.

She drew back as if he'd slapped her. "I'm sorry."

Now he felt like a complete heel. "We're friends. That's all."

"But —"

"But nothing. I know it made you happy when Lavina and Mary Elizabeth brought David and then Sam back to the community. But everyone doesn't get a happy ending."

Happy ending. That sounded like Rose Anna and the romance novels she loved to read. Did all women see life through rose-colored glasses?

"Look, I'm tired, and my mind was wandering, and I really need to get home, get cleaned up, and get some rest. I worked a lot of hours today."

"Have you had supper? I can fix you something."

Pile on the guilt, he thought. He'd bitten off her head, and she was going to feed him.

"*Mamm,* don't be nice to me after I snapped at you." He rubbed at the tension in his neck and muttered under his breath. "Don't be a doormat."

"Don't talk like that!" she said, getting to her feet, her eyes flashing. "I won't have a *sohn* of mine talking like that!"

He stared at her. "So, you do have a backbone."

"I always have," she told him, her voice firmer than he'd ever heard it. "I'll admit I should have spoken up to your *dat* sooner,

286

but a *fraa* doesn't do that."

"Even when he mistreats their *sohns*. Even when he mistreats you. Did you think I didn't hear the night he struck you? And still you did nothing."

Her hand flew to her throat and the color drained from her face. A keening cry came from her, one that sounded like a wounded animal. She shook her head, tried to speak but couldn't seem to form the words. She fled, running into the house. The door slammed behind her, loud as a gunshot.

A moment later David came out. "John? What just happened? What did you say to *Mamm*?"

"Something I should have said years ago." He turned and hurried to his truck, starting it and stomping the gas, sending up a flurry of gravel.

Thank goodness there was no one else on the road. He was so miserable he hadn't stopped to look before he pulled out.

"John did what?" Rose Anna stared at Lavina.

"David said he had Waneta in tears." Lavina plucked a ripe zucchini and added it to the basket beside her. She got to her feet and lifted the basket. "I think this is it for today. The others need another day or two to ripen."

Rose Anna picked up her basket of vegetables and followed her *schweschder* into her *haus.* "What was he doing here anyway? It wasn't a workday."

"*Nee.* It was last night."

She'd half-hoped John would stop by but he hadn't. So this is where he was . . .

"So he just walked into the house and picked a fight with her? That doesn't sound like John."

They went into the kitchen and set their baskets on a counter. "She was sitting on the front porch getting some fresh air after supper and apparently he was driving past."

"It's all so strange."

"I know. I thought John had a problem with his *dat,* not his *mudder.*"

Lavina glanced at the door to the *dawdi haus.* "I don't think we should talk about it here."

"I thought you said Waneta and Amos were at Sam and Mary Elizabeth's this morning."

"They are, but I worry they could come back and walk in on us talking about them." She filled the sink with water and began washing the vegetables. "Get a dish towel out and dry these, will you?"

Rose Anna did as she asked, trying to

puzzle things out. "I doubt they'll walk back in." She bit her lip.

"You haven't talked to him about it?"

She shook her head. "He had to work at the horse farm this morning. Then he was supposed to come here to help." She wondered if he'd come now.

They sat at the table cutting up vegetables for the jars of chowchow they'd be canning that day.

She cut the cauliflower, peeled and sliced the carrots, snapped green beans, and added wax beans and kidney beans to two huge bowls. Finally, she could no longer put off cutting up the onions. It always seemed to her that her eyes teared more than anyone else's when she performed such a chore.

"I can do those," Lavina offered.

"Nee, it's *allrecht."* Doggedly she cut them and felt the tears streaming down her cheeks. Not much more to do . . .

Waneta and Amos came in.

"You're back already!" Lavina exclaimed.

"It got a little too warm for Amos," Waneta said.

He walked over to the sink for a glass of water and drank it thirstily.

Not two minutes later John walked in. He took one look at the tears streaming down Rose Anna's face and his expression turned thunderous. He glared at his *dat*. "Did you say something to upset Rose Anna?" he demanded.

"I'm not the one who throws around harsh words," Amos snapped. "You owe your *mudder* an apology."

Rose Anna stood so abruptly her chair fell back landing on the floor with a loud crack. "John! Your *dat* didn't say anything bad to me! Can't you see what I'm doing?"

She held out the onion in one hand, the knife in the other. She set them down on the cutting board, bent to pick up the chair, and sat again. Grabbing a paper napkin from the basket on the table, she wiped away the tears on her cheeks.

Anger faded from his face, replaced by embarrassment.

"It's always my fault, isn't it?" Amos said.

John nodded. "It was most of the time. My *bruders* and I wouldn't have left home if things had been different."

"We don't talk about family matters in front of others!"

"Lavina and Rose Anna *are* family."

Amos muttered as he stalked to the *dawdi haus*. He turned, his hand on the doorknob, and looked back at his *fraa*. "Are you coming?"

Waneta stood there, still as a statue, her

fingers pressed against her lips. The older woman's face was drained of color, her eyes haunted as she stared at her *sohn.*

Amos went into the *dawdi haus* and slammed the door.

Rose Anna's gaze flew to John. She jerked her head at his *mudder,* sending a silent message, and he looked at her.

"I'm sorry I didn't stand up to your *dat* more," Waneta began haltingly as she stared at John. "You don't know how I've wished I'd done more. But I can't change that now. Can you forgive me?"

He sighed, nodded, then he was closing the distance between them and taking her into his arms. "*Ya.* Don't cry, *Mamm.* Don't cry."

Rose Anna felt tears slipping down her cheeks, tears that didn't come from cutting onions. She looked at the *dawdi haus* door.

Lavina reached across the table and touched Rose Anna's hand. "It'll be *allrecht.* It'll just take time."

She knew Amos and his two older *sohns* had healed their differences. But how long would it take for Amos and John?

16

Rose Anna took a walk after supper.

A long walk. She'd always found it helped when she was restless or upset. Now she found herself upset and not sure what to do about it.

Thank goodness John had to stop by the horse farm after he helped at David and Lavina's today. It meant she didn't have to talk to him until she sorted out how she felt about things.

She just didn't understand this . . . tension in John's family. There had been quarrels in her family. You couldn't have three *dochders* without having the occasional fuss. Especially when the oldest two considered it their duty to tease the youngest. Their *mudder* had refereed as best as she could, but Lavina and Mary Elizabeth weren't stupid. They'd done some of their best work when their *mudder* was out of hearing range. It hadn't been that long ago that *Mamm* had said Rose Anna had to stand up and speak up more for herself. Then maybe the teasing would stop.

Rose Anna knew her *mudder* was a wise woman, but she didn't think anything was going to stop her *schweschders* from teasing.

And her parents had occasionally disagreed, but they had never behaved like John's parents in front of their *kinner.*

But it had been more than tension that had been a problem in the Stoltzfus *haus.* All three of the *bruders* had confided in the Zook *schweschders* how their *dat* had berated them constantly. No matter what they did, no matter how hard they worked on the farm, nothing was ever *gut* enough for Amos.

She knew things had gotten pretty bad for David, then his *bruders,* to leave their home, their community, their church, and live in town.

But she hadn't really understood that John blamed his *mudder,* not just his *dat,* for what had led to their leaving.

What would it feel like to think that *both* your parents had failed you?

And what if Waneta had not only failed to stop Amos from verbally abusing their *sohns*

— but had failed to stop him from hitting them?

She stopped dead in her tracks. John had never said his *dat* hit him. But would he? Lost in her thoughts, she didn't realize that she was just a few blocks from Sam and Mary Elizabeth's farm. She walked on to their back door and went inside.

Mary Elizabeth stood at the kitchen sink doing dishes. "Rose Anna! What a surprise!"

"Where's Sam?"

"Out in the barn. Why?"

"I need to ask you something."

"*Schur.* Want something to drink? Iced tea?"

Distracted, she nodded. "I'll get it. You want some, too?"

"*Ya, danki.*" She dried the last dish and sat at the table. "It's been a long day. Waneta and I canned all those." She waved at a couple dozen jars sitting on a kitchen counter, then took a sip of tea. "So what do you want to ask me?"

Rose Anna glanced at the door, then at Mary Elizabeth. "Has Sam ever said if Amos hit him or his *bruders*?"

Mary Elizabeth stared at her, shocked. "*Nee.* Did John say he had?"

She shook her head. "It's just that he and Waneta had an argument last night and

294

when she walked into Lavina's today, he said something . . ." she trailed off, lifted her hands, let them drop into her lap. "Apparently he said she should have spoken up to Amos, and she apologized to him today in front of Lavina and me. He was so upset — *she* was so upset. It made me wonder if more than yelling — more than verbal abuse — had gone on."

"Oh, my," was all Mary Elizabeth could manage. "Are you going to ask John?"

Rose Anna found herself staring at the glass of tea in front of her. "I have to, don't I? First chance I get." She took a sip to ease her dry throat. "He went from Sam and Lavina's *haus* to his job at the horse farm, so I couldn't today."

They heard feet stomping on the back porch, then Sam walked through the door.

"Well *gut-n-owed*. I didn't know you were here," he told Rose Anna.

"Sam, Rose Anna has something she'd like to ask you," Mary Elizabeth said. She rose and fixed him a glass of iced tea.

"*Allrecht.*" He sat at the table, looking wary. "What is it, Rose Anna?"

"Sam, did your *dat* ever hit you or your *bruders*?"

He didn't react with shock as his *fraa* had. Instead, he sighed heavily. "Did John tell

295

you that?"

"*Nee.*" She related what had happened earlier.

"*Mamm* never spoke up against *Daed.* He never hit me, but I can't speak for John. Or David for that matter."

"But wouldn't they have told you?"

"I'd hope so. But I can't be *schur* of it. *Bruders* don't tell each other everything. Do *schweschders*?"

Rose Anna looked at Mary Elizabeth. "*Ya,*" she said. Then, as she looked at her and thought about it, she shook her head. "*Nee,* maybe not. But something so important. Wouldn't John have come to you to help him?"

Sam shook his head. "John always wanted to stand on his own two feet. He didn't like being the *boppli* of the family."

They *schur* had that in common, thought Rose Anna.

"Why worry about it now? It's in the past."

"*Nee,* it's not. It's part of why John hasn't come back, don't you see?" she asked him. "It isn't just the way your *dat* treated you that's bothering him. It's your *mudder,* too."

Tears welled up in her eyes. John had held so much inside. She hurt for him, for the boy he'd been, for the man he was now.

He needed her. And she needed him. She

296

needed to love away all his pain and show him that someone cared about him.

She stood. "I have to talk to him."

Sam rose. "Let me drive you home."

"*Nee,* I can walk. It's not that far."

"But it's almost dark."

"Rose Anna, let Sam drive you home," Mary Elizabeth said quietly.

She looked at him. It was obvious that she'd upset him asking about whether his *dat* had ever hit John. He wasn't the oldest *bruder,* but maybe he wished he'd looked after him more. Protected him.

"*Allrecht,*" she said. "*Danki.*"

The drive home was silent. It was just the two of them. Mary Elizabeth had asked if they minded if she stayed behind to finish cleaning up the kitchen. Seeing how tired she looked after a day of canning, Rose Anna insisted she stay home.

Sam seemed absorbed in his own thoughts. Rose Anna didn't feel up to making conversation. It was a *gut* thing the trip was short. She thanked him when they arrived at her *haus,* and she was grateful her parents nodded when she said she was tired and was going to bed early.

She got ready for bed and climbed into it, welcoming its softness after a long day.

Then the thought struck her: could a man

who'd only witnessed an unhappy marriage, grown up feeling unloved, be able to make a happy union with a woman? Could he be a *gut dat*?

Sleep didn't come for hours.

Shoveling manure was a part of every day for John. Today it particularly suited his foul mood.

What could be lower than to give your *mudder* a hard time and break her heart? he asked himself as he dumped a shovelful of soiled hay into the wheelbarrow.

When Neil poked his head in to say hello, he raised his eyebrows when all he got was a grunt.

"Don't leave without your paycheck."

"Won't." John dumped another shovelful in the wheelbarrow, propped the shovel against the wall, and pushed the wheelbarrow outside.

Hard work dampened his shirt but didn't improve his mood like it usually did. Only when he finished and leaned on Willow's stall to take a brief rest did he realize he'd been so grumpy he hadn't given any of the horses the attention he usually did. Willow bumped her head against his arm as if to rebuke him, so he stroked her nose and watched as the newly named Fiona pranced over and pushed her nose playfully at his hand. He went down the stalls and gave each of them some time. To his surprise, even Midnight, who usually didn't seek attention and merely tolerated it with the air of an equine prince, shook his head and allowed him to pat him.

He left the barn, making sure the door was secure before he walked up to the main house. Neil always said just walk in, but he thought that was presumptuous so he knocked. And knocked again. Neil had told him to be sure to get his paycheck. Neil finally came to the door looking pale and tired.

"Sorry, didn't mean to keep you waiting," he said. "Did you need something?" He gestured for John to come in, so he stepped inside.

"You told me to get my paycheck before I left, but it looks like you're not feeling well. I can get it tomorrow."

"No, no, it's here somewhere." Neil waved a hand at the kitchen table and frowned. "I was just writing out checks for bills earlier. It's here somewhere." He riffled through some papers scattered on the table and then swayed.

John grasped him by his arms before he fell and gently pushed him down into a chair. "What's wrong?"

Neil shook his head as if to clear it. "Dizzy. Chest . . . hurts." He fumbled in his shirt pocket. A pill bottle slipped from his fingers and clattered to the floor.

John scooped it up, saw it was Neil's heart medicine, and put it back in the older man's hands. But Neil couldn't seem to twist the cap so he took it back, opened it, and tipped a tablet into his hand. "Here. Do you need some water?"

"No, no." He wiped at the sweat on his forehead and seemed to struggle for breath. "It's the third — the third I've taken. They're not working."

John reached for his cell phone and realized he'd left it in his truck. "Give me your cell phone."

When Neil didn't immediately respond and clutched his chest, John reached into the man's shirt pocket and plucked it out. He dialed 911.

"What are you doing?"

"We need to get you to the hospital."

"Don't need —"

John shushed him and answered the 911 dispatcher's questions. It took only minutes for paramedics to arrive, but they were the longest minutes of his life. He found himself praying — something he hadn't done for a very long time — as they swarmed into the kitchen and took over.

"Come with," Neil croaked as they loaded him onto a gurney.

"Of course," he said, locking the door as he followed the paramedics to the ambulance.

He watched as Neil was given oxygen and hooked up to monitors in the ambulance. As the ambulance doors were closed, he realized he was still clutching the bottle of nitroglycerin in his hand. He handed it to the paramedic who was trying to get a medical history from Neil and told him what he could.

The grim look the paramedic watching a monitor had on his face told John that the news wasn't good. He glanced at John. "Good thing you called us. They'll be waiting for us at the hospital."

"I'll call your son," he told Neil.

But the older man shook his head. "Big case. Don't — bother." He frowned as the ambulance accelerated down the driveway and the siren wailed. "Such a fuss. It'll pass."

The paramedic kept his eyes on John and sent him a silent message. John didn't need it. He intended to call Brad, but there was no need to argue with Neil.

Then it happened. Neil coded in the ambulance.

The two paramedics went into action, keeping their balance as the ambulance sped toward the hospital. One spoke to the hospital and administered drugs into the intravenous drip while the other did CPR.

John prayed harder.

When the ambulance arrived at the hospital, the doors were opened and he stayed out of the way as Neil's gurney was pushed rapidly through the emergency room entrance.

He wasn't allowed inside the treatment room. It was a tough call as to which was worse: watching as the vital man he knew and admired went into cardiac arrest or waiting and not being able to see what was happening.

So he walked into the waiting room and used Neil's cell phone to call his son.

"Hey, Dad, can I call you back? I'm going into court right now," Brad said before John could speak.

"Brad, it's John Stoltzfus," he said quickly. "I'm calling about your father. I'm at the emergency room. He's had a heart attack."

He relayed what had happened and told him how Neil had insisted he didn't want Brad called, saying he was involved in a big case.

"It is," Brad said, and he sighed gustily. "Listen, I have to walk into court and talk to the judge, tell him I have a family emergency, and get a postponement. I should be on the road in fifteen minutes."

"I won't leave until you get here."

There was silence, and John wondered if Brad had hung up. "I appreciate that," he heard him say.

"Call me when you're on the road, and I'll let you know what the doctor says if I hear anything more."

"Will do."

A half hour later a doctor appeared in the doorway. "John Stoltzfus?"

He stood. "That's me."

The doctor walked over and sank down onto the sofa. "Have a seat. I haven't been off my feet for hours. Well, Mr. Zimmerman had a heart attack as you know. We're taking him in for a cardiac catheterization in a few minutes. That's a test to see how bad the damage is, see if we need to do surgery. I called his cardiologist, and he's on his way."

"I just called his son. He'll be here as soon as he can." John hesitated, but then he had to ask. "Is Neil going to make it?"

"We're doing everything we can." He stood. "I'll say this. You did the right thing getting him here when you did. Too often either the patient or the family doesn't recognize what's going on."

"I'm not family."

"That's not the impression I got from Mr. Zimmerman. I'll know more after we do the catheterization."

"Thanks, Doctor."

John walked down to the cafeteria for coffee, considered a sandwich, and decided against it. He wasn't entirely sure his stomach could even handle the coffee.

An hour passed. The doctor came out again and explained that one of Neil's arteries was 90 percent blocked and he needed something called a stent.

"Does that mean surgery?"

The doctor nodded.

John wrote down Brad's number and asked that he call him and explain. The doctor took the number and agreed. "You can see him for a few minutes if you like."

Neil frowned at him when he walked into his cubicle. "Heard you called Brad," he grumbled. "Told you not to."

"Well, he had a right to know. Said he was going to ask the judge for something called a postponement. He's on his way here."

"That just drags things out." He plucked at the blanket covering him. "Well, guess I should thank you for insisting on calling for an ambulance. Doc said I might not have made it if you hadn't gotten me here when you did."

He shrugged. "I'm just glad you're going to be okay." He paused. "I wish you'd have let me tell Brad earlier about your heart. I think this was a shock."

"He'd have worried. Tried to talk me into going back to Philadelphia." He shifted in bed. "Well, guess you can be going."

John shook his head. "Told your son I'd stay until he got here."

"You don't have to."

"I want to."

Neil studied him. "You're a good man, John. I'm lucky I hired you."

"*I'm* lucky you hired me. Best job I ever had," he said honestly.

They came to wheel Neil into surgery, so John returned to the waiting room. Restless, wanting to do something, he found himself wandering down the hall. On his way to the cafeteria, he'd passed a chapel.

Maybe God paid more attention to prayers said in such a place.

It couldn't hurt.

When John missed supper, Rose Anna got worried.

"Did you check the answering machine?" her *mudder* asked her as they did the dishes.

She nodded. "I went out there twice." She bit her lip and glanced at the clock on the wall.

"Go check it again. I'm *schur* he just got held up at work."

Her *mudder* was right. There *was* a message from John. It was a long one explaining he'd spent most of the day at the hospital with Neil. He'd be spending the night at the farm — maybe the next few days — until Neil got out of the hospital. He left his cell phone number and asked her to call him back.

She thought about doing it, stood there for a few minutes staring at the telephone.

And then she got an idea.

She walked back to the house and told her *mudder* what had happened. "*Mamm,* would you mind if I took some leftovers from supper and dropped them off to John at the farm?"

Linda wiped her hands on a dish towel. "*Schur.* Why don't you do the same for Neil's son in case he's staying there?"

"*Gut* idea."

She got out plastic containers, packed the food, and loaded it into a tote bag. She added a Thermos of iced tea, some cookies, and fruit.

"Drive careful," her *mudder* said as she headed for the door.

She kissed her cheek. "*Danki*. And I'll be back soon."

Her *dat* was in the barn doing evening chores. He looked surprised when she told him she was taking the buggy out but quickly helped her hitch up the horse to it.

The air was still heavy and warm. A late afternoon rain shower hadn't cooled things down at all. Most of the fields that lined the roads had been harvested. Summer was nearly over.

Time was rushing on.

John's truck was parked outside the barn when she got there. She knocked on the door of the barn and then slid the door open.

"Rose Anna!" John turned from filling a water bucket. "What are you doing here?"

"I got your message. I thought maybe you hadn't eaten supper." She held up the tote.

"*Danki*, I haven't eaten all day." He waved a hand at a nearby bale of hay. "Have a seat."

She sat down. "I'm sorry about Neil. I know how much you like him. How is he doing?"

"He came through the surgery fine. His

son is with him." He took a seat on another bale of hay near her.

She handed him a plastic container of chicken and noodle casserole. "*Mamm* suggested I pack extra in case he was staying here."

John opened the plastic container and his eyes lit up when he saw what was inside. "Your *mudder*'s chicken and noodles are the best."

"I made it."

"Oh, well, I'm *schur* it will be very *gut*."

"It's *allrecht*. I used her recipe." She glanced around at the interior of the barn. It was clean and orderly just like the other time she'd been inside.

She'd have expected no less of John. His *dat* had certainly been a stern taskmaster about keeping the barn clean. She knew animals got sick if their stalls weren't cleaned well. Disease could spread from one to another, and suddenly a farmer was spending large amounts of money on veterinary bills or worse, having to replace stock if his animals died.

She watched with satisfaction as John ate every bite of the chicken and noodles. It wasn't much, just leftovers, but he'd obviously been ravenous. He ate a couple of cookies and then poured cold tea into a plastic cup.

"Want some?" he asked, holding out the glass.

"Maybe just a sip," she said, taking it.

She supposed she should go. The bishop was stern about a single man and a woman being alone together.

The barn was quiet except for the occasional horse shifting in its stall.

When she heard the foal whinny, the sound tentative and high-pitched, she couldn't help smiling.

"Did Neil name her yet?"

He nodded and filled the glass with cold tea again. "Fiona. I have no idea why."

"How sweet. It suits her. She's so delicate."

"She'll grow up to be a big horse like her *mudder.*"

"True. But it'll still suit her with those big brown eyes." She paused. "Speaking of *mudders . . .*"

He winced. "Do we have to?"

She nodded.

"I didn't realize you blamed your *mudder* as well as your *dat.*"

He nodded. "I guess I made that obvious."

"Do you really think she could do anything? Women of her generation were taught that the *mann* is the head of the *haus.*"

309

"It doesn't mean that if he's cruel that she shouldn't speak up."

"I heard that the bishop talked to her and took your *dat*'s side."

John sighed. "He did."

"Then what could she really do, John?"

They heard a vehicle pull up on the gravel drive outside and sprang apart.

A few moments later, the barn door slid open.

"Brad! How's your father?"

"He's resting comfortably. They told me to go home and come back in the morning."

"Brad, this is Rose Anna."

"Nice to meet you."

"It's a good sign when they send family home," Rose Anna told him. "I brought you some supper in case you didn't get anything to eat at the hospital."

He looked surprised as she handed him the tote. "That's very thoughtful. No, I didn't want to leave Dad, and on the way out, I saw the cafeteria was closed."

"It's just chicken and noodles, some cookies, and fruit."

"Sounds wonderful. I'm starved."

A horse neighed, and Brad jumped and stepped several feet away from where she'd been standing.

"I hope you have a key," John said. "I locked up and left the porch light on as we left with the ambulance this afternoon, but I didn't think about the fact that I don't have a key if you needed to get in."

"It's okay. I do." He held up the tote bag. "Thank you for dinner, Rose Anna. I appreciate you thinking of me."

"You're welcome. I'll say a prayer for your father tonight."

"I — that's very kind. Thanks." He looked at John. "And thank you for all you did for my dad today. The doctor said your swift action probably saved his life."

Rose Anna watched a flush creep up John's neck. "No need to thank me. It's no more than anyone would do."

"I disagree. Well, I'm going to go eat this and get some rest. I'll see you later, John. And Rose Anna, again, thank you."

She nodded and watched him leave. "He seems like a nice man."

"*Ya*. I didn't think so at first. He wasn't the friendliest to me when we met. I think he was a bit jealous of the relationship I have with his father. They don't share a love of horses."

"I noticed he looked nervous being in here." She stood. "Well, I should be getting home."

"*Danki* for coming."

"It was just supper."

"It was more than that. You knew Neil's become a friend. A *gut* friend."

She wondered if he'd become the *dat* John never had, but now wasn't the time to say it.

He walked her out, and they stood for a moment beside the buggy. Fireflies winked on and off in the distance. Honeysuckle was blooming somewhere near, and the scent carried on the sulky summer breeze.

The night was perfect for a long drive in the country. But John had looked exhausted in the light inside the barn, and she'd told her *mudder* she wouldn't be out late.

"See you tomorrow."

She nodded. "Tomorrow."

He kissed her, a light kiss but one whose heat lingered. She got into the buggy, picked up the reins, and began the ride back home. And when she glanced back and saw him lift his hand and wave to her, she was glad she'd come. He looked lonely.

When she was a block away, she touched her lips and felt the promise in his kiss all the way home.

17

Rose Anna went to bed with the windows open to a warm, late summer evening breeze wafting in.

She woke to a definite nip in the air and hurried to shut the window. After dressing quickly, she brushed and put her hair in a bun and pinned a fresh *kapp* on.

Her *mudder* had breakfast cooking when she got downstairs. She turned and smiled at her. *"Guder marlye."*

"Guder mariye. I can't believe how cool it is this morning."

Linda nodded. "I thought oatmeal would be *gut.*"

Rose Anna sprinkled brown sugar on top and then added some milk. "I wonder how Neil is doing this morning. His son looked worried last night."

"So he was there at the farm?"

"Ya, he arrived just after I got there. I'm glad you suggested I take some food for

him. He and John hadn't eaten. John said he might come over later today."

Her *dat* walked in, poured himself a cup of coffee, and sat at the table. Linda set a big bowl of oatmeal before him and pushed the pitcher of milk closer. Then she glanced at the door that led to the *dawdi haus*. "Seems like Abraham gets up later and later these days."

Rose Anna frowned. "Are you worried about him?"

"A little, after the news about John's boss."

"I can go wake *Grossdaadi* up."

"Nee, I'm *schur* he's *allrecht."* She brightened. "I know how to do it without knocking on his door."

Rose Anna watched her *mudder* curiously as she went to the refrigerator. She got a package from the freezer, walked to the stove, and turned on the oven.

"Cinnamon rolls?" her *dat* asked, perking up.

"Sticky buns." She slid the pan in the oven.

Soon the scent filled the air.

Before the timer dinged, the door to the *dawdi haus* opened and *Grossdaadi* shuffled out looking sleepy. "Something smells *gut."*

"Hey, we only got oatmeal," her *dat* pretended to complain.

"You can have a bun, dear," Linda told him. "*Guder mariye,* Abraham. Here, have some coffee. Sticky buns will be out in a minute or two."

The timer went off, and she pulled the pan out. She used a spatula to place the rolls on a plate. Both men insisted on taking one before they were cooled enough and then tossed them from hand to hand so they could take a bite. Linda just gave them both an indulgent smile.

Rose Anna took a bun and found she still had room for it after the oatmeal.

"Abraham, why are you rubbing your chest?" Linda asked him.

His hand dropped. "Don't know what you're talking about."

"You were rubbing your chest."

He shook his head. "Just your imagination."

Linda looked at her *mann.* Jacob shrugged.

"I saw it too," Rose Anna said. "*Grossdaadi,* is your heart bothering you?"

"The two of you need to stop fussing. I'm fine. Just had a twinge or two. Now it feels like I have some pressure, like I have to cough and then I don't. Maybe just need a little Pepto-Bismol for indigestion."

Linda got up and checked the calendar on

the wall. "Today's a clinic day. I think we should go have it checked out."

Abraham took a big bite of his roll. "Women worry too much. Man can't get any peace in his own *haus*."

Rose Anna thought about Neil and how John had said the man hadn't wanted to go the doctor . . .

"*Grossdaadi,* we could take a quick trip to the clinic and then stop by the Zimmerman horse farm, take John some of these buns. They have a new filly."

He cocked his head to one side and considered what she had said. "John, eh?"

She nodded. "And a new filly. You know how you used to love helping with the horses."

"*Allrecht,*" he said. "After I have another bun. Can't get through a morning on just one bun you know." He took it and left the table. "I'll put on my *gut* shirt."

"And shoes," Linda called. "You've got on your house slippers." When he went into the *dawdi haus* and shut the door, muttering about being nagged, she chuckled. "Well, that was nice maneuvering, Rose Anna."

Rose Anna grinned and found a plastic container for four of the buns.

"She learned from the best," Jacob said as he reached for another bun.

"What's that supposed to mean?" Linda demanded with a huff.

"Why, she learned from Miriam," he said innocently.

His *fraa* gave him a narrow glance.

Giggling, Rose Anna escaped from the kitchen. She got her sweater and purse, rounded up *Grossdaadi* who pretended he didn't know he still had on his house slippers, and went out to the barn to hitch up the buggy.

Her *dat* was already there doing the job for her. When she thanked him, he grinned. "Seemed a *gut* time to get out of the kitchen."

She laughed. "*Mamm* knew you were teasing."

He kissed her cheek. "You call if the doctor is concerned about *Grossdaadi, allrecht?*"

"I will."

She was disappointed when she didn't see John's truck parked at the farm on the way into town.

"Why aren't we stopping?"

"John's not there. We'll check back on our way home." She saw him glance at the back seat. "*Nee, Grossdaadi,* the buns are for John and Brad."

"Who's Brad?"

317

"Mr. Zimmerman's *sohn*. He's here because his *dat* had a heart attack and is in the hospital."

"That why your *mudder* and you over-reacted about me this morning?"

"We didn't overreact," she said mildly. "It won't hurt to have you visit the clinic."

"Waste of time," he muttered, frowning.

"You're worth it," she told him and grinned at him. To her delight he grinned back, reached over, and patted her hand.

"You're a *gut grossdochder*," he said.

The news from the clinic doctor was mixed. "Mr. Zook has a mild arrhythmia," he told Rose Anna. "But we have a medication that should help. I'd like him to take it for two weeks then come back and see us."

Relieved, Rose Anna left the clinic with *Grossdaadi,* and they started home. John's truck was still not at the farm so she left the box with the buns on the porch of the farmhouse.

Something felt wrong. Very wrong.

John came instantly awake when he heard a noise outside the barn.

He slid the door open and saw Brad standing beside his car.

"Neil?" he mumbled, sitting up and blinking. "Oh, Brad. I thought you were with

318

your dad. Where are you going?"

"You're still here."

He ran his hands through his hair. "Yeah. What's wrong?"

"The hospital. It's Dad. I've got to go back. He's — he's having some sort of setback." He stopped as if unable to go on.

"Let me drive you."

"I can drive myself," he said, his voice shaking. Then he dropped his car keys, and John had to pluck them up.

"Get in the truck." To his relief Brad didn't argue.

"They wouldn't say much. Just said to come right away."

John floored it. He'd risk a ticket. He glanced over and saw Brad's face was leached of color as they passed under a streetlight. "Hang in there. We'll be there soon."

Neil was already gone when they got there.

"I don't understand. I thought he was doing well when I left." Brad stood by his father's bedside staring down at his father's still form with disbelief.

"The doctor thinks he may have had a blood clot," a nurse told them. "He'd be here to talk to you, but he's with a patient. He'll be in as soon as he can. You stay with your father as long as you like." She patted

319

his shoulder before leaving the room.

John had lost *grosseldres*, but they were so much older than Neil. It didn't seem possible that the man was gone.

He couldn't imagine how Brad felt. "He was the best man I ever knew," John said, feeling awkward.

"I wouldn't have left if I'd thought this would happen."

"You came when he needed you. You spent hours with him after you got here."

Brad sank down in a chair beside the bed and took his father's hand. "He was a wonderful father." Tears were running down Brad's cheeks. "I didn't tell him often enough."

"He knew. He was so proud of you."

"He talked about me?"

"A lot."

Brad lifted his father's hand to his face. Grief overcame him.

John felt tears burning at the backs of his eyelids and tremors were shaking his body. He was ashamed of how relieved he was when the doctor — a different one than he'd met before — walked in just then to talk to Brad.

He stepped outside and waited. The doctor came out a few minutes later and strode on down the hall. Long minutes passed.

John debated going back inside and felt doing so would intrude on the other man's grief.

When Brad finally came out his eyes were swollen, but he seemed a little calmer. "Sorry. I forgot you were out here."

"We'll stay as long as you need to. Do you want me to go get you coffee or something?"

He shook his head. "I guess we can go. There's nothing else I can do for him now."

They walked out of the hospital, down silent hallways and out to the truck. Brad seemed in a daze when John pulled into the drive.

Dawn was streaking the sky. It seemed unreal to John that a day was being born and Neil wouldn't be in it. How many times had the older man come out to say hello as he worked in the barn?

"He loved this place so much." He sat there staring blindly through the windshield. "I wanted him to stay near me, but he wanted to be here with his horses."

He seemed to gather himself and opened the truck door. "Your girlfriend left some sticky buns on the porch earlier. You want to come up to the house and have some with some coffee?"

"Sure."

So they sat in Neil's kitchen and drank

coffee made in the fancy coffeemaker he loved, and neither of them ate the buns.

"Why don't you try to get some sleep?"

"*Try* is the operative word," Brad said without enthusiasm.

"Do you need to call a funeral home or anything? I know the ones in the area."

Brad shook his head. "Dad made pre-arrangements. That's the good part of being a lawyer. You think of all that stuff when you're in this line of work." His face contorted. "He took me to the office all the time when I was a kid, made me fall in love with the law. I just wish I could have fallen in love with horses." He looked at John. "Guess he had you for that. We'll talk about it later," he said cryptically. Then he left the room.

John turned off the coffeemaker, put the cups in the dishwasher, and left, locking the door behind him. He mechanically went about the morning chores and then headed to his own place to get some sleep.

When he woke it was late afternoon. He lay there for a few minutes, feeling disoriented at finding himself in bed when the light was different than morning. And then he remembered, and grief swept over him again.

Guilt came in a wave right after it. Would

he feel the same if it had been his *dat* who'd died? Not that long ago he'd been in treatment for the cancer, and that had been a real possibility. But John hadn't been able to get past his anger at his *dat* to reconcile with him the way his *bruders* had.

He knew the blame wasn't all his. Each time the two of them were in the same room, he still felt his *dat* picked at him.

Feeling older than his years, he sat up, swung his legs over the side of the bed, and stood. He'd told Rose Anna he'd see her today, and he supposed he should go by and at least tell her about Neil and beg off eating supper with her and her family. And it seemed to him that he should see if there was something he could do for Neil's son.

Neil would want that.

So he showered, dressed, and drove over to Rose Anna's *haus*.

"Oh, I'm so sorry," she said when he told her. She put her arms around him, and it helped. And then she told him that she agreed, that he should go sit with Brad and see if there was anything he could do for him.

Before he left, she insisted that she put together some food for them. When Brad opened the door, he looked surprised to see him. "Rose Anna fixed something for us to eat. We don't have to eat together if you'd rather be alone."

Brad held the door open. "No, come inside." He sat at the table and watched John unpack the containers in the tote bag Rose Anna had given him.

"She's a very kind woman, isn't she?"

Surprised, John nodded.

"Are you getting married?"

"I don't know. I'm not really in a position to do that."

"Why?"

John remembered his conversation with Neil. "I don't have a career like you. I probably don't even have a job here anymore. I expect you'll want to sell the place since you don't like horses." Then he stopped. "Of course, I'll stay on as long as you need me. You don't need to worry about your Dad's horses or someone to take care of the place until you get a buyer."

Brad stared at him for so long he felt like a jerk bringing it up. Brad nodded, then picked up an envelope from the table. "I found your paycheck sitting here. You didn't even ask if he'd left it."

"I didn't even think about it." Numbly he took it and remembered how Neil had looked for it. Had it only been yesterday? "Thanks."

"I'm going to have a memorial back in Philadelphia. That's where most of Dad's friends and associates are. I'll let you know so you can come if you want." He frowned into his coffee. "I'm picking up his ashes tomorrow from the funeral home. He told me once he wanted them scattered here on the farm."

"He'd be proud of you doing what he asked."

"It's the last thing I can do for him."

John rose and got the coffeepot, refreshed their cups. "I think there's one thing we can do for the people we love when they die. It's to live and be happy and be grateful for the time we had with them." He stopped. "Sorry. I don't want to preach. You don't need that."

Brad ran a hand through his hair and made the expensive *Englisch* cut stand on end. "No, I know Dad would hate us to sit around miserable."

Neither of them ate much. John opened the container of cookies Rose Anna packed, and Brad took one.

Brad eyed the cookie. "Your girlfriend made these?"

He nodded.

"I found a container with a couple left in it when I opened the cabinet looking for coffee. There were other containers, too, empty ones."

"Neil liked her cookies. She didn't use to be such a good baker, but she got a lot better this past year."

Brad hadn't eaten much supper, but he ate two cookies. They put the dirty dishes in the dishwasher, and John insisted on leaving the leftover casserole in the refrigerator in case Brad got hungry later.

"Guess I should be checking in with my office," Brad said, but he seemed lethargic and just held his cell phone in his hand and stared at it.

"See you tomorrow."

"Tomorrow."

John left, sorry he couldn't think of anything more he could do for Neil's son.

Rose Anna hurried outside when she heard John's truck pull into the drive. She climbed into the truck.

It hurt her heart that he tried to smile and couldn't. She waited until he pulled out onto the road, and then she reached for his hand and held it.

"How is Brad doing?"

"Not *gut.*" He sighed heavily. "He feels guilty he didn't stay with him that night at the hospital. But Neil and the staff told him to go home."

"He came when he was needed, so he shouldn't feel that way."

"I told him that, but I don't think he believes it."

"I wasn't there when *Grossmudder* died, and I felt guilty, too." She stared out the window. "*Grossdaadi* said that we never feel we have enough time with our loved ones. He's right. Neil was what, in his late sixties? I'm *schur* Brad was hoping he'd have him longer, get to do things with him."

"I can tell he wishes he shared Neil's love of horses and lived closer. But he told me his *dat* taught him to love the law, and he took over his practice."

He fell silent. The longer he didn't say anything the more Rose Anna sensed something more was wrong.

"What is it?"

"It hit me yesterday that Brad won't be staying."

"Well, of course, he'll be going back to his job at the law firm."

John pulled into a parking lot and turned to her. "No, I mean I'm *schur* he's going to put the farm up for sale. I'm going to be out of a job."

Shocked, she pressed her fingers to her lips and stared at him. "I hadn't thought of

327

that. Oh, *nee,* John! You've been so happy working with those horses!"

"It's selfish of me to even think of such a thing."

"*Nee,* don't say that. Of course you'd be upset. You love the horses and the farm. It doesn't mean you cared any less for Neil. He'd be sorry that you don't want to lose your job there. What are you going to do?"

"I told Brad I'd continue taking care of things until he found a buyer. Maybe it'll take a long time to find one."

"If only . . ."

"What?"

"If only you had the money to offer to buy it from him."

"You're such a dreamer," he said harshly.

"John!"

He hit his hand on the steering wheel. "I'm sorry. That didn't come out the way I wanted."

She blinked furiously, trying to hold back her tears and rummaged in her purse for a tissue.

"I know you meant well. But there's no way."

"Maybe you could do what Sam and Mary Elizabeth are doing."

"What do you mean?"

"They talked to the owner of the farm

they live on, and they pay her, not the bank."

He put the truck in gear and pulled out of the parking lot. "The horse farm is bigger. It has the horses. I'm *schur* it's way out of range for me."

"You don't know what God has planned for you," she told him. "You need to have faith in Him." Her heart ached at how miserable he was, how he sounded without hope. "I know now's not the right time to bring it up with Brad. But you should at least talk to him at some point. Otherwise you'll never know if he might have agreed to what you want."

"True."

"Where are we going?"

"I don't know. Where do you want to go?"

"Someplace quiet. So we can talk."

He headed toward town. "Arc you hungry?"

"Not particularly. But you probably haven't eaten."

"Not much," he admitted.

"Why don't you pull in there and get some burgers and fries, and we'll go somewhere and eat them in the truck?"

"Allrecht."

They went through the drive-through and got the food and soft drinks. He drove to a secluded little park where they sat and watched the sun go down over a little pond. The sky was crowded with pinkish-orange clouds. "You're not eating."

"Doesn't taste as *gut* as I remember."

"Nothing does when we're upset."

"True."

She tried to think of something to cheer him up and knew she was talking too much. Finally she lapsed into silence.

John put the half-eaten hamburger and fries back into the paper sack and set it on the dashboard. She gave up on eating and did the same. "John?" she said and put her hand on his arm.

He turned to her with a groan and pulled her toward him. She let him embrace her, sensed his utter need for comfort, and just held him. Then he turned to kiss her, and she knew she'd do anything to assuage this desperate void in him.

Vaguely she remembered something Emma had said about being careful not to become intimate, that she'd be sorry later.

She tried to pull back, and he resisted. "John, we can't."

For a long moment she didn't think he'd heard or that he wouldn't stop kissing her and holding her too tightly.

And then he released her, rested his forehead against hers. "I'm sorry, I'm sorry.

Everything feels so overwhelming right now."

She touched his cheek. "I know, *Lieb*. I know." She hesitated then plunged ahead. "John, come to church with me this Sunday. Just come. Maybe it'll help you sort through all this. It always helps me at difficult times. No one's going to pressure you."

"You can't promise that."

"I'll get between them and you. I won't let them," she promised rashly.

He took her hand and pressed a kiss in her palm. "That's my Rose Anna."

"Just think about it."

"I will." He turned away and started the truck.

"Promise?"

He looked at her for a long time. "I promise," he said finally.

Pleased, she sat back. They drove past the horse farm on the way back to her *haus*. Brad's car was parked in the drive.

"When's the funeral?"

"Brad's going to have a memorial later, in Philadelphia. He said he'd let me know. He's going to scatter his ashes on the farm tomorrow."

"I'll bring some food over."

"That would be nice. Brad doesn't seem in any shape to do any cooking for himself right now. He found a container of cookies you sent Neil and liked them. There were only two or three left."

"The chocolate chip? I'll bring some more, then."

He pulled into the drive of her *haus.* "Rose Anna?"

"Ya?"

He stared straight ahead, not looking at her. "I love you."

Her heart soared. "I love you, too."

"I'll see you tomorrow when you come over."

"*Gut nacht.* Get some sleep."

He turned to her then. "Sweet dreams."

She hoped she'd dream of him, but she didn't tell him that. She got out and went inside. And felt hope blooming inside her.

18

Rose Anna was up bright and early the next morning, cooking before her *mudder* got into the kitchen to fix breakfast.

"Where's your *mudder*?" her *dat* asked when he came in for coffee after his chores.

"Right here," she said as she walked into the room. "Rose Anna, you're up early." She set a platter of bacon and eggs on the table. "I'm making some food to take over to Brad." She told them what John had said about his plans to scatter his *dat*'s ashes. "We'd take food after a funeral, so this is kind of the same thing. And he has no family or friends here."

"I'll help you," Linda said as she sat at the table. She glanced at the door to the *dawdi haus*. "Jacob, eat the bacon quickly. *Grossdaadi* really shouldn't have any."

"Sorry, I forgot," Rose Anna said. She sat and ate her breakfast quickly.

"Take some bread over, and there's a

pound cake in the freezer. I put a ham in the refrigerator to thaw. You can bake that, and I'll make something else for our supper. Then Brad and John will have leftovers for sandwiches."

Rose Anna glanced at her *dat*. He loved ham, but he didn't ask if she was going to cut some off for him before she took it to the other men. He was a generous man for *schur.*

"I'm baking some chocolate chip cookies. John said Brad found some I'd sent for his *dat,* and he liked them." She frowned. "John said he doesn't think Brad will keep the farm. Brad has a law practice in Philadelphia and doesn't like horses."

"It won't be hard to find a buyer," Jacob said as he polished off another strip of bacon. "It could go to an Amish buyer or an *Englisch* one since it's right at the edge of our community. Neil bought it when the Hostettler family put it up for sale. All an Amish family has to do is take out the electricity."

"John loves working there with the horses so much. I told him he should talk to Brad about buying it when the time is right. Do what Sam and Mary Elizabeth did — ask the owner to hold the loan."

"You're a smart *maedel,*" her *dat* said with

334

approval. "What did John say?"

"He wasn't very optimistic. I think he's still too much in shock from Neil dying. He really cared for him."

She stopped, not *schur* she should voice her thoughts. "I think Neil became a real friend to him not just a boss. Maybe even a *dat*. He's never said he was like a *dat*, but I saw them together when I went there one day," she rushed to say. "That was my impression."

The oven timer dinged. She got up and took two trays of cookies from the oven. Without being asked she took a spatula, lifted two from the tray, then transferred them to a plate and set it before her parents.

No one was surprised when the door to the *dawdi haus* opened and Abraham shuffled out sniffing the air.

Rose Anna quickly checked the platter. Not a strip of bacon had been left on it. "*Grossdaadi*, I made scrambled eggs. And you can have a chocolate chip cookie still hot from the oven."

She finished transferring the cookies to a rack to cool then set about spooning the remainder of the dough onto the trays and setting them into the oven.

She loaded a big wicker basket into the buggy several hours later. John's truck wasn't in the drive of the horse farm, but she saw Brad's car so she carried the basket to the farmhouse. Brad opened the door looking haggard and seemed surprised when she handed him the basket.

"You didn't have to do this," he said as he took it.

"John said you're not eating much. I baked a ham, and there's fresh bread and a pound cake. And the cookies your father liked."

"Dad told me his Amish neighbors made him feel at home here, but I thought he was exaggerating." He put the basket on the kitchen table.

That was when Rose Anna saw the urn she knew was used for cremated ashes. "Your dad was a wonderful man," she said. "John said he spoke of you often, how proud he was of you."

"No one ever had a better father."

Rose Anna nodded. "He didn't just care for his family. He was incredibly kind to John, and I'll always be grateful to him for that. John's father . . . is difficult."

"I'm sorry to hear that."

She bit her lip. "I shouldn't have said anything. But he was very, very different from Neil. All three of the Stoltzfus brothers left home because of their father." She glanced at the clock hanging on the wall. "I hope you'll join us for supper some night before you go back home. Just stop by any evening. We eat kind of early — about five-thirty or six."

"Thank you for the invitation. I think I'll be heading back home tomorrow."

"It's been nice to meet you," she said. "I'm so sorry it was under such sad circumstances."

"Thank you. And thank you for baking cookies for my father."

She smiled. "It was my pleasure. Take care, Brad. I hope we'll see you again soon."

As she walked away from the farmhouse, she saw John's truck pulling into the drive. He didn't see her as he got out and began unloading big bags of horse feed and started for the barn.

"Guder mariye!" she called and his head shot up.

"Guder mariye," he said, smiling as he set the bag on the ground by his feet. "What are you doing here so early?"

"I brought a basket of food. I just gave it to Brad." She paused. "It's so sad, John. He has one of those urns people keep ashes of their loved ones in sitting on the kitchen table. He said he was going to scatter them later. He looks so exhausted and so lonely."

John nodded. "I don't think he's slept since he came here, and he barely eats."

"Maybe you could go up and join him and get him to eat something. I brought baked ham, bread, one of *Mamm*'s pound cakes, and some cookies."

"I'll go see what I can do."

"Well, I have to head off to quilting class."

"Have a *gut* time."

"I told Brad we'd love to have him come to supper before he leaves. He said he thinks he's going home tomorrow. Maybe you can persuade him to come over with you tonight."

He glanced up toward the farmhouse. "Maybe. I'll see what I can do."

She walked to her buggy, her steps lighter, and climbed inside it. Just as she lifted the reins, she saw Brad walk down the path from the house, carrying the urn in his arms.

How sad to see that, she thought. Although the Amish buried their dead she understood why some of the *Englisch* cremated theirs. But it seemed so sad that all Brad had of his *dat* right now was an urn of ashes. She sighed. Well, the Bible said, "for dust thou art, and unto dust shalt thou return."

John called to him and Brad stopped. Then they walked toward the creek together.

She stood there watching until they were swallowed up by the trees.

John met Brad on the walkway to the house.

His heart sank when he saw Brad carrying the urn with his father's ashes.

"So you went to the funeral home this morning."

Brad nodded. "He wanted them scattered here on the farm."

John hesitated, and then he made himself speak. If he didn't, he'd never get the chance again. "Would you like me to show you his favorite spot?"

To his relief, Brad nodded.

"There's a small creek that winds through the property," he told him, pointing ahead as they walked. "Your dad used to like to walk here and sit on a log and watch the water."

They approached the spot, and John felt tears sting his eyes. He blinked furiously at them.

"It's nice here."

"He'd sit here," he said, indicating the log then wondering if he sounded stupid to be pointing out something so obvious. He kicked the little can near the log. "Neil liked to smoke a cigar once in a while, and I think this was his favorite place to do it and think."

Brad took a seat on the log. He looked so like his father at that moment that it made John miss Neil even more. "Maybe you want to be alone."

"No, sit. Thanks for showing this to me."

"We came out here and sat just like this and talked a few times."

"I'm glad he had friends here." He stared at the water, and for a long time the only sound was the gurgling of the water. A dragonfly darted around and then landed nearby.

Brad sighed then stood and opened the urn. He scattered ashes along the bank of the creek then turned to John. "Here, you do some, too."

Touched, John did as he asked then handed the urn back to Brad. They sat again.

"I'd say a prayer, but right now I'm feeling pretty angry at God."

"I can say one if you want."

"Yeah, that'd be great."

John stood up and said a simple prayer. As he spoke, he felt Neil's presence, felt some peace thanking God for having known the man.

"That was good," Brad said quietly when

he finished. "This would be the kind of church and service Dad would like. I'll still have the memorial back in Philadelphia for his friends there. But this feels like what would please Dad most."

John nodded. "I don't blame you for being mad at God. I've been feeling angry at Him myself for taking Neil. But God and I haven't gotten along for some time."

"Why? Did he take someone you loved, too?" They sat again.

"In a way." Feeling he should explain, he turned to Brad. "I envied you your dad. Mine was — is — a hard man. I never could do anything right for him."

He saw understanding in the other man's eyes. "That's gotta be rough. Dad never told me he was disappointed in me even when I messed up."

He rested his arms on his knees and stared out at the water again. "I didn't like you when I met you. You probably picked up on that. I didn't want to share my dad. I was an only kid, and I didn't like it when he began talking about you and asked me to come meet you." He gave a short laugh. "I liked you even less when he showed me the codicil."

"Codicil? What's that?"

"He told me he didn't tell you. Said he

341

wouldn't until I was okay with it." He paused. "I told him when I was at the hospital after I found out what you'd done for him. You know how you said you'd look after the farm while I looked for a buyer?"

John's heart sank. He nodded.

"I won't be looking for a buyer for the farm."

John's spirits lifted. "You're going to keep it? Neil would love that."

Brad shook his head, and his expression looked rueful — and maybe held a little regret? "No, my life's in Philadelphia. And you know how I feel about horses. Dad understood. He really did. John, I think you'll be glad you're sitting down. I have something to tell you."

There was a rushing noise in his head. Like the creek was suddenly swollen like a river overwhelming its banks. Brad was talking, but he couldn't understand the words.

Neil had done what?

"John?"

"What?"

Brad grinned. "Nothing could have told me better that you didn't work for my dad with an eye to gain. Dad left you the farm because he knew you loved it the way he did. The way I never could. I told him I was okay with that the day he had the heart at-tack."

It didn't seem possible that life could take such a sudden turn. This was more than he could have ever dreamed possible.

Rose Anna had told him that God had a plan for him that was bigger than he could ever envision for himself.

Brad was talking, but the words were coming in a blur. He stood. "Let's go back to the house and we'll talk some more. The log's kind of hard to sit on for a long time."

He grinned and held out a hand to steady John when he stood and found he had no knee caps.

They went back to the farmhouse. Brad put coffee on, and they sat down with the paperwork.

There, in black and white, in this "codicil" thing he saw that yes indeed Neil had said he wanted the farm to go to John.

He shook his head. "It's not right. This is part of your inheritance."

"Dad left me a lot. His practice was really successful. He set up a trust for me years ago, too. I don't need or want the farm, John. I want to do what my father asked. This is what he asked me to do."

He got up and poured them coffee. "It'll be good to know someone carries on the work he loved. I'll do it at the law practice, you'll do it here on the farm. Listen, if it makes you feel any better, you can do what we call 'pay it forward.' "

" 'Pay it forward'?"

"Do something for someone else."

"Someone came to talk to Neil not long ago about offering riding lessons to underprivileged kids. He said he'd get back to him if we could figure out a way to do it. I've been working a couple jobs, so it wasn't possible before." He stopped and thought about it. "That might be a good thing. Pass along Neil's love of horses."

"I agree." He stood and went to look in the refrigerator. "First time I've felt hungry since I got here. I think I'll make a sandwich out of that ham Rose Anna brought. I'd invite you to join me, but I think you should go share your news with her, don't you?"

"Yeah. Yeah," he repeated, and he stood on legs that still didn't feel steady.

He crossed the room and had his hand on the doorknob, and then he turned back and wrapped his arms around Brad. "Thank you. Thank you so much."

"My father did it." Brad's words were muffled against his shoulder.

John released him. "He wouldn't have if you'd minded. I think he raised a son as generous as he was."

"Get out of here," he said, ducking his head.

But John saw that his eyes were damp. "I'll be back in a little while to finish my chores."

Brad transferred the ham to the counter, found a sharp knife in a drawer, and began slicing it. "I won't dock your pay."

John had trouble keeping the speed at the limit as he drove to Rose Anna's *haus.*

And then he slammed on the brakes, pulled the truck to the side of the road, and thought. When he pulled back onto the road a few minutes later, he took a slightly different direction.

The bishop's *fraa* answered the door and greeted him as if he hadn't been away from church for as long as he had. Her *mann* — a different bishop than the one who had spoken to his *dat* — was just as friendly and delighted to sign John up for the classes needed to join the church.

When John climbed back into the truck, he took a deep breath and drove to Rose Anna's.

"Hi, John," Linda said when she opened the door.

"Is Rose Anna home?"

"She's due home any minute. Come on in and have some coffee."

He followed her into the kitchen and took a seat at the table where he'd joined the family for so many years and wondered if he could keep his *gut* news to himself until Rose Anna got home.

"Something going on?" she asked when she served him a cup of coffee.

He realized he'd been tapping his fingers on the table. "*Nee.* Just thinking."

"I'm sorry about your friend."

"*Danki.* He was a *gut* friend. A really *gut* friend."

The back door opened and Rose Anna walked in. "John! I saw your truck. Is everything *allrecht*?"

"I'm going upstairs to the sewing room," Linda announced.

"More than *allrecht,*" John said. "Can we go out on the porch and talk?"

"*Schur.*" She set her purse and tote bag on a counter and preceded him outside.

"Please, sit," he said, gesturing at a rocking chair. He took the seat next to her and grasped her hand. "You'll need to sit."

Rose Anna stared at John. "You're joining the church?"

"I am. I want us to get married."

She found herself struggling to breathe. "You — you want us to get married. In

346

November?"

"*Ya.* I stopped on the way here and talked to the bishop." He grinned.

"You're not joking?"

"*Nee,* I'd never do that." He sat in the chair beside her.

She took a breath, then another. "Of course I'll marry you." She studied him. Something was going on. There was a strange energy about him . . . a suppressed excitement.

Neil's death had been such a shock, had such a profound effect on him. She knew grief had a strange effect on people sometimes. Didn't they say there were seven stages? Was he wanting to connect to another human he knew cared about him? What stage was that?

"What's wrong?" He was staring at her.

"It's just so sudden. I mean, you've told me you love me. But I didn't think you felt ready to get married." *Yet you've been working on him,* her conscience reminded her.

"And church. I asked you to come this week, and you were reluctant."

"I was."

Baffled, she shook her head as if trying to clear her muddled brain. "So what changed?"

"Something big. Something . . . God."

"I don't understand."

"I don't quite, either. But after I tell you what happened, you get to say, 'I told you so.' "

"I never do that."

He laughed. "You won't be able to help yourself."

"John!"

"Brad and I scattered Neil's ashes today. Down by the creek where he liked to sit."

She put her hand over his on the arm of the rocking chair. "I'm so sorry. It must have been a sad time for you."

"It was, but I was glad Brad included me. And I felt Neil was there with us. It was very peaceful." He paused, and his hand gripped hers. "Until he told me about his *dat*'s codicil."

"Codicil? What is that?"

He laughed, and then he was leaping out of his chair, picking her up and swinging her around and around until she was dizzy.

"John!" she cried. "Put me down!"

"What's going on?" Jacob asked as he climbed the steps to the porch.

He set her down and faced her *dat*. "I just asked your *dochder* to marry me."

Her *dat* looked at her for confirmation.

"It's true, *Daed.*"

Jacob held out his hand and shook John's.

He turned to Rose Anna. "Does your *mud-der* know?"

She shook her head. "He just asked me."

Jacob walked over to the front door, opened it, and bellowed her name inside. A few moments later she appeared. "Jacob? What is it? Are you hurt?" She stepped outside looking worried.

"Rose Anna and John are getting married."

"Mein Gott!" she cried and rushed over to hug Rose Anna and John. "This is *wunderbaar* news! John, have you told your parents?"

"Nee. Not yet."

"They'll be thrilled."

"I have more news. I was just about to tell Rose Anna."

"There's more?" Linda asked.

"I didn't feel I had anything to offer Rose Anna before," he said. "No way of providing for her."

"I don't want to hear such talk!" she told him. She stamped her foot for emphasis. "You have everything to offer, and I don't need someone providing for me. I just want you to be happy doing work you love. And you've been so happy since you started working at the horse farm."

"And I'm about to be even happier."

"I don't understand."

"We'll let you young people talk," Linda said, tugging her *mann*'s hand and jerking her head at the front door in a signal he was ignoring.

"*Nee,* stay. This is such *gut* news I can't keep it inside any longer." He took her hands in his. "Brad told me his *dat* left me the farm."

"Nee!" She stared at him, shocked. Then she wondered if he was so grief-stricken that his mind had been affected.

"You told me I should talk to him about buying it, but Rose Anna, I don't have to do that. Neil left it to me. He signed a change to his will and left it to me."

"He didn't leave it to his *sohn.*?" Linda asked him. "How does Brad feel about that?"

"He said Neil discussed it with him, and he doesn't want it. Said he doesn't like horses, and his home, his work as a lawyer, is in Philadelphia."

"Are you sure this is legal?"

John turned to her *dat.* "Brad showed me the paper. He's a lawyer just like Neil was. He said he'll help me with any paperwork to change the ownership of the property."

He looked at Rose Anna. "Are you ready to say 'I told you so' now?"

Grinning, he turned to her parents. "When I said there was no way I could find the money to buy Neil's farm, she said I didn't know what God had planned for me and that I had to have faith in Him. She was so right."

She smiled, and then she began crying. God was so amazing.

As they stood there staring at each other, she was barely aware that her parents had tiptoed away and they were alone on the porch. She couldn't believe how utterly happy she felt.

"I need to get back to work. Brad told me to come tell you about the farm, but I wasn't finished with my work. I have more to do with the horses."

"Go," she said, releasing his hands.

"He's going back home tomorrow, so I'm going to stay and see if he needs anything."

"Please tell him thank you for me. If you can persuade him to come for supper, I can thank him in person."

"I will. But I expect he'll want to go through his *dat*'s papers, maybe start packing up some of Neil's things he wants to keep."

They exchanged a quick kiss after glancing toward the road and making *schur* no one was passing by. And then she watched him run down the porch steps and climb into his truck.

She remembered how that truck had been passed down from one Stoltzfus *bruder* to another. Now she guessed it would go to someone outside the family.

Family. She wondered when John would tell his family. Amish couples didn't always tell their families until just a short time before the ceremony. It was just late August, months before they could get married after the harvest.

She wasn't worried about their reaction. They'd be overjoyed that their *sohn* would be returning to the church, to the community.

John and his *dat* still hadn't reconciled their differences. But she was *schur* they'd find a bridge over them.

Hugging her newfound happiness to her, she fairly danced inside her *haus*.

19

Rose Anna was in the kitchen garden on the side of the *haus* when she saw a car pull into the drive. *Was that Brad's?* she wondered. It looked like the car he'd parked in the farm's drive.

She wondered what BMW stood for. It *schur* looked shiny and expensive.

Wiping her hands on her apron, she walked to it. "Brad, hello!" Before she could frame a thank-you for what he'd done for John, he held out a tote bag she'd sent over with food.

"Apparently my father never remembered to return your plastic containers," he told her.

She laughed. "That was no problem. We have plenty. He always said he liked my cookies, and believe me, I'm not the best baker."

"Tasted pretty good to me."

"Have you come to eat lunch with us?"

"No, sorry. I'm heading back home. I'll be back in a week or two, get some personal things out of the farmhouse, help John with the paperwork transferring the property to him."

Tears sprang into her eyes. "Brad, we will never be able to thank you enough for what you've done."

"Dad did it," he said.

"If you'd objected, he wouldn't have. John told me that."

He shrugged and looked a little embarrassed. "It's the right thing to do. It's what Dad wanted."

"He was such a sweet man. And he raised a good son." She clutched the handle of the tote bag with the containers. "John said he invited you to the wedding. I hope you'll come."

"I will."

"If you won't stay for lunch, let me pack you something."

He patted the insulated container on the passenger seat. "I made sandwiches of that wonderful ham you brought over. I'm good."

"Coffee?"

"I can get some on the road."

"Give me just a minute? I have a surprise for you I was bringing over later. Please?"

"Okay. I'll just check my messages," he said as he pulled out his cell phone.

Rose Anna ran inside, washed her hands, and found a Thermos. Her *mudder* had just made a pot of coffee, so she poured it into the Thermos. She took one of the plastic containers from the tote Brad had returned, saw he'd returned it clean, and filled it with the cinnamon rolls she'd made before going out to garden. Two were missing. Either *Grossdaadi* or her *dat* had been in the kitchen. She rushed back outside and handed the tote to Brad. "Cinnamon rolls and coffee. I hope you enjoy them."

"I love your cinnamon rolls," he said, taking the tote from her. "Thank you, Rose Anna."

"And thank you to your father and you for having such generous hearts," she told him fervently. "I'll pray for you to have a safe journey home. See you soon."

He nodded. "See you soon."

She stood there for a long time, watching him head down the road. Then she went inside, climbed the stairs to the sewing room, and found her *mudder.* And burst into tears.

Linda dropped the quilt she was sewing and held out her arms. "What is it, *kind*?"

"I'm so happy," she sobbed.

"I know. I know." She patted her back.

"I told John to believe God would help him, but I never dreamed — I never dreamed —" she broke off.

"You never dreamed God could make something so *wunderbaar* happen?"

"I guess I didn't." She reached over to pluck a tissue from the nearby table and wiped her eyes.

"I thought much the same thing the day I married your *dat,*" she said, smiling reminiscently. "And then the first time I held my *boppli* in my arms. Then I was amazed each time another came along."

She smiled and picked up her quilt. "There have been other times, of course. But those were the biggest miracles, signs God loved me and had *wunderbaar* plans for me as a young woman."

Rose Anna returned to her chair and picked up her own quilt, then set it down. Restless, she prowled the room.

"How is John doing?"

"I think he's just overwhelmed. And he's happy about the farm, but it came about through the loss of a good friend. It's been a mixed blessing."

Linda nodded. "Life's like that sometimes. Sunshine and shadow. I suppose that's why it's always been one of my favorite quilt patterns to work with."

Rose Anna continued to pace the room.

"You know, it's not too soon to start thinking about the wedding."

She stopped and looked at her *mudder*.

"What, this is a surprise?"

"I guess everything's just been moving so quickly. John just came to me two days ago with such amazing news."

Linda set the quilt down again. "Let's go down and have a cup of tea and talk about it."

As they descended the stairs Rose Anna thought she heard something. She stopped, took her *mudder*'s arm with one hand, and held her finger to her lips in a signal to be quiet.

Schur enough there was a scraping sound in the kitchen as if a chair was being pushed back from the table, a scuffle of feet, and the closing of a door.

After exchanging a look they continued down the stairs.

The kitchen was empty when they walked into it. Rose Anna looked at the counter where she'd left the cinnamon rolls and shook her head, trying to hold back a laugh. "*Mamm,* I think we have a mouse."

"A mouse?" Linda looked around and then under the kitchen table. "Where?"

"It's a cinnamon-roll-eating mouse," she said seriously. "It's eaten two rolls so far this morning."

Linda straightened up and looked at her. "It eats cinnamon rolls, eh?"

"I think I know where it is." She gestured at the *dawdi haus.*

"So it's not the one out in the barn?"

Rose Anna shook her head and stuck her tongue firmly in the side of her mouth. "I heard it scuttle into the *dawdi haus,* didn't you?"

Linda nodded. "It's just I've also caught the one who likes to lurk in the barn stealing sweets."

"Shall we see what's up?"

Her *mudder* nodded. They advanced on the *dawdi haus,* rapped on the door, then walked in. *Grossdaadi* sat at the little kitchen table, and he was trying to hide something under a napkin on a plate. "*Ya?* Did you need me?" he asked, trying to look innocent.

"*Grossdaadi,* you have icing on your beard," Rose Anna chided.

He picked up the napkin and wiped at his beard. Then he looked down at the remnants of the cinnamon roll on the table.

Linda made a tsking sound. "We found the cinnamon-roll-eating mouse, Rose

Anna. But it's a very elderly mouse. What do you suppose we should do about it?"

"Catch him, *Mamm*, and hug him!" she cried, advancing on him and hugging him.

He chuckled. "It wasn't my fault. You shouldn't leave such things out if you don't want a man to eat them."

"They were cooling, *Grossdaadi*."

"Now you won't want lunch."

"It's ready?" He stood.

Linda laughed. "You know it isn't. You just sneaked out of the kitchen. It'll be ready in ten minutes. Then we'll see if you have any appetite for it."

They walked back into the kitchen and worked together to fix sandwiches and heat vegetable soup from the day before.

"After lunch I think we need to take a ride into town," Linda walked to the back door, then turned to look at her. "Let's go pick out the fabric for your wedding dress."

Rose Anna smiled as she sat at the table. "I bought it some time ago," she said. "I'll go get it."

His.

John walked around the property still feeling a little dazed. It had been three weeks, and it still felt unreal. He found his steps taking him to the creek. Sinking down onto the log, he stared at the gently flowing creek. He sat there for a long time absorbing the peace and quiet as the horses grazed.

"Figured I'd find you here when you weren't in the barn."

John spun around on the log. "Hey, did you get lost? Thought I'd see you an hour ago."

"Traffic was bad." Brad took a seat beside him.

He was glad to see that most of the grief and stress had faded from Brad's face. "You're wearing jeans," he approved. "So, are you going to give me some help?"

"I'm not going near that barn no matter what you say." He looked at the creek, up at the horses grazing nearby, and sighed. "Sure is peaceful here. So, how are the wedding plans going?"

"Rose Anna's taking care of all that."

"She's not dragging you into plans? I was briefly engaged about a year ago, and I had to go everywhere with Bridezilla."

John stared at him. "Your fiancée's name was Bridezilla?"

Brad laughed. "Sometimes I forget about the difference in cultures. No, that's a nickname for brides who get a little too caught up in all the arrangements and get crazy. She had a list a mile long a week after

I gave her the engagement ring. We had to pick the place to get married, the officiant, the reception. Talk about the theme. Only good part was sampling the different flavors of wedding cake."

"Theme?"

He sighed. "Don't ask."

"Well, here — in the Amish community — things are pretty simple. We hold church services in our homes, so couples get married at the bride's house. We have a big meal, get together and socialize, play games, and then we eat again, and only when it's getting dark does everyone leave."

"An all-day celebration?"

"Yes."

"Sounds fun. Especially the food. No one cooks better than the Amish."

"Rose Anna's already brought over food for our supper. I told her you were coming this weekend."

"Sounds good." He squawked and jumped off the log, spinning around to stare at Fiona. "Oh, it's you." He held out a tentative hand, and the filly stepped closer and sniffed at him. When she found he didn't have any treat, she walked over to John and nudged his arm.

"You could be popular with the ladies if you kept these on hand." He held out a plastic baggie of apple slices and offered one to Brad. "Here, give it to her. C'mon, she won't bite."

Brad took the slice and held it out to Fiona. She stepped forward and nipped it carefully, chewing as she gazed at him with big, liquid brown eyes.

"She's grown a lot since I was here last." He studied her. "She's pretty. For a horse, I mean. What's her name?"

"Your dad named her Fiona."

"He — really? That was his sister's name. She died a few years ago."

"That's nice. Family was obviously important to him." He took another slice of apple and offered it to Fiona. When Willow wandered over, John saw Brad's eyes widen as he backed up two steps.

"Brad, stop!"

"Make *her* stop!"

"You're going to land in the creek if you take another step."

Brad looked behind him and came to a screeching halt.

"That's Willow, Fiona's mama. Give her some apple." John walked over to put several slices of apple in his hand.

"She's got really big teeth."

John saw his hand shaking and took pity on him. "Hold your hand flat, and she'll

362

take them off."

"And how many fingers will she take with them?" he asked nervously.

"None."

Sure enough Willow lapped up the apple slices and chomped on them not Brad's fingers. When Willow bumped his shoulder he paled a little, but John took his hand and showed him how to stroke her nose.

"Horses are big, but they're really gentle creatures."

"So you say." He looked at Willow. "Is she — is she batting her eyelashes at me?"

He chuckled. "Yes. You sure are fickle," John admonished Willow. "I thought you were my girl."

"Did Dad ever tell you why I don't like horses?"

"No."

"He put me up on one at my fifth birthday party. The horse put her foot on his and wouldn't get off. I can still hear him yelling bloody murder for someone to help him. And then when he saw he was scaring me, he told me everything was going to be okay and not to be frightened."

"I can see how that could scare you." But John had to bite firmly on his inner cheek so he didn't laugh. He could imagine Neil yelling and trying not to scare his kid.

"I think if you hung out with Fiona and Willow you'd lose that fear."

"But not Midnight?" he asked, watching him warily as he strutted about a hundred yards away.

"No, he's a handful and likes to intimidate. I'll probably never use him for those riding lessons for underprivileged kids and veterans we talked about. I met with some people about that last week, by the way."

Brad resumed his seat on the log.

"So what happened to Bridezilla?"

"The wedding plan nonsense showed me we weren't the match I thought we were. My parents kind of spoiled me for marriage. They were very happily married for more than forty years. I wanted that, and I saw I wasn't going to have that with Tiffany."

"How long did you know her?"

"I proposed to her after we dated six months. How long have you known Rose Anna?"

"All my life."

"I guess that's the advantage of living in a small community."

John laughed. "It can be a disadvantage, too. News can travel fast on the Amish grapevine."

"Funny thing," Brad said, and his tone became thoughtful. "An old college friend came to Dad's memorial service, and we had dinner afterward. We've been seeing each other since then, and she's been great about cheering me up. We lost touch and went in different directions after law school, but she's back in Philadelphia. So who knows." He glanced at John. "Dad always liked her."

John picked up a pebble and tossed it into the creek. "That's a good sign." Then he frowned. "My dad's always liked Rose Anna. I'm sure he'll be especially thrilled when he hears we're getting married."

"You haven't told him yet?"

"No. Couples often don't tell their families until just before the church announcement."

"Interesting."

They sat there silently for a few minutes.

"I brought some more boxes to pack up some of Dad's personal things, and we can go over that paperwork you called me about. If you're done with horse chores."

John laughed. "Yeah, I'm done with them for the morning."

They got the boxes from Brad's car and took them into the farmhouse. "Do you want some help?" he asked when Brad stood in the middle of his father's bedroom and seemed unable to move.

"No, it's okay." He picked up some framed

365

photos and began putting them into a box.

"You don't have to rush doing this."

"I don't think it's going to get easier if I wait." He sat on the bed and looked at the photo in his hand. "Anyway, there's not much I'm going to take. He didn't bring much here. Called it downsizing after he sold the house in Philadelphia. I'm going to take one or two of his sweaters to remind me of him and donate the rest of his clothes. Maybe you could drop those off to some charity you know can use them."

"Sure."

"Can I say something?" Brad asked after a long moment. "You can tell me to mind my own business if you want."

"Okay."

Brad lifted his gaze from the photo to look at him. "Things can just change so fast. I hope that you can fix the rift between you and your father. We just never know how long we'll have someone, you know?"

He sighed. "I do know. My *dat* had cancer and beat it, but I know it can come back. He just makes things so difficult."

"Didn't you tell me once that your brothers worked things out with him?"

"Yeah. They have more patience I guess."

"You seem pretty patient to me."

John grinned. "My dad would disagree

366

with you. He always acted like I couldn't hold a job after I left home. He didn't seem to understand how hard it was to find a full-time job."

"You were looking for the right one. And it found you."

"You sound like your dad."

Brad grinned. "That's a great compliment."

"I meant it that way."

"What's it like to have a brother?" he asked suddenly as he stood and began packing photos in the box again.

Kind of like the way we're getting along, John wanted to say. But he wasn't sure Brad would welcome that.

"I could show you. I could drag you down to the creek and toss you in. Or we could have a tussle in the mud. One of my brothers did that to me not so very long ago."

Brad glanced down at his expensive jeans and boots. "I think I'll pass on that. Maybe we can have a beer after I finish up here."

"That sounds good. I'll go get some more boxes."

The days got busier as the men harvested the crops and the women canned and froze and otherwise preserved God's bounty.

It was tiring work but so rewarding to

carry all the Mason jars down to store them on shelves in the basement. And after the long, hard, hot summer it wouldn't be long before Rosa Anna's wedding.

The quilting classes were a welcome break, but they were a hive of activity as well. Crafts were being sewn and finished for tourists and locals buying for the Thanksgiving and Christmas holidays.

"I heard the good news," Kate whispered to her as they sat at the front of the classroom.

"You did?"

"I saw John at the courthouse yesterday. He was with Neil Zimmerman's son filing some papers. John told me what Neil did. He was such a nice man. Donated to the policeman's benevolent fund, and Malcolm and Chris went to him about offering riding lessons for underprivileged kids and wounded vets, and he was very receptive. John said he's looking into doing it."

She leaned in closer. "I know I shouldn't ask . . . but does the good news about the farm mean you might be sharing any other good news soon?"

Rose Anna tried to keep a straight face. But this was her *gut* friend. She grinned.

"Oh, I am so happy for you!" Kate reached over and hugged Rose Anna.

"Don't you dare say a word to anyone!" Rose Anna whispered urgently.

"I won't! I promise. I'll zip my lips right now. See, zipped." She looked past Rose Anna. "Lannie!"

The little girl pulled her thumb out of her mouth. "Zipped?"

Kate laughed. "It means be quiet, sweetie."

"Shush," Lannie said with a nod.

"That's right. Shush."

Rose Anna watched her wander off to sit by her *mudder*. It suddenly struck her. Not only was she going to be a *fraa* soon but with luck not that long after it she could be a *mudder* a year or so after like Lavina.

The thought made her slightly giddy. She took a deep breath, then another to calm herself. She couldn't get ahead of herself. That was something she did in the past. She remembered years ago how she'd sat in *schul* daydreaming about becoming John's *fraa* and writing her married name over and over in her composition book.

She and Kate dropped a few boxes of crafts off at Sewn in Hope. By the time she got home, Rose Anna realized she was feeling warm and achy and her head hurt. She walked into the *haus* and sneezed.

"Gesundheit!" her *mudder* said, looking up

369

from her chair in the living room. She set her sewing down and followed Rose Anna into the kitchen.

"Danki." She shed her jacket, hung it on a peg by the back door, and set her purse on the counter.

"You look flushed."

Rose Anna smiled as her *mudder* touched the back of her hand to her forehead. "I'm *allrecht, Mamm.* I'm just probably getting a cold."

"I think you have a fever." Linda left the room and returned with a thermometer. She insisted on taking her temperature. "I thought so. It's 101."

"It can't be. I was fine when I left this morning."

"Why don't you take some aspirin, and I'll fix you some soup for lunch?"

"Danki, but I'm not hungry."

"Some tea, then, and take a nap."

She never napped during the day, but it was sounding like a *gut* idea.

"Colds are going around. It's the time of year for them."

Rose Anna remembered how some of the women had been absent from class earlier in the week. "I think I will lie down. Just for a little while."

She lay on top of her bed and pulled a

throw over herself when she shivered.

Her dreams were vivid and confusing.

She woke, her heart beating fast, her face covered with sweat. Her head hurt even more now, and her pillow felt like a stone. She punched at it trying to get more comfortable, and her journal slid out. Sitting up, she leaned over to put it on her nightstand and dropped it. Leaning over to pick it up was a bad idea. Her head throbbed. And when she went to place it on the nightstand, a piece of paper slid out. Once more she reached down and was sorry as the movement made her poor head hurt even more. Groaning, she lay back in bed and stared at the paper.

It was the list she'd made about how to get John.

She tucked it back into the journal and carefully placed it on the nightstand. Her throat was parched, but she was too tired to get up for water. She got comfortable again and felt herself drifting. She dreamed of walking through the fields beside her *haus* and a scarecrow popped up and shook his finger at her.

"You're a trickster!" he accused. "You don't deserve John!"

She ran from him.

"I'm not a trickster! I love him!" she cried

and pushed her way through the cornstalks trying to escape him.

She ran and ran until she was at the horse farm calling for John.

He came out of the barn, but when he saw it was her he turned and walked away. He closed the barn doors behind him, and no matter how hard she beat against them he wouldn't open them.

She sank to the ground, sobbing.

20

"Rose Anna! *Kind,* wake up, it's just a nightmare."

She woke and blinked. *"Mamm?"*

"You were having a nightmare." She touched Rose Anna's forehead. "Still feverish. I'm going to get you some more aspirin."

"And water?" she croaked.

"And water, of course."

Rose Anna dozed until her *mudder* came back, sat on the side of the bed, and waited while she took aspirin with the glass of water she'd brought.

"Why don't you get into a nightgown and try to get some more sleep. Maybe it'll make you feel better."

She liked the idea but didn't have the energy to climb off the bed. "Never had a cold feel this way," she complained.

"I hope it's not more than a cold. Abraham said the last time you took him to the clinic the doctor told him the flu is going around, too, with the change in seasons. Your *dat* and I promised to go to Lavina's for supper. Will you be *allrecht* for a few hours?"

She glanced at the clock on the nightstand. It was late afternoon already. "*Ya,* of course."

"I'll see if Abraham would like to go, too. Would you like some soup before we leave?"

"*Nee,* I'm not hungry."

Her *mudder* patted her head and left her.

Rose Anna dozed and dreamed, dozed and dreamed one nightmarish episode after another with the same theme — her running from the scarecrow, John not wanting to talk to her. He holed up in the barn of the horse farm and refused to come out.

He'd gotten his dream, and she'd been locked out of his life.

When she woke next, dusk was falling and her throat ached. She drained the glass of water on the nightstand and decided to brave a trip downstairs. Looking in the mirror was a mistake. She looked awful. After she dragged a brush through her hair she went downstairs, drank two glasses of water from the tap, and decided her stomach might take a bowl of soup.

Mamm kept a pot of soup in the refrigera-

374

tor this time of the year. She ladled out some and warmed it on the stove. The knock came on the back door just as she was sitting down to eat at the table.

"John!" She pushed her heavy fall of hair behind her shoulders and tried not to think how wrinkled her dress looked after sleeping in it.

"Rose Anna! Are you sick?"

She leaned against the door jamb. "*Ya*. So you shouldn't come any closer. And not just because you could catch whatever this is."

He leaned in and kissed her. "I wouldn't mind catching germs from you. But you're burning up." He grasped her by the upper arms, moved her into the room, and closed the door. "Get inside, it's chilly."

She walked back to the table and slumped back into her chair. "I'm having soup. Do you want some?"

"*Nee*. Brad and I ate while we went over paperwork."

She tried to swallow a mouthful of soup and found it difficult. The bad dreams she'd had most of the day swam around and around in her head making her miserable.

She let the spoon fall into the bowl and put her head in her hands.

"*Lieb*, if you feel that bad you should go to bed."

"I know. I will." Tears sprang into her eyes, and they weren't all because she was so sick. "John, I can't do this."

"I know, I know," he murmured. "Here, I'll help you upstairs. Or maybe you should lie down on the sofa. Where are your parents?"

"Over at Lavina's *haus*."

"I'll call them," he said as he got out his cell phone. "I don't think you should be alone."

"John! Please, listen to me." She swallowed, and her throat hurt. But she had to tell him. "I can't marry you."

He pulled out a chair, sat down, and reached out to touch her forehead. "You're not making any sense. You're out of your head. I'm calling your parents and taking you to the emergency room."

She grasped his arm. "I'm not out of my head. Today when I was upstairs in my room, I came across this list in my journal, and it made me remember just what a manipulative person I am. I had a plan, John. A plan to make you fall in love with me and come back home."

He stared at her. "Are you saying you don't love me?"

She shook her head and it pounded. "*Nee*, but I tricked you. I deliberately set out to

376

trick you into marrying me."

He got to his feet. "Look, if you don't want to marry me just say so. Don't be making up some bizarre excuse." He paced the room then turned to her. "Is it Peter? Did you decide to go back to Peter?"

Rose Anna felt her heart leap. He'd just given her the perfect excuse, one he'd believe. *"Ya,"* she said. *"Ya,* I just realized it recently. I'm so sorry."

"I can't believe this." He took off his cap and ran his hand through his hair. "Here I thought my life was going in the right direction and this happens."

Looking disgusted, he spun around and headed for the door, and just as he opened it, Linda walked in.

"John, *gut-n-owed."*

He muttered something and strode out.

"Rose Anna? What's going on?"

She picked up the bowl of soup she hadn't been able to eat and put it in the sink. "We broke up."

"Nee! Why?"

"I don't want to talk about it right now. *Mamm,* I think I'm going to throw up."

Linda pushed her into a chair, grabbed a plastic bucket from under the sink, and put it into her hands. "Use this if you need to." Turning, she wet a clean dish towel with cold water from the faucet and pressed it against her face.

"I just want to go back to bed."

"*Allrecht,* then that's where you'll go." She wrapped her arm around her waist, and they climbed the stairs. Then she helped Rose Anna take off her dress and pull on a night-gown.

Linda bustled around the room, filling the water glass and putting a box of tissue on the nightstand. "If you feel sick in the night use this," she said, putting a plastic waste-paper basket beside the bed.

"I will." Weak tears ran down her cheeks.

"Now don't you cry or you'll get your head all stuffed up," Linda said as she pulled the quilt up to Rose Anna's chin. "You still feel very warm. I'm going down to get the thermometer and fix you a cup of tea with honey. I'll be right back."

A cup of tea with honey would soothe her throat, but it *schur* wasn't going to heal her heart. But she just nodded and watched her *mudder* leave the room.

Linda frowned after she took Rose Anna's temperature. "It's up a bit more," she said. "If you're not feeling better in the morning, I'm calling the doctor."

Rose Anna managed to drink the tea and then fell into a restless sleep. Once she woke and thought she heard John's voice. She told herself it was her imagination, a remnant of a bad dream.

She felt her *mudder*'s cool hand on her fevered brow, smiled when her *dat* bent down and kissed her head and his beard tickled her cheek.

"Don't worry, she'll be fine in the morning," he said, his voice rumbling. "Let's go to bed."

"Rose Anna, you call me if you need me."

"I will," she murmured and closed her eyes. And tossed and turned all night.

John ripped off the "For Sale" sign he'd taped on the truck and tossed it into the back seat.

"Did you sell it?" Brad asked him.

"I'm not selling it."

Brad set the box of clothes he'd been carrying in the trunk of his car. "Why not?"

"There's no point."

"Wait," Brad said when John started past him. "Didn't you tell me you had to give it up to join the church?"

"Yes."

"Have they changed the rules?"

"No. Look, I need to go check Midnight's hoof." He was in a foul mood, so it was best if he hid out in the barn until it passed. He figured going to the barn would stop a discussion he didn't want to have.

He figured wrong.

Brad followed him inside, his steps slowing as John opened Midnight's stall door. "So are you saying you're not joining the church?"

"I'm not sure."

"Don't you have to join to marry Rose Anna?"

John bent to examine Midnight's right front hoof and pretended he didn't hear the question.

"I can wait."

He looked up. "I can open the stall door and let you talk to Midnight if you're so eager to have a discussion."

"Now that's just mean." Brad folded his arms over his chest and waited. "Did you have a fight with Rose Anna?"

"Lawyers are just full of questions, aren't they?"

Brad grinned and looked unoffended. "You bet. I make my living asking them."

John grunted and used a pick to clean Midnight's hoof, then worked on the other three.

"Come on, something's obviously wrong. Maybe I can help."

He lifted his head and stared at him. "I've

known Rose Anna all my life, and I haven't figured her out. I don't think you can."

"Well, I'm no expert on women, that's for sure." Brad hitched up his carefully ironed jeans and took a seat on a bale of hay — the one furthest from the stalls. "If I were, I'd have figured Tiffany out long before I put a diamond on her finger." He stretched out his legs and crossed his ankles. "The thing is, sometimes it helps to get another point of view. Tell me what happened. It's obvious something did."

John finished with Midnight and left the stall. He put the pick up on a shelf and walked over to the barn sink to wash his hands.

"She broke up with me." It felt like someone had driven the hoof pick into his heart just to say it. "I didn't think I ever wanted to get married, but she changed my mind about that. And now she doesn't want to marry me."

"No way! She loves you. Anyone can see that."

"See, I told you that you didn't know her." He turned and dried his hands on a bandanna, but he wouldn't look at Brad. He didn't need the man's pity.

"What reason did she give you?"

"She said she was in love with another

man, okay? I don't want to talk about it."

"And you believed that?"

"Why wouldn't I?" he snapped. "It's the same guy she saw while I was away from the Amish community."

Brad tilted his head and studied him. "But John, I've watched the two of you together, and I can see she loves you. I'm a pretty good judge of character. I make my living being good at this type of thing. I have to be able to know when a client's lying, know what potential juror is a problem."

"That doesn't mean you know Rose Anna. You said yourself you didn't know Tiffany."

"Ouch. But I *did* figure her out in time to save myself from a lot of unhappiness."

"Well, Rose Anna just saved me from it, so that's done."

"Is it? Do you want it to be? No, don't answer. If you did you'd be happy and dancing around celebrating your freedom. Instead you're acting like you've lost your best friend."

"She *was* my best friend before I fell in love with her." He sank down onto a bale of hay and stared at his hands. "I don't see what I can do. I went back that night because I was worried about her. She was really sick. Her mother said she's better but doesn't want to see me."

He rubbed the knot of tension in his neck.

"Okay, let's take this step by step. You say she got you to change your mind about marriage. You act like she manipulated you. Well, friend, we all use manipulation every day of our lives. It's like my mother always said: you get more flies with honey than vinegar. So what's her motive, what is she trying to get?"

"Rose Anna loves to get her way. She's usually charming about it but . . . she said she tricked me into asking her to marry me." Funny, he had a flash of memory where they'd argued once about this very thing, and she'd denied she was after marriage like so many Amish *maedels.*

"But John, isn't it what you wanted, too? So what's wrong? We know she wasn't after you getting the farm."

John's head came up. "How do we know that?"

"Because it should be obvious to even a dunderhead like you that she was in love with you *before* you got the farm. She seemed as surprised as you when you inherited it. I remember how she looked days after when I stopped at her house on my way home. She looked dazed."

"True." He thought about that. "Then what is going on?"

"Maybe it's just a little guilt. Or cold feet? It's a big step even if you want to do it and know it's the right decision. And you did hit her with a lot at once. Returning to the church, the proposal, the farm, after, what, more than a year of your waffling around."

"I didn't waffle."

Brad just looked at him. Then he stood and brushed off his jeans. "Maybe I can find out what's going on with her. With my analytical skills and witness interrogation abilities, I bet I could pry it out of her . . ." he broke off as John snorted. "I beg your pardon."

"Sorry, Mr. Big Shot Attorney, in a match-up of the two of you, I'm afraid Rose Anna could outthink and outmaneuver you."

Brad narrowed his eyes. "You want to make a bet on that, Mr. Horse Whisperer?"

"Yeah." He thought about it and grinned. "You find out what's going on with her, and I'll wash that fancy car of yours before you head home and make sure you have another of those hams Rose Anna baked you that you love."

"The second part's her doing."

"Well, do you want it or not?"

"Sure."

"And if you don't win, you have to take a

384

ride on Midnight."

Brad paled. "That's not just mean. That's criminal."

"Okay. On Patsy. She's so old and tame a toddler could ride her." He grinned. "Well? You up for it or are you going to chicken out? Chick, chick, chicken," he jeered.

He shook his head. "Oh, that's mature."

"We'll see how mature you are when you get up in the saddle on Patsy."

"Go put the sign back up on the truck. You're going to be selling it and getting the proverbial ball and chain on your ankle very soon, pal."

John had heard a man once say, "From your lips to God's ear."

He hoped God was listening.

Rose Anna glanced at Brad as she buckled the seatbelt in his car. "You're positive John won't be at the farm?"

"I promise. He's off at some horse auction with a friend."

"I'm not sure how much help I can be to you. We don't have very fancy things in our house."

"Dad wasn't into fancy. But I thought we could go through some of the things he brought here and see what I want to keep, what you and John can use, and what we should donate to charity."

"Brad, whatever you want you should take and not worry about leaving for John. And I told you, there is no John and me. But I'm happy to help you pack and drop things off at a charity."

"Fine."

She saw John's truck parked in the drive at the farm. The "For Sale" sign was gone.

"He went with a friend," Brad assured her. "Come on, I'm not allowed to lie."

"A lawyer who doesn't lie?" She gave him a skeptical glance.

"Hey, you're too sweet to make cracks like that."

She laughed. "You don't know me well. I get in trouble all the time for being a smart aleck."

They went inside, and he poured them glasses of iced tea. "I thought we could start in the kitchen."

They filled a box with mismatched plates and cups and glasses. Evidently Neil hadn't cared about fancy matching sets. Brad saved an old glass pitcher he said his mother had loved. He tenderly wrapped it in old newspapers and placed it in a box. They moved from room to room with boxes marked "Brad," "John," and "Donate."

Brad's hands shook as he took down a

framed photograph of his father with one of his horses. She patted his back as he packed it into a box to take with him. A few other personal things went into his box from the living room and dining room, and then he looked around. "The rest is for you and John and charity."

"That's all you're taking?"

He nodded. "I cleared out his bedroom and took photos and a few of his books. John helped me take Dad's clothes to a thrift store the other day."

"I don't think I was much help."

The kitchen door opened. "Brad?" John called out.

"In the dining room."

"You said he'd be gone."

"He must be back early." Brad shrugged.

John walked into the room and stopped dead when he saw her. They both turned on Brad and gave him accusing looks.

"I think the two of you could benefit from my mediation skills." He sat at the head of the table and gestured at the other chairs.

"I think you could benefit from a cold dip in the creek," John growled.

"Now that would be assault and battery —" Brad began.

"I have money saved. I'll pay for a lawyer to get you off," Rose Anna offered.

"The court wouldn't look kindly on such an act of aggression," Brad told John. "I'm just trying to mediate a painful situation between two people I care about."

"He's just trying to manipulate us," John told her. "Like you said you did, Rose Anna."

She winced.

"But isn't it true that you did it out of love, Rose Anna?" Brad asked her.

Without waiting for an answer, Brad turned to John. "And isn't it true that you asked her to marry you, that she didn't ask you?"

"Well —"

"And isn't it true that there isn't another man, Rose Anna?"

When she hesitated, he looked at her sternly. "You're under oath here."

The corners of her mouth lifted, but she schooled her expression. "No, there isn't another man."

"And isn't it true that both of you have been miserable since you sent him away the other day, Rose Anna?"

She nodded, and tears slipped down her cheeks. "But I did set out to bring him back home. I wanted him to come back to the church. Back to me."

"Because you love him."

It was a statement, not a question.

"Yes," she whispered. "Yes."

"Then I pronounce you guilty, Rose Anna. The sentence is a lifetime with this man. For better or worse, for richer or poorer . . ."

John barely heard Brad as he moved to take her into his arms.

They never heard him leave the room.

Rose Anna and John clasped hands and waited for the minister's signal. Then they walked down the aisle toward him.

Friends and family sat on each side of the big room in her *haus* created by pushing the movable interior doors.

There was Kate, sitting on the women's side, crying as she always did at weddings. She had to put on a tough look in her job as a police officer, but she confessed to melting at weddings. Her husband sat on the opposite side with the men, and he was looking at her with such love it warmed Rose Anna's heart.

Jenny and Matthew Bontrager were both in attendance. Rose Anna had been young when they married, but she still remembered how brave Jenny had looked as she struggled to walk without a cane not that long after surgery to repair damage from the overseas car bombing that had sent her here to recuperate. Another love story, thought Rose Anna. Jenny had reunited with Matthew, the boy next door to her *grossmudder*'s *haus*. Now their *kinner* and their *grosskinner* were there.

So many friends. So many love stories better than the romance novels Rose Anna loved to read. Hannah and Chris, Naomi and Nick, Mary Katherine and Jacob, Anna and John. The two sets of twins Rosie and Katie, Ben and Mark, and Rosie's *mann*, Jacob.

And Leah and so many cousins and friends who attended church as well as some *Englisch* friends like Carrie were here.

As Rose Anna and John drew closer to the front of the room, she saw Lavina and David and little Mark and Mary Elizabeth and Sam and her parents and *Grossdaadi*. And of course Waneta and Amos who beamed from their seats on each side of the aisle. John and Amos seemed to be getting along better.

Brad had brought a friend, a woman he introduced in a way that told Rose Anna that she was very special to him. And she felt Neil's presence as surely as if she saw him in the flesh.

Rose Anna and John stood here in her childhood home before friends and family and listened as the minister began the ceremony to join them.

The road to this time and place had seemed so long and hard. Rose Anna had so often doubted she'd ever stand here and be married.

She remembered how she'd decided that God needed a hand and sat down on her bed to write in her journal and begin a list to plan how she would convince John to return to the community to marry her.

Her *schweschders* had reacted with mock-horror and relentless teasing when she'd slipped and said God needed her help. But she was glad she'd done it now, even if it had caused her and John to almost break up.

She glanced at Brad, and as if he knew what she was thinking, he gave her a wink that reminded her so of his fun-loving *dat*.

There were hymns and prayers and finally it was over. They were *mann* and *fraa*.

Men began moving the hard pews that were taken from *haus* to *haus* for biweekly services and converted them to tables. Women began loading the tables with baked chicken, *roasht,* vegetables, breads, and so much more.

Rose Anna and John sat at the *eck,* the corner of the wedding table, and enjoyed the good wishes of friends and family.

Kinner darted around, laughing and playing and being lured to join in games in a corner of the room.

The day passed in a happy blur. She ate but had no idea what as John gazed at her with such love.

After the evening meal guests began to drift out, heading home. Brad and Joanna were among the first since they had to drive back to Philadelphia because of their work schedules.

"I felt like your father was here today," she whispered to him as she stood and hugged him.

"I did, too."

He and John exchanged the hug and slap on the shoulder that told her they'd become more like *bruders* than friends.

She turned to Joanna and clasped her hand. "I'm so glad you could come."

"Me, too. It was lovely. Just lovely. I hope we'll see you again very soon."

Rose Anna glanced up and saw Brad watching them. He nodded and winked at her, and she understood his silent message. They would see them soon, and she felt they would have their own happy news to share.

She sighed. It wouldn't be much longer before she and John could start their new life at the horse farm. How lucky they were. So many couples had to live with their parents and wait to buy or build their home.

God was so *gut* bringing them together and in giving them a beautiful place to live for years to come and hopefully raise many *kinner.*

"I have a surprise for you, *Lieb,*" John told her. He led her outside, and there in the drive sat a brand new buggy. Willow was hitched to it and wore white ribbons woven into her mane.

"I bought it with the money from the sale of the truck. And a little more cash."

"I hope you won't miss the truck."

"Never," he said. "Never." He helped her into the buggy. "Let's go home."

"Home," she said. "That sounds just perfect."

■ ■ ■ ■

Favorite Amish Recipes from Lancaster County, Pennsylvania

■ ■ ■ ■

AMISH YUMASETTA

1 1/2 pounds ground beef
Salt to taste
1/4 teaspoon pepper
8 ounces wide noodles, cooked and drained
1/2 cup diced celery
1 (10 1/2-ounce) can cream of chicken soup
1 (10-ounce) can tomato paste
1/2 pound Cheddar cheese, grated

Preheat oven to 350 degrees.

Brown meat and season with salt and pepper. Drain grease. Cook and drain noodles.

Place a layer of noodles in a 2-quart casserole, then one layer each of meat, celery, soup, tomato paste, and cheese. Repeat until all the ingredients are used, ending with a layer of cheese. Bake uncovered for 1 hour.

Serves 6

CREAMED CELERY

(often served at Amish weddings in Lancaster County)
1 quart finely chopped celery
water
1/2 teaspoon salt
1/2 cup sugar
2 tablespoons vinegar
1 tablespoon flour
1/2 cup milk
2 tablespoons mayonnaise

Cover celery with water in a saucepan, and add salt, sugar, and vinegar. Cook until tender. Drain. Combine flour and milk and bring to a boil. Cool. Stir in mayonnaise. Add cooked celery and mix until blended. Serve hot.

Serves 6

ROASHT

(Chicken Filling or Dressing)
4 tablespoons butter
1 cup chopped celery
1 loaf bread, cubed
1 1/2 cups cooked chicken, diced
3 eggs, beaten
1/2 teaspoon salt
pepper to taste

Preheat oven to 350 degrees.

Melt butter in a large skillet. Add celery and saute until soft. Toss bread and chicken together in a large bowl. Pour celery and eggs over bread mixture. Sprinkle with salt and pepper. Mix well.

Pour into a greased roaster or a large baking dish. Bake uncovered for 1 1/2 to 2 hours. During baking, stir occasionally, stirring bread away from sides of pan to prevent overbrowning or burning.

Serves 6

AMISH APPLE BUTTER BARS

1 cup butter, melted and divided
1/2 cup chopped nuts
2 cups whole-grain flour, divided
2 cups apple butter or pear butter
1/4 teaspoon baking soda
1/2 cup rolled oats
1/4 teaspoon salt
1/4 cup oat bran

Preheat oven to 350 degrees.

Mix together 1/2 cup butter, chopped nuts, and I cup flour. Press into an 8 × 13-inch pan. Bake for 10 minutes. Remove from oven and cool slightly. Leave oven on.

Top cooled crust with apple or pear butter.

Mix together the remaining butter, baking soda, oats, the remaining flour, salt, and oat bran. Press mixture gently onto apple or pear butter. Bake for 25 to 30 minutes or until toothpick inserted in the center comes out clean. Cool, cut into bars.

PUMPKIN WHOOPIE PIES

3 cups all-purpose flour
1 teaspoon salt
1 teaspoon baking powder
1 teaspoon baking soda
2 tablespoons ground cinnamon
1 tablespoon ground ginger
1 tablespoon ground cloves
2 cups firmly packed dark-brown sugar
1 cup vegetable oil
3 cups pumpkin purée, chilled
2 large eggs
2 teaspoons pure vanilla extract, divided
3 cups confectioner's sugar
1/2 cup unsalted butter, softened
8 ounces cream cheese, softened

Preheat oven to 350 degrees. Line two baking sheets with parchment paper or a nonstick baking mat. Set aside.

In a large bowl, whisk together flour, salt, baking powder, baking soda, cinnamon, ginger, and cloves; set aside. In another large bowl, whisk together brown sugar and oil until well combined. Add pumpkin puree and whisk until combined. Add eggs and 1 tsp. vanilla and whisk until well combined. Stir flour mixture into pumpkin mixture and whisk until fully incorporated.

Using a small ice cream scoop, drop heaping tablespoons of dough onto prepared baking sheets, about I inch apart. Bake until cookies are just starting to crack on top and a toothpick inserted into the center of each cookie comes out clean, about 15 minutes. Let cool completely on pan.

For the filling: Sift confectioner's sugar into a medium bowl. Set aside. Beat butter until smooth. Add cream cheese and beat until well combined. Add confectioner's sugar and remaining vanilla, beat just until smooth. (Filling can be made up to a day in advance. Cover and refrigerate; let stand at room temperature to soften before using.)

Assemble the Whoopie Pies: Line a baking sheet with parchment paper and set aside. Transfer filling to a disposable pastry bag and snip the end. When the cookies have cooled completely, spread filling on the flat side of half of the cookies. Sandwich with remaining cookies, pressing down slightly so that the filling spreads to the edge of the cookies. Transfer to prepared baking sheet and cover with plastic wrap. Refrigerate cookies at least 30 minutes before serving. Cookies may be refrigerated for up to 3 days.

SHOOFLY PIE

2/3 cup firmly packed brown sugar
1 tablespoon solid shortening
1 cup all-purpose flour
1 teaspoon baking soda
3/4 cup boiling water
1 egg, beaten
1 cup molasses
1 (9-inch) pie crust, unbaked

Preheat oven to 375 degrees.

Mix brown sugar, shortening, and flour, and set aside 1/2 cup for topping.

Combine soda with boiling water, then add egg and molasses. Stir well to create a syrup. Add crumb mixture, except for 1/2 cup reserved mixture. Pour into unbaked pie crust and cover with reserved crumb mixture.

Bake at 375 degrees for 10 minutes, then

reduce heat to 350 degrees and bake for an additional 35-45 minutes (until firm). When cut into, the bottom may be "wet." This is okay. It is also called a "wet bottom shoofly pie."

Serves 6–8

GLOSSARY

ach — oh
aenti — aunt
allrecht — all right
boppli — baby
bruder — brother
daed — dad
danki — thank you
dat — father
dawdi haus — a small home added to or near the main house into which the farmer moves after passing the farm and main house to one of his children
dippy eggs — over-easy eggs
dochder — daughter
eck — the corner of the wedding table where the newly married couple sits
Englisch — what the Amish call a non-Amish person
fraa — wife
Gott — God
grossdaadi — grandfather

411

grossdochder — granddaughter

grosseldres — grandparents

grosskinner — grandchildren

grossmudder — grandmother

grosssohn — grandson

guder mariye — good morning

gut — good

gut-n-owed — good evening

haus — house

hungerich — hungry

kapp — prayer covering or cap worn by girls and women

kind, kinner — child, children

kumm — come

lieb — love. Term of endearment

maedel — young single woman

mamm — mom

mann — husband

mein — my

mudder — mother

nacht — night

nee — no

newehocker — wedding attendant

onkel — uncle

Pennsylvania *Dietsch* — Pennsylvania Dutch. A dialect spoken by the Amish in Lancaster County, Pennsylvania

roasht — roast. A stuffing or dressing side dish

rumschpringe — time period when teenagers are allowed to experience the *Englisch* world while deciding if they should join the church

schul — school
schur — sure
schweschder — sister
sohn — son
wilkum — welcome
wunderbaar — wonderful
ya — yes

DISCUSSION QUESTIONS

Spoiler alert! Please don't read before completing the book as the questions contain spoilers!

1. Many Amish believe God has set aside a marriage partner for them. Do you believe this? Do you believe in love at first sight?

2. Rose Anna has been waiting for John, the man she feels God has set aside for her, for a long time. Have you ever become upset with God when His timing isn't yours? What did you do?

3. John left home after he couldn't get along with his father. He's had to find whatever jobs he can to support himself. Have you worked at a job you didn't like or felt is not what you want to do with your life? How did you handle it?

4. What was your relationship with your parents when you were growing up? Good? Troubled with conflicts? How do you get along with them now as an adult?

5. Have you ever had to walk away from a relationship with a family member or a good friend who felt like family? Why? What happened? How did you handle it?

6. Rose Anna finds her work volunteer teaching quilting classes to be fulfilling. Have you ever volunteered? What did you do?

7. Rose Anna gets a second chance with John, and their relationship seems back on track. But John doesn't feel he has anything to offer her — Amish men are traditional and believe they should support their wives. What did you think of Neil's advice?

8. John finds a mentor — a father figure — in Neil. Have you ever had a mentor or been a mentor to someone else? How did this relationship change your life?

9. When Neil has a sudden health crisis, John and Neil's son must come together.

Have you ever had a situation where you had to do this? What did you do?

10. Neil's death changes John's life. Have you ever lost a parent or parent figure?

11. Sometimes family is made up of our mother, father, and siblings. Sometimes it's made of friends or others like Neil and Brad who become family. Do you have friends who are family to you? How did this happen?

12. Rose Anna feels guilty when she reflects on how she manipulated John into marrying her. Do you think she did? What would you say to her?

ABOUT THE AUTHOR

Barbara Cameron has a heart for writing about the spiritual values and simple joys of the Amish. She is the best-selling author of more than 40 fiction and nonfiction books, three nationally televised movies, and the winner of the first Romance Writers of America Golden Heart Award. Her books have been nominated for Carol Awards and the Inspirational Reader's Choice Award from RWA's Faith, Hope, and Love chapter. Barbara resides in Jacksonville, Florida.

The employees of Thorndike Press hope you have enjoyed this Large Print book. All our Thorndike, Wheeler, and Kennebec Large Print titles are designed for easy reading, and all our books are made to last. Other Thorndike Press Large Print books are available at your library, through selected bookstores, or directly from us.

For information about titles, please call:
  (800) 223-1244

or visit our website at:
  gale.com/thorndike

To share your comments, please write:
  Publisher
  Thorndike Press
  10 Water St., Suite 310
  Waterville, ME 04901